"Are you trying for spontaneous combustion?"

Sam felt about to burst into flames, the way Laurel kissed him lightly, then deepened the kiss. He tried to ease away from her. "A bedroom is a very intimate place, where things can get out of hand real quick."

Like the way their argument suddenly turned into a romantic duel. He wanted to keep her away from the action tonight, where she'd be safe. She wanted to go with him, where she felt she belonged. Neither of them reached an agreement, not once she came into his arms.

Laurel looked up into his eyes—and he saw innocence and trust. "You wouldn't do anything I didn't want you to do, Sam."

"How do you know?" He ground out the words.

"You're too honorable."

But as she brought her mouth back to his for another feast, he barely had the time or the will to speak.

"I wouldn't be too sure about that."

Dear Harlequin Intrigue Reader,

Need some great stocking stuffers this holiday season for yourself and your family and friends? Harlequin Intrigue has four dynamite suggestions—starting with three exciting conclusions.

This month, veteran romantic suspense author Rebecca York wraps up her special 43 LIGHT STREET trilogy MINE TO KEEP with *Lassiter's Law*, and Susan Kearney finishes her action-packed HIDE AND SEEK miniseries with *Lovers in Hiding*. Julie Miller, too, closes out the MONTANA CONFIDENTIAL quartet with her book *Secret Agent Heiress*. You won't want to miss any of these thrilling titles.

For some Christmastime entertainment, B.J. Daniels takes you west on a trip into madness and mayhem with a beautiful amnesiac and a secret father in her book *A Woman with a Mystery*.

So make your list and check out Harlequin Intrigue for the best gift around…happily ever after.

Happy holidays from all of us at Harlequin Intrigue.

Sincerely,

Denise O'Sullivan
Associate Senior Editor
Harlequin Intrigue

LASSITER'S LAW
REBECCA YORK

RUTH GLICK WRITING AS REBECCA YORK

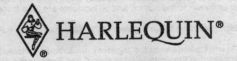

TORONTO • NEW YORK • LONDON
AMSTERDAM • PARIS • SYDNEY • HAMBURG
STOCKHOLM • ATHENS • TOKYO • MILAN • MADRID
PRAGUE • WARSAW • BUDAPEST • AUCKLAND

ISBN 0-373-22641-1

LASSITER'S LAW

Copyright © 2001 by Ruth Glick

This edition published by arrangement with Harlequin Books S.A.

® and TM are trademarks of the publisher. Trademarks indicated with ® are registered in the United States Patent and Trademark Office, the Canadian Trade Marks Office and in other countries.

Visit us at www.eHarlequin.com

Printed in U.S.A.

ABOUT THE AUTHOR

Award-winning, bestselling novelist Ruth Glick, who writes as Rebecca York, is the author of close to eighty books, including her popular 43 LIGHT STREET series for Harlequin Intrigue. Ruth says she has the best job in the world. Not only does she get paid for telling stories, she's also the author of twelve cookbooks. Ruth and her husband, Norman, travel frequently, researching locales for her novels and searching out new dishes for her cookbooks.

Books by Rebecca York

HARLEQUIN INTRIGUE

HARLEQUIN SINGLE TITLE

JO'S GRILLED BEEF
WITH PEPPERS AND ONIONS

Makes 3 to 4 servings

1 1/2 lb sirloin steak, cut one inch thick
1/2 cup chopped onions
1/2 cup olive oil
1/2 cup red wine vinegar
1 tbsp Italian seasoning
1/2 tbsp Dijon-style mustard
2 tsp chopped garlic
1 tsp salt

Place steak in a plastic food storage bag. In a small bowl, combine onion, oil, vinegar, Italian seasoning, mustard, garlic and salt. Stir to mix well. Pour into bag with steak, distributing evenly over meat. Seal, lay on a large plate and refrigerate 6 to 8 hours or overnight.

Adjust rack 5 inches from broiler. Preheat broiler. Transfer meat to broiler pan. Broil meat for 11 to 18 minutes, turning once, until desired degree of doneness is reached.

Adapted from *Fabulous Lo-Carb Cuisine* by Ruth Glick

CAST OF CHARACTERS

Sam Lassiter—An ex-cop haunted by nightmares from his past.

Laurel Coleman—Afraid to trust Sam—or trust herself?

Eric Frees—Was he a grieving husband or a monster?

Teddy Frees—A small boy with big problems.

James Ripley—Would he be the death of Sam, Laurel and Teddy?

Arnold Naylor—Was he planning to double-cross Sam?

Dallas Sedgwick—A desperate man willing to use desperate methods.

Lucas Somerville—Was he playing straight with his friends?

Cal Rollins—One of Sedgwick's bitter enemies.

Alex Shane—Willing to risk his life to help Sam and Laurel.

Carlton Jones—Was he the key to the Dallas Sedgwick mystery?

Dear Reader,

I've had a wonderful time writing MINE TO KEEP, a trilogy within the 43 LIGHT STREET series. In *Lassiter's Law*, I've tied up all the mystery elements left from *The Man from Texas* and *Never Alone*. Getting it all to work out was a challenge, since there were so many threads woven through the three stories.

While wrapping up the overall mystery, I was determined to keep the focus of this book on Sam Lassiter and Laurel Coleman. They are just the type of hero and heroine I love to write about—wounded people whose love for each other heals them.

Sam lost his wife and child in a horrible automobile accident that comes back to him again and again in his nightmares. To deaden the pain, he turned to alcohol. He's been dry for over a year, but he still sees himself as damaged. And he's still afraid to let himself love again.

Laurel is coping with her own problems—a painful past that haunts her present. How she comes to trust Sam with her secrets—and to trust herself—is also central to the story.

In the MINE TO KEEP trilogy, Alex Shane has been a strong secondary character. I've been chomping at the bit to tell Alex's story. And I'm going to do it in my next Harlequin Intrigue novel, *From the Shadows*. Like most of my heroes, Alex is coping with personal issues. When he's sent on a special assignment by Randolph Security—back to his hometown of St. Stephens, Maryland—his private life and his job come crashing into conflict. So look for that title in early 2002.

Until then, happy reading!

Best,

Ruth

Ruth Glick writing as Rebecca York

Chapter One

It had been years since Laurel Coleman had enjoyed a sound sleep. Which was probably what saved her life that August night.

One moment she was dozing in the queen-size bed. In the next, she heard a harsh male voice, low and menacing.

Was the sound from one of her bad dreams? She had them often enough to think it could be.

But this felt different. Real. From the here and now. Pushing herself up, she strained her ears. Then she heard Cindy, her voice rising in fear. "No, Eric. No. What are you doing?"

"Quiet, you bitch."

Eric?

Eric Frees, Cindy's husband, was supposed to be on one of his business trips. He was rarely home, and he wasn't due back for another three days.

Yet the voice she heard down the hall sounded like his. "Where's the kid?" he demanded.

"In his room."

"I checked. He's not there."

"Then I don't know."

"Can't you even keep track of your son, you stupid bitch?"

Laurel looked toward the opposite side of the bed. Five-year-old Teddy was curled on his side, his mop of blond hair wreathed around his head. Earlier he'd awakened from one of his own nightmares, and instead of going all the way down the hall to his mother's room, he'd come to Laurel for comfort, because he'd known she'd understand. She'd rocked him in her arms, told him that everything was okay. And when he'd asked to stay in her bed, she'd agreed. "Just this once," she'd said.

At the other end of the hall, Eric's voice rose in anger. "You're lying! I want that kid, and I want him now."

The resounding smack of flesh contacting flesh made Laurel cringe. Then Cindy screamed, a high desperate sound.

Teddy's eyes snapped open, widened in terror. "Laurel?"

She was across the bed in seconds, pressing her hand against his mouth. "Teddy, honey, don't make a sound."

As she hovered over the trembling boy, Eric was issuing orders to unseen companions. "Get that kid. And find the nanny, too. I don't want any witnesses."

"Eric, please. You're hurting me. What's going on? Don't! Oh, God, you're not—" The sentence was cut off by the sound of a slap, then another scream.

Seconds later, Laurel heard something heavy thumping down the long curving staircase.

A body.

Paralyzed by sick fear, she cringed from the horrors beyond the door as vivid pictures flashed in her mind. Eric Frees, a harsh man under the best of circumstances, had gone crazy. He had pushed his wife down the stairs. And now he was looking for her and Teddy.

As if in confirmation, she heard doors slamming up and down the long hallway.

The bursts of sound galvanized her. Frantically she considered her options. There was only one. Scooping up the boy in her arms, Laurel shoved her feet into the tennis shoes beside the bed, moved toward the window and pushed up the sash. "Come on. We're going to play a game of hide-and-seek," she whispered.

"Is that Daddy?" the boy whispered back. "He sounds angry. Is he going to spank me again?"

"I won't let him," Laurel answered.

"We can't go out in our pajamas."

"It's okay. Everything's okay," she soothed automatically as she looked down at her clothing. A big T-shirt over underpants. But the shorts she'd discarded the night before were draped over the back of the chair. She dragged them on, then took more precious seconds to open the bottom desk drawer and remove the wad of cash she'd been saving. After stuffing it into her purse, she hustled Teddy toward the window.

Her room was over the wide front portico of the antebellum-style mansion that millionaire Eric Frees had built in Howard County, Maryland. After lowering Teddy three feet to the porch roof, she stepped onto the shingle-covered surface. Clutching the boy's small hand in hers, she led him toward the large maple tree whose branches hung over the porch.

Slinging her purse across her chest, she squatted.

"Climb on my back," she said. "And wrap your arms around my neck."

Teddy whimpered. "Laurel, I'm scared."

"I know, honey. I am, too. But we've got to get out of here. So come on. Climb aboard."

As his small weight settled on her back, and his arms tightened around her neck, Laurel breathed out a little sigh. Cindy had told her about Eric's harsh punishments—punishments that had made the boy afraid of his father. The knowledge had sickened her. Tonight she was grateful, since it meant Teddy wasn't protesting their escape.

She maneuvered onto a branch, feeling his skinny arms tighten around her neck as she lowered herself downward.

After jumping the last few feet to the ground, she shifted Teddy to her arms and dashed away from the front of the house toward the Mustang that Cindy was letting her use. There was no time to belt him into his booster seat. She simply scooped him into the car as loud shouts shattered the stillness of the night.

"Over here. The bitch is over here."

Laurel leaped into the driver's seat, slammed the door and turned the key in the ignition as she floored the accelerator.

Ear-splitting explosions tore through the air, and something pinged against the side of the car.

Gunshots.

They were shooting at her. Wide-eyed, her hands fused to the wheel, she spun down the driveway and onto Holly Thicket Pass, pressing her foot to the accelerator in a mad dash for safety.

After several miles, when it looked as if no one had immediately picked up her trail, she slowed to a more moderate pace and glanced in the back seat. Teddy was curled into a tight ball, his arms clasped round his knees. When she softly called his name, he didn't answer, and she hoped he was sleeping.

Turning back to the road, she drove on, her mind reeling. Though she'd hardly known Eric Frees, she'd never liked him and she'd stayed out of his way as much as possible. But there had been no way to totally avoid him. Not when her old friend, Cindy Frees, was the only person willing to give her a job—as Teddy's live-in nanny.

Her hands clenched on the wheel. Over the past six months, she'd done her best to stay out of trouble. Now trouble had reared up on its hind legs and sunk its teeth into her throat.

Lord, had she done the right thing by spiriting Teddy away? In her mind, she went slowly back over the events that had propelled her dash for safety. There was a slim chance that she'd misinterpreted what was going on out in the hall. But she hadn't made up the gunshots that had followed her down the driveway.

Which led back to the conclusion that Cindy was dead.

Laurel wanted to pull over to the side of the road and cradle her head in her hands. God, now what?

Drive to the nearest police station? The thought of turning the problem over to someone else was so tempting that she wanted to cry with relief. But when she pictured herself trying to explain what had happened to a uniformed officer, she went cold and sick inside. What had happened to her at the hands of the police was too vivid, too raw for her to dare risking it again.

No. She was on her own.

She made a harsh sound that was something close to a laugh. Ironically she knew what to do because she'd talked to enough women who had been on the run. If she didn't want Eric Frees and his gunmen to find her, then she had to do something about her car.

So what was she supposed to do? Steal another one? God, no. She couldn't go that route—even if she knew *how* to jump a car. But maybe she could get another set of license plates.

She'd been driving aimlessly, with no real idea where she was going. Now she thought vaguely that she was in Catonsville. In a working-class neighborhood. When she turned the corner, she came to a house that looked abandoned. In the yard was a car with the side bashed in. But she could see a license plate on the bumper.

Pulling up along the curb, she cut the engine and twisted around to look at Teddy. He was still curled on his side, but his eyes were open.

"Laurel, where's Mommy?" he asked.

She felt her heart turn over. For a moment she hesitated, but she couldn't voice her fears. "She's at home."

"Then why are we here?"

"I'm afraid your daddy wants to hurt you. So I need to take you somewhere safe."

"Where?"

Where indeed? She didn't know yet, but she came up with an answer. "A motel."

"Then are we going home to Mommy?"

Again she wondered how to respond. She didn't want to lie, but she certainly didn't want to share what she was really thinking. Compromising, she said, "We're going to do what's best. And right now I'm worried that the men who were at your house with your dad will find us. So I'm going to try to fool them. You stay in the car and I'll be back as soon as I can."

Teddy whimpered, pushed himself up and reached across the seat to grab her shoulder. "Laurel, don't leave me alone."

"I'm not. I'm going to get something out of the trunk. Then I'm just going over to that car." She pointed to the wreck.

After a moment's hesitation, the boy scooted back onto his seat.

"I'll be right back," Laurel promised again as she popped the latch on the trunk. After getting out the tool kit Cindy had insisted she carry for emergencies, she closed the trunk again, then headed for the wrecked car.

She had just tackled the rusty bolts on the license plate with a screwdriver, when a high-pitched voice rang out from the Mustang.

"Laurel, watch out."

Her head jerked up in time to see a tall, thin man coming toward her around the side of the car.

He was looking at her like a glutton confronted with a roasted turkey.

"What do you think you're doing, girlie?" he growled.

Laurel stood up, turning to face him, struggling to keep her body from trembling as she saw his tongue swipe across his lips.

"I..." She tried, but no explanation came to her lips. God, now what was she going to do?

She wanted to close her eyes, to curl into a ball the way Teddy had done. Instead she straightened her shoulders.

"Out kind of late, aren't you? And up to no good in the bargain." Confidently, he took a step closer, reached for her.

It was pure self-protective instinct that had her slashing at the large hand with the screwdriver she still clutched in her fist. She felt the blade connect with flesh.

Cursing, roaring in pain, he made another grab for her, his face contorted with rage. But she danced back, turned and ran to the Mustang.

His feet pounded on the gravel behind her, but she dared not look back. Gaining the car, she slammed the door and clicked the locks.

In the back she could hear Teddy whimpering.

"It's all right. Everything's all right," she chanted, knowing the reassurance was as much for herself as her passenger.

As she twisted the key in the ignition, she saw the man bend and pick up a large rock in his beefy hand.

Frantically, she gunned the engine, and the rock struck the rear fender as she jerked away. Gravel spewed out from under her tires as Laurel barreled down the street, barely missing a parked car as she careened around the corner. She slowed as she drove deeper into the neighborhood, making frequent turns, splitting her attention between the road ahead and the rearview mirror.

There was no sign that the man had followed. Still, her pulse was drumming so loudly in her ears that it was several miles before she was aware of another sound in the car—a small boy's sobs.

"Oh, honey."

Making sure the street was clear, she pulled to the curb, cut the engine and scrambled across the seat into the back. The will to survive had kept her going until now. But she had reached the end of her emotional reserves. As she took the sobbing boy into her arms, her eyes filled, and her own tears began to flow.

SAM LASSITER MADE a strangled noise and tried to claw his way toward consciousness. But it was no good. It was happening again. He was a captive of his nightmare. And there was nothing he could do to stop it.

Jan was behind the wheel because he'd been driving for ten hours straight, and she'd insisted on giving him a break. Ellen was asleep in the back seat. And then a car was hurtling out of the darkness, crossing the median, heading right for them. A car whose grill looked like a grinning death mask.

He screamed a warning. "Jan…Jan…"

But it was too late. Too late for his wife and daughter. The car slammed into them like a derailed train as the sound of rending metal filled the air. The phantom impact jerked him awake. His eyes snapped open, and he sat there in his easy chair, breathing hard, sweat pouring off his body as he struggled back to reality.

Then a rustling sound filled the sudden silence in the room, and he blinked down at the loose papers that had slipped off his lap and cascaded across the tweed carpet.

Eighteen months ago this had been Ellen's cozy bedroom, decorated in soft pink and green. Sam had ruthlessly stripped off the kiddy wallpaper, pulled up the rug, carted the little-girl furnishings to Goodwill—and replaced them with an oak desk and a couple of fake-leather easy chairs.

He got down on the tweed carpet and began shuffling the papers together. He'd fallen asleep over his notes on the Dawson-Somerville case. His friends Hannah Dawson and Lucas Somerville—who were being chased by a crime lord named Dallas Sedgwick, bent on their destruction. Somehow the case was wound up with a drug bust in Baltimore that had gone bad, a drug bust in which a kid had been killed. And the boy's brother had come after the police officers involved—including Hannah.

Like Sam, Hannah's traumas had driven her to quit the police force and join the Light Street Detective Agency. That was how she'd met Lucas, who had been an undercover operative for a super-secret government agency called the Peregrine Connection. He'd ended up with amnesia and a suitcase full of Sedgwick's money. And he'd hired her to find out who he was and who owned the cash.

Tonight Sam had tried to slip in some background reading on the case. But now he silently admitted that he'd been pushing himself past any reasonable level of coherence because he was afraid to climb into bed and lie down.

Not smart to drop off to sleep—when he had a new client coming.

He looked at his watch and winced. He had fifteen minutes to get ready for a man who had wanted to meet him at home where they'd have more privacy, instead of at the office.

It flicked through his mind that a glass of bourbon would settle him down. Yeah, right.

He had won his war against the bottle and he wasn't going to throw it all away to steady his nerves.

Angry that the thought had even crossed his mind, he dragged himself down the hall to the bathroom and splashed water on his face, then ran a finger along his lean jaw. It was covered by dark beard stubble. But there wasn't time to shave now. Still, he could look a little more presentable. A quick combing took care of his dark hair.

Then he stripped off his sweat-soaked white shirt, grabbed a clean one and shoved his arms through the sleeves. He had just tucked the shirttails into his waistband when the doorbell rang.

"Coming," he called as he pulled the bedroom door shut.

"Sam Lassiter?" the man on the front porch asked. He was of medium height. Medium weight, with dark hair just beginning to gray at the temples.

"Yeah. Come on in."

"Eric Frees." He held out his hand, and they shook.

It was a firm grip, designed to impress with its sincerity.

"I appreciate your seeing me at home, because I've got to keep this strictly confidential."

"No problem," Sam assured him, taking in the man's tense face. His cheeks were sunken, his thin lips pressed together. But his blue eyes burned with an unnerving intensity.

Suddenly uncomfortable, Sam turned away and led his guest down the hall to the office.

"So what do you want to talk to me about?" Sam asked, taking the armchair on the far side of the lamp table.

Frees sank into the opposite chair. "My wife's death. My son's disappearance."

"This happened recently? I don't remember seeing anything in the paper about it."

"A few days ago. The police believe Cindy's death was an accident. I'm not so sure."

"Based on what?"

"Based on the criminal record of Laurel Coleman, the nanny my wife hired."

Sam sat up straighter. "You didn't investigate her background before you hired her?"

"Cindy knew about the girl's past. They'd been best friends in high school. By the way, Coleman's not her real name. She plucked that from thin air after she got out of prison. She used to be Laurel Ames. Cindy told me Laurel turned rebellious in high school."

"Why?"

"I figured she didn't like sticking to the rules. Anyway, she got in with the wrong crowd. Cindy thought she'd had a bad break. When Laurel couldn't get a job after she got out of prison, Cindy hired her."

"In prison for what?"

"Kidnapping. She claimed her boyfriend tricked her into it." His voice turned hard. "My wife trusted her. Now she's dead, and my son's missing."

"And you've talked to the police about your suspicions?"

The man's face contorted. "I can't prove Laurel had anything to do with Cindy's death. She fell—or was pushed down the steps. And the issue with my son is kind of delicate. Cindy's parents never approved of me. If they learned Teddy was missing, they'd blame me, even though it's not my fault. So I want you to locate him before they find out."

"Surely with their daughter dead, they've asked to see their grandson."

"They're on a wilderness-camping trip in Alaska. I've got ten more days before I have to produce the boy."

Convenient, Sam thought. And not entirely convincing. Eric Frees wasn't exactly acting like a grieving husband and father. He was acting more like a man whose plans had gotten derailed—and he wanted them back on track.

"If I agree to work for you, I'll want as much information as I can get about the nanny." He looked down at the notes he'd taken. "Laurel Coleman."

"I've written up a report on her with all the facts I know. And pictures."

Efficient. "I'll want to know more about you, too."

Frees spread his hands. "Just ask."

"Did you and your wife get along?"

"Yes."

"You didn't resent her parents' attitude toward you?"

His lips thinned, and he looked down. "Of course I did. I still do. But that has nothing to do with Cindy's death."

Sam would have liked to see his eyes. He was making a show of being cooperative, but the more he talked, the less convincing he sounded.

Opening the folder, Sam riffled through the contents. On top were several photographs. Most featured a boy of about four or five. A cute kid with light-brown eyes. Sometimes he was alone. Sometimes he was with a young blond woman.

"This his mother?" Sam asked, pointed.

Eric silently nodded.

Sam studied the image. She appeared to be at least ten years younger than her husband.

There were other pictures—of a pretty brunette with delicate features, liquid brown eyes and shoulder-length, layered hair.

"Coleman?"

"Yeah."

She looked older than Cindy Frees. Or perhaps it was more that her face reflected a kind of bruised wariness. Prison had probably done that to her.

"How old is Coleman?"

"Twenty-four."

Sam spread out several of the pictures on the table. In the soft lamplight she looked very feminine and very vulnerable, almost as if she was expecting trouble to reach out and grab her. He shook off the notion, warning himself not to identify with her too closely.

Whether or not Eric Frees was telling the whole truth and nothing but the truth, she'd gotten herself in trouble by disappearing with the man's son.

Frees was speaking again, changing the subject adroitly. "I got as much information on you as I could, too. When you were in the Baltimore Police Department you were a real straight arrow. People talked about 'Lassiter's law.'"

He'd heard that phrase himself. He knew what it meant to him, but he was curious about Frees's perception. "Which signifies what as far as you're concerned?" he asked.

"That you see things in black-and-white terms. No gray areas. You know what's right, and you do it."

Sam nodded. He did try to do what was right. But he hoped his own experience in sinking into the depths of hell had given him a perspective he'd lacked when he was on the force.

"Okay, I'll read over the material on Coleman, do some checking on my own. Then I'll tell you if I can take the case."

Frees's face contorted. "I told you, I'm on a deadline. I was hoping you could give me an answer tonight."

"Yeah, well, that's the problem with seeing things in black and white. You've got to be sure before you leap off a cliff."

Frees's mouth opened and closed. He was silent for several seconds. When he spoke, his voice was low and controlled. "Don't take too long making your decision. If you can't help me, I'll have to find someone else who can."

LAUREL CAREFULLY SPREAD peanut butter on a slice of day-old bread. Grape jelly went on another slice. After placing the sandwich on a paper towel, she opened a small foam ice chest, pulled out a carton of milk and shook it. Still half-full.

"Lunch," she announced cheerfully, cutting the sandwich into quarters with a plastic knife. Then she set the food and milk on a small plastic tray beside the boy.

It was a late lunch, because Teddy had slept until after ten. She'd let him stay in bed because that shortened the long day she knew was stretching in front of her. Now he was watching cartoons.

At least the news of Cindy's death hadn't made much impact up here in Western Maryland. One night on the news, and that was all. But she'd already known her friend was dead before she'd heard the report. And she'd kept her grieving strictly private to spare Teddy.

Without turning from the TV, he picked up a sandwich quarter and began to eat. She'd told him they were having "an adventure—like in a movie," and he seemed to accept that version of reality. He didn't seem to mind the dismal room. He wasn't worried about the police or his father finding them. And he wasn't concerned that their supply of money was dwindling dangerously. Even up here in western Maryland, where prices were rock bottom, they were going to run out of funds pretty soon unless she found a way to earn some more. And there weren't too many options on that front.

A shadow crossed in front of the window, and she stiffened, expecting the door to burst open and men to come charging in. Men with guns. She'd been expecting it all along. And the terror hadn't lessened after a week on the run.

Whoever was outside moved down the sidewalk, and she let out the breath she'd been holding.

They were still safe. But for how long?

One thing she knew for certain: She couldn't leave Teddy alone. And she couldn't come up with a social-security card, either. So anything she did was going to be part-time, off the books.

God, what a mess!

She stood for several seconds with her eyes closed and the heel of her hand pressed against her forehead as she fought a sudden surge of emotion—part panic and part despair as she felt the unknown future closing in on her and Teddy.

If there were somewhere safe she could leave him, she could—

With a shake of her head, she cut off that line of thought. Teddy was the child she'd never had. The child she was sure she'd never have. Perhaps that was why she'd bonded with him so quickly, so solidly, and why she would do whatever it took to protect him.

Turning back to the dresser she was using as a makeshift kitchen counter, she made herself a sandwich.

She'd thought about going back to Frostburg, but she'd discarded the idea. Eric knew where she and Cindy had grown up. Probably he had men there looking for her right now. But Grantville made a pretty good substitute. She knew the area, understood the kind of people who lived here, understood how to get along.

For example, she knew that several of the local churches maintained stores where families could pick up used clothing at almost no cost. That was where she'd bought a couple pairs of jeans and some T-shirts for herself and Teddy as well as shoes and socks.

She also knew that the supermarket down the road stocked a shelf with dented cans and baked goods past their pull date where she could replenish her food supplies. And she was hoping that there'd be a package of cinnamon buns that she could give Teddy for dessert.

"Want to go to the store?" she asked.

He looked up from the cartoon he was watching. "Okay."

She felt a twinge then, at his calm acceptance of her suggestion. Normally he was a high-spirited little boy. But he'd been so good during the past few days. Too good. As though he had shut down part of his mind and spirit.

Telling herself that his cooperative behavior was a blessing, she waited until he'd finished his sandwich, then found the tennis shoes and socks he'd left beside the bed.

After grabbing her purse, she opened the motel door and stuck her head out, trying to project a sense of confidence she didn't feel. Last night the parking lot had been crowded. This afternoon there were only a few cars outside, since most of the guests were travelers passing through, and they'd already moved on.

Taking Teddy firmly by the hand, she turned to close the door in back of her.

Too late she caught a flash of movement.

Before she could regain the safety of the room, a tall, dark man had crossed the distance between them and clamped his hand on her shoulder.

"Just act naturally, and everything will be all right," he said, his voice low.

He held a gun in his right hand, held it shielded by his body where Teddy couldn't see it. But it filled Laurel's field of vision as if the image of the weapon were projected on a giant movie screen.

Chapter Two

Laurel's muscles went rigid as the man moved her back into the room, turning quickly to lock the door and slide the safety chain into place. The scraping of metal against metal was like the clank of a prison door slamming shut.

Instinct urged her to turn and scratch his eyes out. It didn't matter what happened to her now, but if he killed her, then he'd have Teddy.

"Laurel?" the boy asked in a shaky voice. "Laurel, what's going on?"

She was trying to dredge up some words when the man spoke in a surprisingly warm voice.

"It's okay, Teddy. I'm a friend. I've come to help you and Laurel."

He looked from the boy to her, then spoke in a barely audible whisper. "We don't want to cause any undue alarm, do we?"

"No," she managed to say, his features burning themselves into her brain. Dark hair. Dark eyes. A mouth that might have been sensual if the lips hadn't been grimly compressed.

"I'll bet you were watching cartoons in here," the man continued, addressing the youngster again. The casual observation made Laurel realize he must have been the presence she'd sensed outside.

The gun was still hidden from Teddy as their captor marched her across the room and turned on the television set. "You keep watching your show while Laurel and I talk."

"Okay," the boy answered with the passivity that she'd found so disturbing.

"We're going into the bathroom where we won't bother you. But we'll keep the door open."

Laurel closed her eyes, trying to send Teddy a silent message. *Run. Get out of here. Run.* But the boy only settled back against the pillows. Damn!

Her mind was still clawing for an escape plan as her captor grasped her arm and moved her into the bathroom.

"So you found us. Are you one of Eric's goons?"

"I'm a private detective. Eric hired me to find you."

She couldn't prevent a shiver from traveling over her skin, and she knew he'd caught the movement. Forcing a calm she didn't feel, she stared up at him through her lashes. He had told her he was working for Eric. Yet his face didn't match her mental picture of the men with the harsh voices who had searched the mansion looking for her.

And he'd spoken softly to Teddy, although she wasn't going to give him any points for that. Not frightening the boy was simply expedient.

Still, he hadn't hustled them straight out of the motel room and into his car. He said he wanted to talk. About what?

His eyes smoldered with leashed emotion. Anger. But not just that. Sadness, too. Something profoundly bad had happened to this man, she thought with a sudden glimmer of insight.

Could she twist what she saw inside him to her own advantage? She'd never been good at cold calculations. Mostly, she was impulsive—which had gotten her into trouble more than once.

Now she vowed to use what weapons she could muster.

The bathroom was small, and he was only a foot away, taking up too much of the oxygen in the room. At least that was the way it felt when she struggled to draw in a full breath.

Forcing herself not to flinch, she saw that he was studying her as closely as she was studying him. She tried to ignore the sensations his scrutiny produced as she took in more details. His cheeks were lean and freshly shaven. His jaw was firm.

Viewed objectively, he looked like a good man. A decent man. But if that was true, why was he working for Eric Frees?

"How did you find me?" she asked.

"Deductive reasoning. I knew you were from Frostburg. I figured you wouldn't go there. But you feel comfortable up here. So I started scoping out nearby towns, asking questions about a woman and a boy."

Silently she cursed herself. By now she could have been in California if she'd had the guts to strike out for parts unknown.

"You have a name?" she asked.

"Sam Lassiter."

It didn't sound made up. But what did she know?

Raising her chin, she regarded him with a lot more boldness than she felt. If she stalled for time, maybe she could figure out a way to get herself and Teddy away. He'd been careful about not frightening the boy. Perhaps she could use that. Or perhaps…there was another way, she decided as she began to work out a plan so desperate that it made her head spin. But she couldn't risk it yet. Not until she knew a little more.

She kept her voice low as she said, "Well, Mr. Lassiter, I guess you're pretty proud of yourself. I suppose Eric's paying you a fat fee to bring us back so he can kill us."

His eyes registered a moment of shock. Then he laughed, a harsh, raspy sound in the confines of the small room. ''Nice try.''

''You think I'm making that up? Why would I climb onto the portico roof with Teddy and spirit him away if I didn't think we were in danger?''

''Because you knew you had a chance to pull off the same kidnapping scheme you did before.''

Her throat was suddenly so constricted that she could barely breathe, but she managed to say, ''If you know about that, you know I was tricked into helping Oren.''

''That was your story.''

''I testified against him.''

''Criminals will testify to anything to get a lighter sentence. You got off pretty easy, I'd say.''

''And once a criminal always a criminal?''

''You said it, not me.''

Fighting a surge of despair, she asked, ''What did Eric Frees tell you about the night I escaped with Teddy?''

''That he came home and found you and his son missing. That he found his wife lying at the bottom of the stairs. He thinks you stole money from her, and the two of you fought. Either she fell down the stairs or you pushed her. Then you scooped up Teddy and split.''

The words made her feel sick and dizzy. *That* was Eric's story?

Ignoring Lassiter's stony stare, she took a shallow breath, then another. When she could speak, she lowered her voice. ''I did not kidnap Teddy for any kind of personal gain. I took him to keep him safe.''

''Uh-huh.''

''That night…I was in my bedroom. Noises in the hall woke me up. Eric was out there—and other men. He was shouting at Cindy. Then I heard…I heard her scream, heard something like a body thumping down the stairs. After that, he told his men to find me and Teddy. Luckily Teddy had had a nightmare, and he was sleeping with me. I got the two of us out the window.''

He regarded her with interest. ''That's a pretty amazing story.''

''It's the truth. You have to believe it's the truth,'' she added, hearing the pleading sound of her own voice. ''Eric killed his wife. He wants to kill me and Teddy.''

''Why?''

''We're witnesses.''

''You maybe, but to go after his own son? Your story doesn't make sense.''

Despair threatened to drown her, but somehow she made her voice soft, feminine. ''Please. I'll do anything.''

His eyes had brightened as though he was waiting to find out just what she meant by that.

''Please,'' she said again. ''Help me.'' She put desperation into her voice, desperation she didn't have to fake because the next move she planned to make was so out of character that part of her was standing back in amazement watching the performance.

The blood was roaring in her ears as she raised her arms and took him boldly by the shoulders.

He tried to take a step back, which put him squarely against the tile wall with a heavy glass sconce above his head. The sconce that was in as bad condition as the rest of the motel.

She told herself she was only doing what must be done in order to save Teddy from Eric Frees. And only for a few desperate moments. Raising up on tiptoe, she pressed her mouth to his, pressed her breasts against his chest and her hips against his middle, like a woman willing to trade intimacy for personal advantage. Although she'd never done that in her life, nor thought she was capable of it.

She tried to keep her mind numb, tried not to think. She

had braced herself to fight revulsion but she didn't feel it. In fact, she couldn't name what she was feeling.

She might have pulled back then—purely for self-preservation—but she stayed where she was. With her lips and her body making promises she wasn't prepared to keep, she reached up and over his shoulders toward the heavy glass light fixture.

The cover was loose. She'd been worried about it and tried to fasten the screws. Now she was glad that her efforts to shore it up had been only partially successful. In one swift motion she grasped the globe, wincing as the hot glass burned her hands. Ignoring the pain, she wrenched the fixture from the wall and brought it down on the back of Sam Lassiter's head.

He cried out, staggered backward against the wall. While he was reeling from the shock of the blow, she shoved him to the side, into the tub, where he went over the edge and collapsed like a wounded stag.

His groan of pain sent guilt stabbing through her. Lord, what had she done? But she wasn't about to stop and help him. Not when he worked for Eric Frees and her only goal was to get herself and Teddy away from him.

Seconds later she was out of the bathroom, slamming the door behind her as she focused on the boy, who was staring wide-eyed at her.

"Come on," she screamed, grabbing his hand, pulling him off the bed and toward the door. Then she remembered the car keys. They were in her purse, and she knew she wasn't going to get very far without them.

Opening the front door, she gave Teddy a little shove. "Run to the car."

"Laurel?"

"Just run, honey. I'll catch up with you. We have to get out of here."

Teddy did as he was told. Laurel found her purse, looked

frantically around the room one more time at the clothing and food she had to abandon. Then she sprinted out the door.

The scene in front of her registered in a second of shocked awareness. Teddy, following her directions, running headlong across the parking lot, all his attention focused on the car. So much so that he didn't see the truck that had just turned in—the truck that was bearing down on him because the driver was as oblivious as the small boy dashing into his path.

"Teddy, watch out!"

The shout came from behind her. From Sam Lassiter. Oh Lord, he was already out of the bathroom.

After what she'd done to him, he was probably ready to kill her. But she couldn't worry about him now.

Time seemed to speed up, like a movie on fast forward. There was no thought of her own safety. All she knew was that she had to save Teddy. Sprinting forward, she made a frantic leap into the path of the truck, her arms outstretched as she grabbed Teddy by the shirt and pulled him back, just as two tons of metal rolled over the spot where he'd been standing.

Brakes squeezed. A door slammed open, and the driver rushed toward her. "Lady, I didn't see the kid. Lady, are you okay?"

She nodded as she clutched Teddy to her, rocking him in her arms. At first he must have been too stunned to react. Then he began to sob.

"It's okay. It's okay," she soothed, knowing that nothing was okay. And maybe it never would be again.

CURSING AT HIS OWN STUPIDITY, Sam had staggered out of the bathroom and made it to the doorway of the motel in time to see the truck bearing down on Teddy.

There was nothing he could do. He was too far away

and too unsteady on his feet. His only option had been to shout a warning to the boy, then watch incredulously as Laurel dashed into the path of the vehicle and, with only agonizing seconds to spare, snatched the boy out of harm's way.

Leaning against the door frame, he watched the kneeling woman and the boy who clung to her for dear life.

He could see her breath trembling in—then out again.

"You're sure you're all right?" the truck driver was saying as he moved to Laurel's side.

Sam pushed away from the doorway and shambled unsteadily into the parking lot.

"Everything's under control," he answered, clamping his hand on the woman's shoulder. It was a slender shoulder, the bones too close to the surface. And it flashed through his mind that she was all tension and nerves. She raised her head and looked at him across the boy's tousled hair.

"Hey, I—" The driver's voice intruded on the silent message that passed between himself and Laurel.

"I'll take over from here," Sam said.

The driver hesitated uncertainly for a moment. Finally he moved back, climbed into his truck and steered the vehicle toward the motel office.

Sam, Laurel and Teddy were left alone at the edge of the parking lot. And Sam was left trying to reconcile Laurel's mad dash into the path of the truck and Teddy's turning to her for comfort with the image he'd formed from reading the files on her.

She looked so innocent, so shaken by what had just happened to the boy. Like a woman in need of someone to protect her.

But that was all a lie, he told himself as he fought against the reaction—and the pounding headache she'd given him.

She wasn't sweet and innocent. She was dangerous and immoral. He'd learned that from her dossier.

In high school, she'd gotten into several minor scrapes. Shoplifting. Drinking. Pot. Then she'd left home and moved in with a low-life creep named Oren Clark. She claimed that Clark had duped her into the previous kidnapping. She'd been eager to testify against him, but a jury had convicted her as an accessory after the fact.

Of course, she'd broken the destructive pattern when she was incarcerated at the women's prison in Jessup. She'd been so good that she'd gotten parole the first time she came up for a hearing.

Okay, so she'd be able to stay on her best behavior because she wanted to get out of the joint. He could understand that. Now that she was free, she'd gone back to her old behavior patterns.

Because no woman with a shred of moral fiber used tricks like the ones she'd just played on him. He reached to rub the back of his head, wincing as his fingers encountered bruised flesh, wondering if she'd given him a concussion when she'd bashed him with that heavy glass and shoved him into the tub.

God, what a jerk he'd been, letting down his guard like that. But she'd taken him by storm—then dulled his awareness of everything besides the pressure of her lips and body against his.

Guilt, chagrin and emotions he didn't care to explore waged a war inside his throbbing skull. Setting his teeth, he reminded himself that this wasn't about him and what he was feeling. It was about her. She was a kidnapper. A criminal. A woman who would shamelessly use her body to get what she wanted from a man.

Yet the image directly in front of his eyes didn't square with that assessment, not when she was curled so protectively around the child, and he was clinging to her as if she was his last best friend.

She held the little boy against her breast, soothing her hands over his hair and shoulder. But she raised her face to Sam, staring at him like a wild creature afraid to trust humanity.

"Don't hurt him," she whispered.

"I have no intention of hurting him. I'm planning to return him to his father."

"Eric will hurt him," she mouthed, the words barely audible.

"I don't believe that."

Her face contorted. "How can I convince you that he will?"

"Let's see…by sleeping with me?" he asked, his voice pitched almost as low as hers.

She squeezed her eyes shut for a moment. When she opened them again, they were full of such abject despair that he almost felt himself falling for her act.

"I made a mistake," she whispered, sounding as if she was trying to hold back tears.

"Which one?"

"All of them. I was scared. I'm still scared," she added, and he could see that the admission was costing her.

"You should be. Eric can get you for kidnapping, and I've got a good case for assault."

"None of that's important."

"Oh yeah?" He took her by the arm and pulled her to her feet. "Come on. We can't stay in the middle of this parking lot." Then, bringing his mouth close to her ear, he added, "Tell him that I'm not going to hurt either one of you."

"You want me to lie to him?"

"It's not a lie. It's the truth."

"Maybe you're not a bad man. You don't seem like the thugs who were with Eric that night. But you're his dupe."

The label grated.

"Laurel, where are we going?" the boy asked, his voice high and frightened.

She looked from him to Sam and back again.

"With Mr. Lassiter. He's not going to hurt us."

"But you told me to run."

"I guess I made a mistake."

"We're getting in my car," Sam said, holding tight to her arm as he walked her to the Chevy he was driving. He felt her muscles tense, and he prepared himself to have her wrench away.

"Let me get Teddy's booster seat."

"Okay." As he watched her unfasten it from her car and reattach it in his, he felt a pang he didn't want to examine too closely.

The kid scrambled into the seat, and Laurel strapped him in, then climbed in beside him. Once they were in the back seat, Sam snapped the child locks that prevented the back doors from opening without his disabling them from the front.

Slipping into the driver's seat, he wrapped his hands around the wheel and sat there with his eyes closed for a moment, thinking that he needed some ibuprofen.

"I thought we were getting out of here," she said from the back seat.

"My head hurts like a son of a bitch," he growled.

"I'm sorry."

"I'll bet."

She slid across the seat so that she was sitting in back of him. "Let me look at it."

He didn't want her to touch him again, not after he'd fallen for her cheap trick, yet he couldn't see the place where she'd bashed him, only gauge the shape of the goose egg. "Why the change of heart?" he asked.

"I told you, I'm feeling bad about...what I did."

"A few minutes ago? Or a few days ago?"

"A few minutes ago. What I did a few days ago was the right thing."

"Uh-huh."

"Let me see how badly I hurt you." Her fingers were gentle as she touched his scalp. "You're cut a little. Not bad. And there's a lump."

"A big lump."

"Yes."

He should go to a drugstore and get some antiseptic. But if he took Laurel inside, she might make a run for it again, and he wasn't going to take another chance on losing her. On the other hand, if he left her in the car, he'd have to cuff her to the hand grip on the side of the door, which might freak out the boy, who didn't exactly seem to be reacting normally. He was too quiet. Too controlled. Too obedient. And too under the sway of Laurel Coleman.

His best bet was to call Eric Frees and tell him that he'd located his son. Yet something was stopping him from pulling out his cell phone. Despite reading Laurel Coleman's record, despite the evidence against her now, she had planted a seed of doubt in his mind when she had dashed into the path of that truck.

So perhaps the best thing was to spend a little more time with them. He swung around to look at Teddy.

"There's a drive-through up the road. How about a hamburger and fries?"

The child looked from him to Laurel. "Is it okay?"

"Yes."

Sam started the car, pulled out of the parking lot and headed for the McDonald's on the highway.

"You want a Happy Meal?" he asked as they approached the speaker.

"How do you know about Happy Meals?" Teddy asked. "Do you have a little boy?"

Sam felt his stomach tie itself in a sudden, painful knot. "I had a little girl," he said in a thick voice.

"Where did she go?"

"She died," he murmured.

"Is she in heaven, like my dog, Peanuts?"

"Yes."

"With God and Jesus."

"Yes."

"Then she's happy, and she gets to play all the time and have fun. But you miss her."

He could only manage a tight nod.

"Your order, sir?"

Realizing from the tone of voice that the person at the other end of the intercom must have asked the question earlier, he swung toward the speaker, cleared his throat and said, "Just a second."

"What do you want?" he asked Laurel without looking at her.

"Fries and a Coke, I guess."

He ordered the same thing, although he wasn't sure he could get any food down at the moment.

After picking up the order, he drove to a spot near some white pine trees and handed most of the food to Laurel without looking at her.

Finally, when he figured he could control his expression, he twisted around. She was spreading a napkin on Teddy's lap and had unwrapped his hamburger. The boy rummaged in the box and brought out a plastic play figure, which he turned in his hand, quietly examining it from all angles.

"Let's eat first," Laurel said.

The kid dutifully took a bite of his burger, swallowed.

Sam watched them together. Laurel appeared downright maternal as she hovered over the child. Probably they would have been totally comfortable together if he hadn't been there.

He watched Teddy flick him a quick gaze, then turn back to his burger.

To ease his dry throat, Sam took a sip of his Coke, then another. "So what are you and Laurel doing up here in this neck of the woods?"

The boy kept his eyes on his food. "We're having an adventure."

"Why? I mean, why did you leave home?"

He watched Laurel tense, watched the kid swallow the food in his mouth. "Something bad happened at my house."

"So what did you do?"

"We went across the porch roof and climbed down a tree. I was scared, but Laurel told me everything was going to be okay."

"Scared of what?"

The boy kept his head bent. "My dad."

"Why?"

"He was in the hall, shouting." Teddy hesitated, leaned closer to Laurel.

"What else do you want to say?" Sam prompted.

"It's okay to tell him," Laurel murmured.

"He was mad. He gets mad a lot."

Sam considered the youngster's answers. They sounded genuine. But Laurel could have coached him, could have suggested what had happened. He'd read about how people could plant false memories in children's minds. There were day-care center workers who had been put in jail for sexually assaulting the children in their care, and it had turned out the suggestions of abuse had come from the well-meaning police and district attorneys who had asked the questions in such a way that the kids had given them the answers they wanted and expected. Something similar happened with troubled adults who had gone for counseling and emerged with memories of childhood traumas that had never happened.

Carefully Sam asked, "Did you see him hurt...anyone?"

"No. Me and Laurel were in her room. But I heard him yelling at my mom."

Laurel raised her chin, giving him a direct look.

The boy's version sounded like the one she'd told. But Sam still wasn't sure.

"Are you a policeman?" the boy asked suddenly.

Sam's gaze shot back to him. "I used to be a policeman. Now I'm a private detective. What makes you think I'm a policeman?"

The boy shrugged. "I saw a show on TV once where the police were after this boy who ran away."

Sam nodded.

"Did Laurel and me do something wrong?"

Sam swiped a hand through his dark hair, trying to sort out truth from fiction. Eric Frees had hired him to find his son and the woman who had kidnapped him. But now that he'd found them, they told a very different version of events from the story Eric had given him. Was his obligation to the man who was paying for his services? Or was it to the boy and the woman in the back seat?

Chapter Three

Laurel held her breath as she waited for Lassiter's answer.

"No," he finally said.

Relief flooded through her. Then she reminded herself that his words meant nothing—beyond the fact that he was trying not to upset Teddy.

The boy nodded and began chomping on his burger again.

When Laurel's nerves were stretched as thin as tissue paper, she cleared her throat.

As the man's dark eyes focused on her face, she almost lost her nerve. But she managed to ask, "So are you going to turn us in?"

"I don't know."

A fraction of her tension eased. He was thinking about what he'd heard, maybe what he'd seen. She wished she knew exactly what was running through his mind.

"What are you going to do?"

He looked at her consideringly. "Sleep on it."

The way he said it sent a shiver skittering over her skin. Was he implying that he was going to sleep with *her?* In the bathroom, she'd probably given him the impression that sex for favors was an option.

She looked down at her Coke, toying with the straw, wishing she hadn't come on to him like that. Her behavior might determine whether he turned her in, and now she didn't know what to do or what to say. Lord, she was in a trap, and she'd sprung it on herself.

She bent the straw in half as she tried to think. Be herself. That was Cindy's advice when she'd said that she didn't know how to act around people.

Be herself.

She was herself with Teddy. She'd been herself with Cindy. But with anyone else it was so hard.

Cindy had told her she'd paid her debt to society. What's more, she wasn't the same depressed, out-of-control girl who'd fled from her stepfather, then let Oren Clark influence her thinking.

She knew that much. She'd changed. Not just because she'd been locked away from society. She'd wanted desperately to change. But that didn't make it easy for her to know what to do and say.

She swallowed and tried to ask Sam what he meant. "You mean, stay up here? With us?"

"Yeah."

"The motel room's paid for."

The moment she'd said it, she wished she could take it back. That was the room where she'd kissed him then made her desperate escape attempt.

"Okay, since your stuff is there." He looked toward Teddy. "You finished with your meal?"

"Can I keep my Coke while we drive?"

"Sure."

She gave Sam points for that. Eric Frees had never let Teddy eat or drink in his immaculately kept car.

It was getting dark as they retraced the route they'd taken, and Lassiter switched on the headlights. Laurel slung her arm around Teddy and focused on the back of the detective's head. He'd had a daughter, and she'd died. Did that mean he also had a wife? She looked at the hands gripping the steering wheel. No wedding ring. But that didn't prove anything.

Her nerves twanged as they pulled into the motel parking lot. It was less crowded today, and Lassiter was able to find a space close to their room. He left her and Teddy in the car while he went around to the trunk. When he came back, he was carrying an overnight bag.

"You've got the key?" he asked as he opened her car door.

Her fingers felt cased in layers of wool, and she almost dropped the key as she handed it to him.

"Go inside," Lassiter said to Teddy after he opened the door and flicked the light switch. "We'll be right there."

The boy did as he was told, and Laurel looked at their captor questioningly. "What?"

"Does Teddy know his mother's dead?" he asked in a low voice.

She shook her head. "No. And don't tell him. Not yet."

They stared at each other for charged seconds, and she would have given ten years of her life to know what he was thinking.

"We'd better go in," he said.

As Laurel stepped into the dim glow cast by the lamps, she was glad then that she'd kept things relatively neat. Their clothing was in plastic bags, all piled in one corner of the room. And the groceries were confined to the dresser. Still, she felt as if Lassiter was evaluating her housekeeping.

"It's hard to keep things neat in one room," she heard herself saying.

"Uh-huh."

She turned to Teddy. "Let's have your bath."

"I don't want a bath. My boat and my rubber clown are back at home."

"But we have the sponges I got you. Those are fun."

"I want my boat and my rubber clown."

Because she didn't want to deal with Lassiter, she started to hustle Teddy into the bathroom.

"Just a minute," he said, pushing past her and entering the small room. She cringed when she saw him inspect the dangling sconce. Then he moved to the window, pushed up the lower sash—she supposed to see how easily it opened—then closed it again.

When he looked meaningfully back at her, she lifted her chin. "I'm not going anywhere."

"You've changed your mind about running?"

"I don't think I'd get very far. You're too fast for me."

"You're learning. But just in case you get any bright ideas, leave your jeans, shoes and socks out here."

"I beg your pardon?"

"Your jeans, shoes and socks."

She stared at him for several seconds. Then, because she really had no choice, she stepped into the bathroom, closed the door partway and shucked off the required clothing. Reaching through the door, she set them on the rug in a little heap.

Without waiting for permission, she turned and closed the door.

"Why did he make you take your pants off?" Teddy asked.

She heaved a sigh. "He wants to make sure we won't run away."

"We won't, will we? I like him."

"I thought you were afraid of him."

"Not now."

She wanted to tell the boy he had poor taste in men, but she settled for murmuring a noncommittal reply. As she started running the bathwater, she realized she'd forgotten to bring in clean underpants and the T-shirt Teddy had been sleeping in. Leaving him standing beside the tub, she opened the bathroom door and stepped out.

Lassiter was lying on the bed by the window, his hands stacked behind his head. His shoes and shoulder holster were off. She glanced around but didn't see his gun. Maybe he'd put it somewhere he knew Teddy couldn't find it.

He looked at her from under hooded lids. A look she couldn't read, yet it fueled the feeling of intimacy that was gathering in the motel room.

She was covered by her T-shirt, she told herself. She was less exposed than if she were wearing a bathing suit. Still, she looked quickly away from him as she found the clothing, darted back into the bathroom and started to close the door.

"I didn't say you could shut the door. Leave it open so I can hear you," the man on the bed called out.

She bit back a sharp retort, then knelt beside the tub, turned off the water and tested the temperature. Next, she helped Teddy into the water.

"No. Don't do anything until I get there," the man who had hired Sam Lassiter said, his voice betraying little of his seething emotions. "I want to be in on the kill."

"Yes, sir."

"I'll be leaving within a half hour." Without further conversation, he set the phone carefully in the cradle. He'd counted on Sam Lassiter's integrity. But he hadn't trusted the man, not completely.

So he'd had men tailing the P.I. at a discreet distance, made possible by the transponder that he'd had attached under the bumper of the man's car. Which was why he knew what was going on up there in Grantville. Lassiter had located Laurel and Teddy, but he hadn't jumped to report the information to his employer.

A bad move on Lassiter's part.

But it wouldn't make any difference in the end. He was going to get all three of them. And this time he had the perfect cover story. He would blame the death of his son and the nanny on the boozing detective. He'd been thinking about how to do it, and he'd come up with a very creative scenario.

OUT IN THE BEDROOM, Sam squeezed his eyes shut as he listened to the sounds from behind the half-open door.

Domestic sounds of a woman giving a small child a bath. The woman using the sponges to squeeze water over the child's head. The child squealing in delight. The two of them giggling together.

Sam felt his throat thicken, felt his eyes burn as he remembered another motel room, another bed, another time when he'd listened to happy noises like that through the bathroom door.

Jan giving Ellen a bath the last night they'd all been together. Of course he hadn't known then that it was the last time. He'd lain in bed, half drowsing, half listening. Half appreciating.

The next day, in a few seconds of terror, his wife and daughter had been snatched away from him. Again the image of a car hurtling out of the darkness assaulted him, and he clenched his hands into fists at his sides and squeezed his eyes shut, willing the memory and the pain to go away.

In that one blinding instant, he'd lost everything that had mattered to him.

And for months he'd taken refuge in a bourbon bottle. He'd been on the wagon now for longer than his drinking bout. Still tonight, with his insides burning, he knew that a glass of bourbon could ease the pain in his gut.

Another excuse for a drink! He gave a little snort. Excuses came to him with disgusting regularity. But he wasn't stupid enough to act on them. Not tonight. Not any night.

And he'd better not forget why the bathroom door was ajar. Because he couldn't trust Laurel Coleman any farther than he could heave her across the parking lot outside. Laurel wasn't Jan. And Teddy certainly wasn't Ellen, his smart, adorable daughter. But being with the boy had stirred up emotions he'd tried to bury.

Laurel was a bundle of contradictions. He knew she was afraid of him, yet she'd hatched a desperate plan to get away.

He thought again of her mouth and body pressed to his. In the moments before she'd bashed him on the head, she'd projected a kind of innocence. That had to be pure fantasy on his part. Laurel Coleman was no innocent. She was a convicted felon.

Still, she might be telling him the truth about the night she'd fled with Teddy Frees. And even if she wasn't, her vulnerability was no illusion. She was in trouble. Which didn't mean she was on the right side of the law, he reminded himself sternly.

Eyes closed, he tried to sort out fact from fiction, reality from illusion. But he still didn't have all the answers he needed.

He kept his ears trained on the bathroom, his uneasiness mounting as the minutes ticked by. They'd been in there an awful long time for a kid's bath. Was she hatching some new scheme?

Finally he heard her pull the plug. Then he guessed that she was drying the kid off.

His insides squeezed as he remembered that wonderful smell of a freshly scrubbed little body.

Through slitted eyes, he watched the bathroom door open as Laurel ushered Teddy toward the opposite bed. She made a show of acting as if there was nobody else in the room as she moved around the small space, turning off all the lights except one.

Her efforts were spoiled when the boy called out, "Good night, Mr. Lassiter."

"Good night," he answered, watching her lean over to kiss the boy's cheek, wondering if she realized she was giving him a tantalizing view of her behind.

"You can't put me to bed without the Big Brown Bear story," Teddy objected.

He heard her sigh, then watched as she eased onto the bed and started talking in a low voice, deliberately excluding him. But he caught the gist of the story. It was about a brown bear who wanted to live in a house, sleep in a featherbed and eat sugar cakes.

Struggling to keep a smile off his face, he listened to the tall tale, thinking that Laurel Coleman was certainly charming and inventive.

When the boy finally drifted off to sleep, she stood, turned away from the bed and started to stretch. But she must have realized that the motion was pulling the front of her shirt against her breasts.

Very nice breasts, he thought, struggling not to react.

Quickly she lowered her arms. "I'm going to take a shower. I hope you're going to let me close the bathroom door."

"The boy's out here. I think you'll stick around. But don't lock the door."

"Why not?"

"I'm reckless, but not stupid."

She didn't answer, only disappeared into the bathroom and closed the door. He listened to the rustling sounds from inside, unable to stop himself from picturing her taking off her clothing. Then when the shower came on, he switched the image to a naked Laurel standing under the spray, water cascading down her breasts, over her nipples. In his imagination he made them plump and pink to go with her pale skin. Then his imaginary gaze swept lower, down the flat plane of her belly to the thick triangle of dark hair at the juncture of her legs.

He squeezed his eyes tightly shut, gathered up handfuls of the bedspread, trying to banish the image. God, he'd been without a woman for too long, he thought, shifting uncomfortably on the bed, trying to ease the pressure of his erection against the fly of his jeans. There had been a few women not long after Jan had died. Several times he'd been half sloshed in a bar and one of the female patrons had taken him home for the night. He could remember disappointing some of them—the amount of alcohol in his system making it impossible for him to perform. But there had been a few wild, uninhibited sexual encounters, sessions that he was glad he couldn't remember all that well.

The water switched off. A short shower. Was she afraid he'd come bursting through the door? Eyes still closed, he listened to more small sounds, imagining the play of the towel across her back, her shoulders and other parts of her body.

The sensual images dissolved in a piercing scream that came from beyond the bathroom door.

Sam was off the bed in the blink of an eye. Sprinting across the room, he pulled open the bathroom door and surged inside.

Laurel was standing in the center of the floor, dressed only in a pair of cotton panties and the least feminine-looking bra he'd ever seen. A towel was pooled around her feet.

Her face was startlingly pale, her eyes large and brown, and she was holding up her right hand, staring at the black streaks across her fingers.

"What happened?" he demanded.

"I…" Her voice hitched and she began again. "I was drying my hair. The sconce started falling, and I couldn't see what I was doing. I reached to push it back in place and—and the insulation must have pulled off the wires when I...when...'' She didn't have to explain the rest. They both knew when the sconce had come loose.

Crossing the room, he took her hand in his, looking down at the black marks and the blisters that were already starting to form. Turning on the cold water, he thrust her fingers under the stream from the faucet, then worked the stopper and pushed her hand into the water filling the basin.

''You got a shock. And a burn,'' he muttered. ''It hurts, but you're lucky as hell the floor wasn't wet.''

She bowed her head. ''I wiped it with one of the bath towels so you wouldn't think the place was a mess when you came in here.'' Her voice quavered on the end of the sentence. He felt her shoulders heave, then a giant sob swelled up from her chest into her throat, low and deep.

He could identify with what she was feeling. Utter helplessness. It wasn't just the fright and the injury. She'd been pushed about as far as she could bend. And now this. Holding her hand in the water, he reached around her with the other arm and gathered her close.

When he felt her stiffen, he murmured, ''It's okay. It's okay to let somebody else do the worrying for a change.''

''Is it?'' The question came out as a gasp.

''Yes.''

She hesitated for another moment, then he felt her unbend, felt her melt against him. He still didn't know whether he could trust her, and he understood that she felt the same way about him. But right now she needed comfort and first aid. He tried to remember what he knew about burns. The cold water would help numb the pain and keep down the blisters.

He ran his hand through her wet hair, pressed her head to his shoulder, trying to give her basic human contact, trying not to react to her near nudity and the wonderful clean scent of her skin.

He felt her shivering in the cool air coming from the bedroom. Lifting her in his arms, he carried her across the carpet, then glanced over his shoulder to look at Teddy. The boy was still sleeping.

When Sam reached the other side of the room, he felt her stiffen again and try to pull away.

"Not the bed!" she gasped between sobs.

"What?"

"Not the bed," she repeated.

"Okay." Lowering himself to the easy chair, he cradled her on his lap. Then he reached forward, pulled the spread off the bed and tucked it around her, giving her warmth as well as some modesty. And giving himself a set of mixed feelings that he was hardly prepared to deal with.

He felt protective toward her and lustful at the same time. There was the part of him that kept remembering his basic knowledge of criminals. Jail didn't mean rehabilitation; it just took the bad guys off the streets for a few years. But as he stroked Laurel's back and shoulders, it hardly seemed right that the philosophy of criminal behavior should be applied to the woman in his arms.

His lips skimmed her hair as he murmured soothing words, and he closed his eyes because he wanted to be totally absorbed in her. He felt her shivering and sobs gradually fade. Twisting around, he handed her a tissue from the box she'd left on the end table.

"Thanks." She blew her nose, and burrowed farther under the spread.

"Does your hand hurt?"

"That's the least of my problems." She turned her head and looked over at Teddy. He hadn't moved. Apparently he was too exhausted to take any notice of what else was going on in the room.

When she started to rise, he put a firm hand on her shoulder. "Stay here."

"Why?"

"I don't want you to feel like you have to run away from me." As soon as the words were out of his mouth, he wondered why he'd spoken them and what exactly they meant.

She stared at him. "Are you saying you've changed your mind about me?"

Had he? Carefully he said, "Tell me why I should."

She sighed, shifting so she could press the heels of her hands against her eyes. "Why should I assume you'll believe anything I say to you?"

"Maybe I want to. If you just play fair with me."

She was quiet for several moments, then said, "You've been assuming I'm the same person I was five years ago when I let Oren Clark trick me into helping him with that kidnapping."

"And you're somebody different now?"

"What happened then has nothing to do with me and Teddy running away. I've changed a lot since...going to prison."

Disappointment surged through him. He'd heard that line before, and he'd expected better from her.

She continued in a halting voice. "I made a bad mistake—trusting Oren...but there were reasons why I started hanging around with him."

"Such as?"

She looked as if she wished she hadn't opened up the subject of the past.

"I'd like to hear them," he prompted.

"What difference does it make?"

"I'm trying to understand you."

She worried her lower lip between her teeth. "If I tell you the truth, you're going to think I'm trying to make you feel sorry for me. I mean, it's an ugly story."

"Let me be the judge of that."

She considered his words, sighed again, then began in a tentative voice. "Okay. The first ten years of my life were nice and normal. You know that unemployment is high up here. But both my parents had pretty good jobs. My mom was a secretary at a lumber company. My dad worked for the phone company. I was mostly happy. Actually, I didn't know how good I had it. Then…" Her voice hitched, and she was silent for several seconds. "Then my dad got cancer and died. For a couple of years it was pretty hard making ends meet on just my mom's salary and the little bit of pension money she got from Dad. Then she started dating Ralph."

She said the name as though it were a curse word, and the implications had every muscle in his body going tense.

"He married her. And she completely changed who she was to accommodate him. He had two kids of his own, and Mom had me. But the way things worked out, his kids got all the advantages. I mean, like new shoes when they needed them, new clothes, toys. What I got was the message that I was lower than dirt. That I didn't measure up. One of them got my old bedroom and I got moved down to the basement. Not a finished basement—just a room with cinder-block walls. And, uh…and, uh—" She stopped suddenly, as if she'd just realized where her story was leading.

Turning her face away from him, she curled her body into itself. "I thought I could, but I can't tell you any more," she whispered.

She sat with her head bowed, looking so small and vulnerable that his heart turned over inside his chest. At the same time he felt a kind of sick fear growing inside him. Fear that he already knew what had happened to her.

"You can tell me," he prompted in a low voice, not wanting to hear what came next but knowing that he had to deal with it because that was part of understanding this woman.

He felt her whole body radiating tension, then in a rush of words, she blurted out, "And Ralph used to come down there to visit me. Convenient for him, having me away from everybody else."

His curse made her gulp back a sob, and he laid a gentle hand on her shoulder.

"He...did things to you? In bed?"

She gave a tight nod. "Things he shouldn't have been doing. Then I'd hear him telling my mom that I was no good. That I was a slut. That I was coming on to boys."

Acid burned in his gut. Again he couldn't hold back a curse. "That bastard. Did he rape you?"

"No." She sucked in a breath. "He just...touched me...and made me touch him. Maybe at first he was afraid that he'd get in trouble if anyone could prove what he'd been doing with a thirteen-year-old kid. Then maybe later he was afraid he'd get me pregnant." She gulped. "By the time I was sixteen, I had to get out of there. So when Oren Clark started acting like he liked me, I...moved in with him."

Sam wasn't sure what was the right thing to do then. So he simply sat there, holding her, stroking her hair as she pressed her forehead against his shoulder.

"Did you tell your mom what your stepfather was doing?" he asked.

"When I finally worked up the guts, she didn't believe me. Or she didn't want to believe. I don't know which."

His hands soothed across her shoulders. "I'm sorry."

"It's not your fault."

"What happened to you should never have happened to any kid."

She raised her head, her eyes seeking his. "You don't think I'm...bad?"

"Of course not!"

"You did. I mean when you first grabbed me and shoved

me back inside the room. I saw it in your eyes. You thought I was the scum of the earth for taking Teddy away from his dad.''

He remembered what he had been feeling then. It was miles away from what he felt now. He'd told her he wanted to understand her. He thought that maybe he did. Maybe because he'd been through so much horror himself, and he knew that it had changed him. Changed the way he looked at life, changed his motivations.

He thought he understood why she'd been desperate to save a small boy named Teddy Frees. Why she'd risked her life for him. Still, he wasn't sure what to say to her. And speech was such an inadequate means of expression. He felt humble before her now. He felt mangled inside. He felt the spirit-crushing weight of the pain and terror and confusion she had endured. Wordlessly, he lowered his head and gently brushed his lips against hers. Then, before the gesture could go any further, he pulled back.

Her small sound of surprise almost undid him. He wanted to gather her close. Instead he stayed where he was, with his hands pressed to his sides.

Her eyes were large and round as she focused on him.

''You don't talk about your stepfather much, do you?''

''No, I don't. I told Cindy. And…and my therapist in prison.''

''And me,'' he added softly.

''I wanted you to stop hating me.''

''I didn't!''

''Well, you believed what Eric said about that night.''

''I had pretty good reasons to believe him.''

''And now?'' she asked, going very still.

''Now I think you ran away with Teddy because you were afraid for his life.''

''Just because of what I told you? Maybe it's a lie.''

He shook his head in denial. ''No. Not from the way

your face looked when you were talking. And then there's Teddy. I watched you with him. I know how you feel about him—and how he feels about you. He loves you and you love him.''

"Thank you for saying that.''

"It's true.''

She looked down at her hands again. "Eric was a strange man. Harsh. And he terrified Teddy. I don't know why Cindy married him.'' She drew in a breath and let it out. "Well, maybe I do. He was rich, and she saw him as a way to get the things she always wanted. But it didn't work out so well for her.''

"Or you.''

"Then you'll help us?''

"Yes.''

She touched her fingertips to his face. "You said you had a little girl. You said she died.''

He nodded because he couldn't speak.

"Are you married?''

"I was.'' He swallowed, thinking she had told him her painful secrets and he could do no less. But it was still hard to force the words from his suddenly dry lips. "Jan and Ellen died when a drunk driver barreled across the median and plowed into us.''

"I'm so sorry.'' This time she was the one who moved forward, the one who touched her lips to his. It was simply a brush of mouth against mouth, but he sensed that the gesture came from her heart.

He closed his eyes and stroked his hand up and down her arm.

Her face was so close that he could see a faint, tiny scar high up on her cheek. It made him wonder if her stepfather or the other jerk—Oren Clark—had hit her.

He wouldn't hurt her. Not physically. He didn't beat up

on women to inflate his own ego. But he needed to tell her that she'd be a fool to trust a guy with his track record.

Pure male selfishness kept him from breaking the contact of her mouth to his. In fact, he was aching to gather her up and take her to the bed. But doing anything so overtly sexual was out of the question after what she'd revealed to him.

So he kept his hands off of her, his mouth undemanding. Her lips were soft, supple, surprisingly unschooled as they moved over his, and he gave in to the luxury of being kissed so sweetly.

"That's nice," she breathed, her voice holding a note of wonder.

He touched her mouth with the tip of his tongue then. Just a small gentle touch. But her lips parted and he stroked along the warm, sensitive flesh on the inside of her lips.

"Oh…that feels good." Her voice sounded breathy, as if she couldn't believe the experience was real.

It had been so long since he had felt this kind of warmth, this kind of sharing. This kind of need.

His blood was humming, and it took all his willpower not to make demands he had no right to make. They had hardly done anything, yet his body felt as though it were on fire. And the roaring in his ears blocked out all sound from the outside world.

Which was why he didn't hear the door open. Didn't hear anything until Eric's Frees's voice penetrated his fogged brain.

"Well, well. I see why my private detective hasn't bothered to call me. He's been too busy making it with the little bitch I sent him to bring home."

Chapter Four

The gun was on the top shelf of the closet, where Teddy couldn't get at it. And there was no way Sam could get to it, either. Not with Eric Frees and two goons standing over him, their own weapons drawn.

Eric reached for Laurel and pulled her up. She made a grab for the spread, clutching it around her.

"Put some clothes on," he growled. "Once a whore, always a whore."

Her face was pale as moonlight as she scurried across the room and rummaged in one of the bags against the wall for a pair of sweatpants and a T-shirt. Teddy was sitting up in bed rubbing his eyes. When he focused on Frees, he gasped, then started whimpering.

Laurel was beside him instantly, gathering him close, speaking in a low, soothing voice, telling him that everything was okay.

Sam doubted it.

Eric turned back to him.

"I expected to hear from you this afternoon."

"I didn't expect you to come bursting in here with guns drawn. You can put them away."

"I don't think so."

Sam's mind was churning. This afternoon he hadn't spotted a tail. Yet Frees had known exactly where to find him.

Which meant that anyone following him didn't need to keep him in sight...Frees must have slapped a transponder on the car.

Sam cut Laurel a glance, knowing she wasn't going to like hearing what he had to say next. But telling Eric Frees the truth didn't seem like the smartest thing to do.

"I was going to call you," he said in an even voice. "But then the chick and I got kind of friendly. You know what they say about all work and no play."

Frees stared at him. "I don't believe you."

"Why not?"

"You're not that kind of guy. And even if you were, Bo and Frank have been keeping tabs on you, like at McDonald's," he answered, confirming Sam's speculation. "It looks like you were just as interested in making friends with the kid. So let's cut the crap and get down to business."

"Bo, break out the good stuff."

One of the men stepped forward and Sam saw that a tote bag was slung over his shoulder. As he lowered it to the table, something inside thunked against the flat surface. With a flourish, he pulled out a fifth of bourbon and set it down. The sound of the glass hitting the wood sounded like a cannon shot in Sam's ear.

"Don't know if this is your brand," Frees said conversationally, "but I do know bourbon's your drink. So I guess you can make do in a pinch."

"I'm not drinking that stuff!" Sam growled.

Involuntarily, his eyes flicked to Laurel. She was watching him with a kind of sick horror on her face.

"I thought you had a craving for it. I mean, isn't that why you got kicked off the Baltimore P. D.? Didn't you disappear inside a bottle after you lost your wife and kid?"

Sam kept his gaze level. "I didn't get kicked off. I resigned."

"A minor distinction," Frees said as he twisted the top and broke the seal on the bottle.

Sam could smell the pungent aroma of the bourbon drifting toward him. His chest tightened, and he felt a trickle of sweat slide down his neck. He hadn't had a drink in over a year, and he wasn't going to start now. Yet the aroma of the booze seemed to tug seductively at him, like a long lost lover who had finally returned.

Frees continued in a conversational tone, "See, everything is going to work out perfectly. It looked like my wife was killed by the nanny who pushed her down the stairs. Only, the two of you were working together. Unfortunately for you, you got yourself sloshed and took my son and his kidnapper for a ride down Winding Mountain. Too bad none of you is going to walk away from the plunge over the side of the cliff."

"In your dreams," Sam snapped, his mind frantically searching for a way out.

As Frees crossed to the bathroom, Sam's mind was still racing, trying to improve their chances. Twisting his body slightly, he reached into his pocket, pulled out his car keys and wedged them down into the chair cushion.

When Frees returned with one of the motel glasses, Sam was sitting with his hands folded in his lap. "You can't get me to drink that."

"Oh, I think you'll cooperate with me," Frees said, turning toward the man who stood over Laurel and Teddy. "Frank, show him what's going to happen if he doesn't take his medicine like a good little boy."

The man pulled Teddy away from Laurel. When she made a grab for him, the thug gave her a shove that sent her sprawling across the bed. Then, taking out his gun, he pressed the barrel against Teddy's head and cocked the trigger.

Laurel made a sobbing sound.

"If you don't want to see the boy get blown away, you'd better start drinking."

"No," Laurel begged, her frantic gaze swinging from the gunman to Sam.

"Pour yourself a stiff one," Frees said, his voice deathly calm. "Or drink it straight out of the bottle. I don't care which."

Concentrating on keeping his hand from shaking, Sam picked up the bottle and poured the amber liquid into the glass because at the moment there was no escape. Not yet.

"Drink it!"

The glass was smooth and cool in his hand, giving him a chill all the way down his spine. He'd sworn he'd never do this again. Now, as he lifted the rim to his lips, he closed his eyes. The first swallow burned his mouth, burned all the way down his throat. The rest went down smoothly, too smoothly.

Fast or slow... Should he do this fast or slow? He wished he knew which would help him keep his wits longer.

Frees was looking at him now like a bright-eyed crow swooping down on roadkill. He was enjoying this. "More," he demanded when Sam had emptied the glass.

He drank again, and this time it was easier. The terror of that almost overwhelmed him. Then a kind of foggy feeling took over.

Vaguely, he remembered what he'd read: Booze hit you faster when you were a recovering alcoholic. Unfortunately, it seemed to be true.

He found he could gulp the stuff like water from the fountain of youth.

Not my fault. Not my fault. The words were like a chant in his brain. He clutched at them like a lifeline, aware that everybody in the room was watching him. He kept his own gaze focused on a stain on the carpet.

"More." Frees's voice came to him from across time and space.

He felt numb, weightless. Detached. Yet somewhere inside the fog, he was still thinking, still making plans that might never come to fruition.

Voices were a blur from outer space. But he assumed someone had told Laurel to get Teddy dressed because he could see her pulling on his shirt.

One thing he knew, they needed to get the show on the road. And fast, before he was too wasted to function.

He made a show of trying to pour, sloshing liquid down the side of the glass.

Frees took the bottle away.

"You said more," he complained, tripping over his tongue, yet slurring his speech even more than necessary. "You son a bitch..." He leaped to his feet, swinging ineffectually at Frees, then let the man punch him in the jaw. He staggered back as Bo—or was it Frank?—came forward.

"You want me to work him over, boss?"

"No. I don't want him to throw up all that nice bourbon and make us have to start all over again. Just get his car keys."

The man felt in Sam's pocket, then turned toward the dresser. "I can't find them."

"Where are the keys?" Frees demanded, giving Sam a shake.

He shrugged, looked confused. "Don't know."

Frees cursed, then strode across the room and picked up Laurel's purse. When he found her keys, he looked relieved. "We can use the whore's car."

Laurel's car. Thank God, Sam thought in some dim recess of his brain, although he couldn't remember why it was important.

"Frank, you drive him up the mountain to the drop-off."

Frank took his arm and led him toward the door. There was nothing Sam could say to Laurel, no way he could tell her what he had planned. All he could do was give her a wide-eyed look as he passed and mumble, "Cooperate."

"What was that?" Frees demanded.

Sam gave him a foolish grin.

LAUREL CAUGHT the look in Sam's eyes, heard his mumbled advice, and hope surged through her. It wasn't over. He was going to try something. But what? When?

Maybe before they got into the car.

The warm night air slapped her in the face as Bo steered her and Teddy toward the Mustang.

Frank led Sam, who shuffled along behind them, hanging back, she thought. Or maybe he was too wasted to do anything. Maybe the part about a rescue attempt was pure fantasy.

Frank inserted the key in the lock. Bo opened the back door and shoved her and Teddy inside.

It was all over, she thought with despair.

Then things started happening faster than she could take them in.

Sam slugged Bo, pulled Frank out of the front seat and slid behind the wheel, slamming the door behind him just in time to keep the thug from reaching him.

Frank was grabbing for the outside door handle when she lunged forward and snapped the locks.

Frees was cursing. His men were banging ineffectually on the windows as Sam turned the key, and the engine sprang to life. Instead of backing up, he shot forward and bounced over the curb, cursing loudly as the rear end of the car thunked against the lip of concrete.

He kept going through a stand of pine trees, spewing out more curses as branches slapped the windshield, then scraped the side of the car.

She wanted to scream at him to watch out, wanted to ask if he knew what he was doing. But she could see his hands clutching the wheel in a death grip, and she understood he had all he could do to cope with the car. Never mind an hysterical woman in the back seat.

So she turned her attention to Teddy, frantically trying to snap his seat belt into place, then her own.

"Laurel, Laurel, what are we doing?" he asked.

"Getting away."

Sam hunched forward, making an abrupt circle that sent the tires squealing on the pavement.

Her heart was in her throat as he came swinging back into the parking lot.

"Sam, we've got to get out of here!" she shouted.

"Gotta keep them here, baby," he shouted back as he aimed the car at the thugs.

She was glad she and Teddy were belted in as the car hit Frank with a thumping noise, sending him flying backward into a porch post. Frees was quick enough to jump out of the way. His gun was in his hand, and Laurel expected the impact of bullets crashing into the car. But doors were already opening along the row of motel rooms. Shooting at them would certainly kill the theory of accidental death.

Teddy had started sobbing. Knowing he must be terrified, Laurel turned her attention to him, holding him close as Sam sideswiped Eric's big black car, knocking out one taillight, then circling back again to ram the other side of the vehicle, driving a fender into one of the back tires.

With the Mustang a moving wreck, he careened toward the strip of motel rooms, sending shrieking people back into their rooms. Overcorrecting, he sideswiped another car with a screech of tearing metal.

"Sam, get out of here! Go! Go!"

Somehow he made it out of the lot, then wove down the

road, headlights off. Twice he drifted across the white line, and she thanked God that no one else was on the road.

Each time he pulled the car back onto his own side of the pavement. A moment later he drifted into the other lane again, just as she saw headlights knifing toward them out of the darkness. Big headlights—from a truck.

"Sam, Sam, get back on your own side of the road," she screamed.

He swerved abruptly right, pulling onto the shoulder as the truck roared by, shaking the car in the backwash of wind.

Sam cursed and slammed on the brakes, jolting Laurel forward, almost catapulting her into the front seat.

"You better drive, baby," he muttered. "I'm wasted."

She pulled up the door locks, ran to the driver's side, but had trouble yanking open the caved-in door.

Finally, when she leaned inside and tried to move Sam out of the way, she found he was immobile and slumped over the wheel. And apparently he hadn't even thought about putting the car in park or pulling up the emergency brake, because it began drifting slowly forward. Frantically, she heaved at the dead weight in the driver's seat.

"Move, damn you. Move!" she sobbed out, pounding his shoulder with her fists as she kept up with the rolling vehicle.

"No need to…get your dander up," he muttered, and heaved himself into the passenger seat and sprawled with his head back, breathing heavily.

She slid behind the wheel, then saw they were drifting into a drainage ditch.

Heart in her throat, she yanked the vehicle to the left, pulling them back on firm ground just as the right front wheel began to drift down the incline.

When they were out of danger, she slammed the door behind her and pressed gingerly on the accelerator. Easing back onto the highway, she tried to turn on the lights. They didn't work. And it was then that she realized that the fingers she'd burned earlier were stinging like the devil.

Gritting her teeth, she leaned forward, straining her eyes, and took the first turnoff from the main highway, a winding road that ascended into the mountains. But she knew the area, knew the road, knew where she was going to come out.

The man beside her made a low sound.

"Sam?"

He didn't respond, and she saw he'd passed out. She soothed her hand over his shoulder. "Thank you," she whispered.

There was no reply.

A small voice came from the back seat. "Sam got us out of there. It was like in the movies. Or in a cartoon."

She swung around to see Teddy huddled on the seat. "Yes."

"Aren't you gonna turn on the lights?"

"They don't work," she answered.

"Where are we going?"

She thought about the answer, and an idea popped into her mind. "Mr. Ripley's lodge," she said.

"Who's Mr. Ripley?" Teddy demanded.

"Mr. Ripley, a man I used to work for. He won't mind if we stay at his place," she said, crossing her fingers as she mouthed the lie. Arthur Ripley would be mad as a swarm of hornets if he knew she was taking liberties with his private property.

"Daddy doesn't love me," Teddy suddenly said.

"Oh, honey." Laurel swallowed, trying to think of what to say. "You know, sometimes people get sick in their minds and they do stuff they never would if they were...if they were normal."

The boy's voice quavered. "How did he get that way?"

Laurel grimaced, way out of her depth now. What could she say that wouldn't worry him more? Grasping at straws, she said, ''I think your daddy took some bad drugs that made him sick.''

Teddy thought about that for a while. ''That's what made him want to hurt me?''

''Yes.''

''Will he kill us if he catches us?''

She wanted to scream out her rage at the bastard. Instead, she gave the only answer she could. ''He won't catch us.''

''Okay.''

When Teddy settled back into his seat, she started thinking about Ripley again. He was a rich guy from Baltimore who came up here to relax—mostly on weekends. When she'd been in high school, there had been a program that had gotten teens into part-time jobs. Making assumptions about her abilities, they'd gotten her work as a maid, and one of her jobs had been cleaning Ripley's lodge. With any luck, they could hole up there for a couple of days. She hoped the key was still in the same place, under a fake rock near the front door. Otherwise, they'd have to break a window.

No, *she'd* have to break a window, she corrected herself.

The scene in the parking lot flashed into her mind again. Sam on a wild rampage of destruction. The car slamming into Frank and sending him flying. Hopefully, the man wasn't dead, because that would add murder to their list of crimes.

She felt an hysterical laugh bubbling up inside her. Wrong, she thought. Eric had already accused her of murder. Frank would just be another victim. Or would they get a chance to plead self-defense?

She steered the car through the night, moving at moderate speed, thankful that there was enough moonlight for her to see where she was going. Every once in a while they passed a car. Sometimes the driver honked at her. Did they think she didn't know she was driving without headlights?

Now all they had to do was keep from meeting a police cruiser. That mental picture had her stomach clenching. Not to mention her fear that the rolling wreck would conk out before she reached Ripley's.

She might have started to sob as she drove through the night, but she didn't have the breath for it.

Finally, when she'd begun to wonder if she was on the wrong road, she saw his wild-duck mailbox looming along the shoulder. Turning in at the long driveway, she headed toward the house.

Again she held her breath, straining her body forward. Relief flooded her when she saw all the lights were off and there was no vehicle near the front door, where Ripley always parked. After pulling into the man's favorite spot, she climbed out and searched the bushes to the right of the door for the artificial rock.

It was in the same place. Luckily Ripley hadn't thought of a new hiding place. Extracting the key, she opened the door, then thought about what to do.

Teddy was still awake. Sam was out like a fighter who'd gone down for the count. Probably it was safe to leave him where he was while she got the boy settled.

Taking Teddy's hand, she led him across the threshold, then waited for her eyes to adjust. There was enough moonlight slanting through the windows so that she could see the bulky shapes of the rustic sofa and easy chairs and the television set in the middle of the wall unit beside the fireplace.

Teddy's hand tightened in hers. "Is it really all right to be here?" he asked.

"Yes," she answered, putting as much reassurance as she could muster into her voice.

"It's spooky."

She felt it too. The dark house, the hulking furniture, the silence, their precarious situation. That was the worst of all. But she wasn't going to let Teddy see her fear. They were safe here, she told herself firmly.

"Why don't we turn on the lights?"

"Because we're hiding. We don't want anybody to know we're here."

"We don't want Daddy to find us," he said, and she could feel him shivering.

"He won't."

She took Teddy to the bathroom, then settled him in the closest bedroom, somehow managing to tell him more stories of the Big Brown Bear to relax him enough for sleep. After he drifted off, she waited another few minutes to make sure he wasn't going to wake up alone. Then she went back to the car.

Through the windshield, she could see Sam sprawled where she'd left him. Opening his door, she leaned inside, catching the aroma of bourbon. It wasn't unpleasant, just strong. He muttered something she couldn't understand.

"Sam?"

He didn't seem to know she was there.

"Sam?" she called out again softly.

This time he roused slightly, and his face contorted. "Swore I'd never...'nother drink," he muttered. "Now...look at me."

"It wasn't your fault."

He lapsed back into sleep, and she wiped the damp hair back from his forehead. God, the poor man. What had Frees said? That Sam had started drinking when his wife and child had been killed. Apparently he'd pulled himself out of hell, and Frees had tossed him back into the pit.

She stroked his shoulder and moved closer so that her cheek was resting on top of his head. It hit her then how extraordinary it was that he'd gotten them to safety. Frees had counted on the booze making Sam docile, but it hadn't worked out that way at all. Somehow he'd held himself together when he needed to. And now it was her responsibility to take care of him.

"Sam, you've got to get up. I can't carry you into the house."

"Go 'way. Let me sleep."

She thought about leaving him in the car. But what if he woke in the middle of the night and didn't know where he was? What if he panicked and hurt himself? She didn't know a lot about drunks, didn't know what to expect. But she did know that *she'd* be frightened if she suddenly woke up out here with no idea of where she was.

"Come on," she urged. "Help me."

"Hum?"

"We've got to get you to bed."

"Bed," he murmured, the tone of his voice turning silky. Apparently his thinking didn't quite match hers. In case she didn't catch his meaning, he added, "Yeah, you sure turn me on, baby."

She sucked in a sharp breath as his hands gently touched the front of her shirt.

"Sam, don't."

"You feel good." He sighed. "And it's been a damn long time…since I wanted anyone."

She should have been terrified by the touch. But she wasn't. Perhaps because she knew he was no threat. Not in his condition. Or perhaps because he stirred something inside her that she hadn't allowed herself to feel before. Gently she removed his hand, stroking her fingers over his. He turned his face, pressed his lips against her cheek, and for a moment she stayed very still, feeling her throat go tight.

Then she reached under his arms and tugged. "Come on to bed."

"With you," he answered, pushing himself up and swaying on his feet.

The tightness in her throat increased. "Uh-huh," she said, thinking—hoping—that he probably wouldn't remember any of this.

He leaned heavily on her as they made their way across the gravel driveway and into the house.

Carefully, she half propped him against the wall, then reached to close the front door behind them, wincing again as her injured fingers closed around the knob.

As she caught her breath, she was sorry that she'd chosen the closest bedroom for Teddy. Sam was heavy, and the thought of taking him all the way down the hall was daunting. It crossed her mind to just deposit him on the sofa. But she knew he was already in bad shape, and she didn't like the thought of him waking up stiff from a night crammed onto the couch.

The few extra steps down the hall were torture. But finally she got him into the bedroom and eased him onto the bed. Next she removed his shoes and socks, feeling the intimacy of touching his feet. For a moment she thought about taking off his slacks, but she was hardly prepared to go that far.

So she stretched him out on the bed still wearing the rest of his clothing, then she worked the covers over him.

The exertion left her breathing hard.

The idea of lying down next to him had a certain forbidden appeal. Most likely, he wouldn't even know she was there. And she might find out if she could handle sleeping next to a man.

On the other hand, the man could take care of himself better than the boy down the hall. Teddy had been through a pretty traumatic evening. If he woke up in the middle of the night, he might be terrified to find himself alone in an unfamiliar place.

She stood there until she was swaying on her feet with fatigue, feeling strangely torn. Finally, she bent and stroked Sam's cheek and tucked the covers up around his shoulders. Then she turned and made a stop in the bathroom. After using the facilities, she rummaged in the medicine cabinet. To her relief, there was a tube of burn salve, which she slathered on her hand.

It was then that she remembered the battered car. Leaving it in the driveway wasn't such a good idea. So she forced herself to go out into the night again and pull the wreck in back of the house.

Then she came back inside and climbed into bed with Teddy.

He stiffened as her weight shifted the mattress. "Laurel?"

"I'm right here."

"Don't let Dad hurt me."

"I won't, honey. I won't," she vowed, praying that she could make good on the promise.

Chapter Five

Sam cracked an eyelid, winced. A shaft of sunlight was slanted through the spot where the curtains didn't quite meet. It felt like a hot poker driving itself directly into his brain.

He lay very still, cataloging sensations and impressions. He was dressed in his clothing, except for his shoes. And his head felt like a team of men with pickaxes were mining for gold.

Careful not to move his aching head, he dragged air into his lungs and let it flow out again. For long moments it was as though he had gone through a time warp—back to the phase of his life where his very existence was too painful to bear. And the only way to stop the torment was to drink until he passed out.

He'd drunk that much last night. He certainly had the headache to prove it. And the parched, achy feeling as well. The physical discomfort was bad enough; the confusion was worse.

Then memories grabbed him by the throat. The scene in the motel. Frees and his two thugs. The bottle of bourbon staring him in the face like an evil goblin. Laurel and Teddy watching his degradation.

He bolted up, shame and terror clawing through him. At the sudden movement, agony burst inside his head.

He remembered some of what had happened after he'd followed Frees's directions and started guzzling the booze, though the scene was shrouded in a bourbon-induced fog. Being led to the car. The damp night air of the parking lot. The wild ride, when he'd been barely in control of the car. The truck that had almost put a finish to the whole escapade.

After that everything was a blank.

He opened his eyes again, this time very cautiously. He was in a pretty nice bedroom. But where were Laurel and the boy?

It was agony to push himself up, but he managed to do it, only to be rewarded with a wave of nausea. Staggering out of the room, he located the bathroom, lurched inside and threw up into the toilet.

The first thing he thought about when his belly was empty was a drink.

He needed a drink. God, no!

Scared and shaking, he stood up and braced himself against the sink. He hadn't wanted the bourbon last night. But once he started, the liquor had soothed him like an old friend. And now he wanted more.

"No!" he said the word aloud, willing it not to be true. He *would not* allow one night of forced drinking to toss him back into hell.

He was in control. Yet his memory of the time when alcohol had taken him by the throat was too strong for him to kid himself.

Cautiously, he rinsed his mouth with water, then flexed his hands. His knuckles hurt from hitting one of those bruisers. Bo or Frank? It was a miracle he remembered their names.

Movement caught the corner of his eye, and he whirled, groaning at the pain. Laurel was standing in the doorway, wearing a clean T-shirt and sweatpants several sizes too large. Her hair was combed, so she must have been up for a while. And her eyes were full of concern.

"Are you all right?" she asked.

"I was going to ask you the same question."

"I'm fine, thanks to you."

He lifted one shoulder, then turned away to the medicine cabinet, avoiding his reflection as he swung the door open, saying a prayer of thanks when he found a bottle of aspirin. With his back still to her, he cupped his hand under the faucet and swallowed two pills.

Her gaze burned into his back, and he wanted to tell her to go away and leave him alone. For the rest of his life.

When she stayed where she was, he finally straightened and turned slowly toward her, thinking that he'd better find out the worst.

"What happened after the parking lot? I remember that much. No. I remember the truck."

"You pulled over to the side of the road and asked me to drive."

He started to nod, then thought better of it. "Uh-huh. So where are we now exactly?"

She looked down at her hands. "This is a hunting lodge where I used to work as a maid. We're, uh, borrowing it."

"Okay."

She sighed. "I promised myself I was going to stop breaking the law."

"You mean, like tearing through a parking lot, bashing into cars and tossing crooks into the air?"

"You were drunk."

He winced.

"Sam, when you drank that bourbon last night, you had no choice. If you hadn't cooperated, he was going to—" She stopped, glanced over her shoulder.

"How is Teddy?"

"Better than I expected. He's watching television."

"Good." He cleared his throat. "So what did I do last night that I can't remember?"

"Mostly you slept. I got you into...bed."

The way she hesitated made him study her face. "Did I do anything out of line?"

"No."

The tone of her voice and the look in her eyes told him she wasn't telling him the whole truth. He desperately wanted to know what she wasn't saying. But he didn't want to embarrass them both by pressing her.

"There's instant coffee. Do you want a cup?" she asked. "And there's food in the freezer. Teddy and I had pizza."

He grimaced at the thought of food. "Coffee would be good. But first I'd like to take a shower."

"I kind of checked around. There are clothes here that would fit you, if you want to change."

He didn't like the idea of stealing clothes any more than she'd liked the idea of borrowing this place. Yet after his shower, he wasn't going to climb back into the sweaty garments he was wearing now.

"Okay. Thanks," he said.

She laid a hand on his arm. "Sam, thank you for getting us out of there last night."

"I got myself out of there, too."

"You could have left us behind before you cut and ran. But you took us with you." She stood on tiptoe, pressed her lips to his cheek. Then, surprising him, she slipped her arms around his waist and wedged her face against his chest.

His arms came up to clasp her, and they stood for long seconds, neither of them moving. She felt warm and pliant in his arms.

"Don't blame yourself for anything bad that happened last night," she whispered.

He wanted to tell her it didn't matter whom they used

as a scapegoat. He'd drunk that bourbon, and he was scared spitless that he was going to need some more. But he didn't explain that to her.

She tipped her head up, her gaze questioning him. "If you didn't call Eric, then how did he find us? He was saying he was keeping tabs on us. Did those guys follow you from Baltimore?"

"I'd be a pretty poor excuse for a detective if they'd stayed behind me all the time. I think he put a transponder on my car before I left Baltimore. That way he knew where I was." He made a low sound. "Maybe I'm a poor excuse for a detective anyway."

"No! When Eric hired you, you had no reason to believe that he was lying to you."

"There was something about him I didn't like. Didn't trust. I should have gone with my instincts."

"Which was why you didn't call him as soon as you found us."

"Yeah."

She looked thoughtful. "The, uh, transponder. That's why you wanted to take my car."

"Yeah," he answered again.

"Where are your keys? You had them when we came back to the motel."

"I stuffed them in the sofa cushion."

"Clever." She grinned, shifted against him, then went very still as if she'd just realized they'd been holding on to each other the whole time they were talking. She gave his shoulder a quick squeeze, then eased away. Before he could close the bathroom door, she was back with a folded pair of pants and a knit shirt, which she thrust at him before disappearing down the hall.

He stood looking after her, then shook himself out of his trance and reached for the shower control. The hot spray and soap did a lot to revive him. And as long as he was already borrowing clothing, he decided there was no point in not taking a disposable razor out of the bag he found in the cabinet.

The pants were an inch too short, and the shirt was baggy, but they'd do. Too bad his gun was still back at the motel.

When he walked into the living room, Teddy looked up. "How are you doing?" he asked the boy.

"Fine," came the automatic answer.

Sam eased down to the sofa beside him. "Kind of scary last night."

"Uh-huh."

"Who were you scared of?" he asked, holding his breath, hoping he wasn't the bad guy.

The kid looked down at his hands. "My dad, and those mean men."

"I was scared of them, too," Sam said. "That's nothing to be ashamed of."

"You? But you got us away."

"I was scared I wouldn't be able to do it."

He felt Laurel's eyes on him from where she was standing in the doorway, holding a mug. "There's sugar and cream. How do you want your coffee?"

"Black and sweet," he said, figuring he could use the calories and the caffeine.

"Got to go to the bathroom," Teddy announced, jumping off the couch.

As soon as he'd gone, Sam glanced at his watch, then changed the channel, looking for the noon newscast. He came in in the middle of the report he didn't really want to hear: "According to Sheriff Andrew Barrington, the FBI has been brought in on the Frees kidnapping case."

"What?" Laurel gasped.

Sam cursed under his breath. "Oh great, the FBI."

"But..." Laurel started to protest as the newscaster continued to speak.

Sam waved her to silence. He needed to hear what was going on. At least the official version.

"This morning Eric Frees appealed to local authorities to help him find the couple who abducted his son, Teddy. Last week, Mr. Frees's son was taken from his home by the child's nanny—after the death of his wife. Frees now says that he believes the sitter and her boyfriend, Sam Lassiter, are responsible for his wife's death."

Sam saw Teddy in the hallway, wondering if he was still ignorant of his mother's death. If so, he wasn't going to let him find out from a television news bulletin "Go get him, and keep him out of here," he ordered Laurel.

She jumped to her feet, intercepted the boy and took him back to the bedroom as the reporter continued. "The couple is armed and dangerous."

Sam felt his skin go cold. Frees had changed his tactics.

The sordid story unfolded as he listened. The nanny had been convicted as an accessory in a previous kidnapping case. The P.I. was her present accomplice.

"Just great!" Sam muttered, pretty sure how the hours after their escape had gone down. Probably Frees and his goons had spent the night frantically looking for them, figuring they couldn't get far in their wrecked car with a drunk at the wheel. Then Frees had gotten frustrated and decided to check in with the local police, who would already be investigating the scene last night at the motel, although they would have no idea what Frees had really been doing there. Maybe he hadn't realized that the cops would immediately call in the FBI because a kid was involved.

And Frees had set them up to shoot first and ask questions later. Even if they didn't, who were the authorities going to believe—a tanked-up P.I. and a convicted felon?

Or the poor man who had lost his wife and was frantically searching for his son?

Sam stood and snapped off the television. No more cartoons, not when a piece of breaking news could preempt Bugs Bunny at any time.

He pressed his fingers against his temple. The headache that had receded into the background was suddenly back in full force.

He needed a drink. Badly.

Then, realizing what he was thinking, he clenched his hands into fists in front of him. God, no!

He'd been sober for over three hundred and sixty-five days. And one night of boozing—even if it wasn't his fault—had wiped out all his carefully constructed self-control. He'd read about that. About how a recovering alcoholic couldn't risk even one drink without craving a whole lot more. And he'd been afraid to test the theory.

He held up his hand, saw it was shaking and made a disgusted sound deep in his throat. When he found himself scanning the room for a liquor cabinet, he let out a stream of curses and strode down the hall.

"Laurel says I can't watch TV anymore," Teddy whined as soon as Sam stepped into the bedroom. "Why not?"

Sam thought of various lies as he crossed the room and sat down beside Teddy on the bed. As he slung his arm around the kid's shoulder, he decided to go with a version of the truth. "Your dad called the police last night."

"But he was the one with the gun."

"Right. But he's your father. So the police believe Laurel and I kidnapped you. There are going to be more reports on TV, but Laurel and I don't want you to get upset by watching them."

Teddy considered that. "Okay," he said in a small voice.

"Thanks for going along with us. That's a big help," Sam said.

The boy nodded gravely.

"I found some paper and pencils," Laurel said. "You can draw pictures."

"Okay."

"Laurel and I will be right out in the living room."

"You don't want me to hear you," Teddy said.

"Right." Sam gave him a forced smile. "You're a smart boy."

They settled Teddy on the floor with pencils and sheets of paper. Just as they were about to leave the room, he looked up. "What's a hor?" he asked.

Laurel stopped in her tracks, her face as white as paste. Sam clasped her arm, then squatted beside Teddy. "That's a word for a bad woman. Your dad used it last night to talk about Laurel because he was angry with her. He was angry that she got you away from him. So he was calling her names."

"Oh."

"She's not anything he called her. And that's not a word I want to hear from you again."

"Okay." The boy looked down at the paper. Then, picking up a pencil, he began to draw. Sam ushered Laurel out of the room, feeling the stiff way she held her body.

"Little pitchers have big ears," she whispered when they'd returned to the front of the house.

"Don't take it personally. Kids are curious about bad words."

She gave a tiny nod, but he saw the slump of her shoulders.

"Nothing Frees said about you had any validity. I've found that out for myself."

She didn't seem to be listening to him. "I'm not a whore. I may be bad, but I'm not a whore."

The despair in her voice tore at him. "Eric was trying to hurt you."

She nodded tightly, paced to one end of the room and braced her hands against the window frame, as though she could no longer hold herself up.

Finally, she straightened, but when she turned, he saw her features set in despairing lines. "You probably think I was sleeping with Oren Clark," she whispered.

He gave a noncommittal shrug. That was exactly what he'd been thinking until she'd told him the story about her stepfather. Then he hadn't been sure anymore.

She stood clenching and unclenching her fists, then blurted out, "I wasn't sleeping with him. I *picked* him because he never put his hands on me. Well, he hit me. But he didn't sleep with me. I don't know why, but I was grateful."

"Oh," he answered, feeling an unexpected surge of relief.

"So I'm not a whore." He saw her swallow, saw her face take on that fragile look that made his heart squeeze. "I'm a virgin. A technical virgin, I guess you'd call it, because Ralph didn't ever…didn't ever have intercourse with me." She ended with a shuddering sob.

Moving swiftly, he crossed the room, folded her into his arms, rocked her against him.

"It's okay. It's okay," he murmured automatically, although he felt like a liar and a cheat for offering reassurances. It was hard to comprehend just what this woman had been through. But God help him, he was glad that nobody had made love with her, because he wanted to be the one to show her how good it could be between a man and a woman. The admission sent a wave of guilt crashing through him. Make love to her! He shouldn't even be thinking such a thing. He should be thinking about how to keep her safe from the cops, the FBI and Eric Frees.

He was still holding her in his arms, still stroking his hands over her back and shoulders. As his mind switched from fantasy to reality, he could feel her struggling to get control of herself. "You're going to think I go to pieces at the drop of a hat," she managed to say.

"You had good reason to go into hysterics when Frees showed up, but you kept your cool."

"And when you were—" She stopped, as though she'd just realized what she'd started to say.

"What?"

"Coming on to me last night."

"I did?"

She pressed her hand to her mouth as if she wished she could take the words back. "I wasn't going to tell you that."

"What did I do?"

"Not much. You said you were attracted to me."

"I am."

"You weren't just saying it because Frees had poured all that liquor down your throat?"

"He didn't pour it. I was lifting the glass myself."

"We both know why." She looked over his shoulder, toward the back of the house where Teddy was drawing.

Sam didn't speak, thinking what Frees had threatened last night. Lord, how could a father even think of something like that! It was beyond his comprehension.

His attention snapped back to Laurel as she looked into his eyes. He saw uncertainty warring with boldness. Then, as if someone had dared her to leap off a cliff, she pressed her mouth to his.

He was too shocked at first to do more than stand there. But when she started working her lips against his as though she were competing in a kissing race, he murmured into her mouth, "It's not a punishment. Don't do it if it doesn't feel good."

She went still, and her mouth softened. "Show me how."

"It's not complicated," he answered, nibbling at her lips, moving back and forth against them, the contact both soothing and stimulating. Lord, he'd just told himself he shouldn't be doing this. It seemed he couldn't help himself.

He had thought he wasn't in good enough shape to become aroused. This woman aroused him. With her mouth and her body. Her frustration and her innocence.

He wanted to stroke his fingers down her spine, find the curve of her bottom, press her against his erection. God, that would feel wonderful. But he kept his hands lightly on her shoulders because he didn't know how far he could go without frightening her.

So he kept the kisses leashed, his tongue playing delicately with the tender flesh just inside her mouth, his teeth nibbling at her succulent lower lip.

One of them moaned. He wasn't sure whether the sound came from her or from himself.

Finally she lifted her head, her eyes dreamy and dilated.

"You do something to me, Sam. When you kiss me I feel things I've never felt before."

"What?"

"Tingly. Edgy. But it's not bad. It's nice. Like my body's singing a song."

God, yes. He closed his eyes, pressed his forehead against hers.

"Is that all right?" she asked.

"You said it feels good."

"Yes."

"Then it is good."

"For you too?" she asked in a halting voice.

"Oh, yeah."

She looked pleased and a little stunned. Then her gaze drifted to his hand where it rested gently on her shoulder. In one swift motion, she grabbed the hand and brought it down, cupping it around her breast.

His whole body clenched as he absorbed the sensation of the beautifully rounded swell. Gently, oh so gently, he moved his fingers, squeezing just the barest amount, then lightly stroking back and forth over the hard button of her nipple.

She sucked in a strangled breath. "That's so good."

He wasn't doing much, barely touching her. Yet his own reaction shook him to the core. If he wasn't careful, he was going to have her flat on her back under him. And he'd already figured out that was a bad idea for a lot of reasons.

He pulled his hand away.

"Please don't stop," she begged in a broken voice.

"We have to."

"Why?"

"Because Teddy could come walking in," he answered, reminding her that the boy was just down the hall. The kid made a good excuse for not jumping into something that neither one of them was ready for.

"Teddy," she repeated, her expression changing to chagrin. "I wasn't thinking."

"I wasn't either. I was just enjoying what we were doing." Actually, he'd been letting lust carry him along. Well, not lust, he corrected. A more tender emotion.

It was a long time since he'd wanted a woman. Now all the sexual impulses he'd buried were surging to the surface, and they were directed toward a woman who had been brutalized. A woman who'd told him she'd never experienced a normal man-woman relationship.

"We'd better talk about the news bulletin while we can," he said.

She nodded. "How bad was it?"

"Bad." As he summarized the parts she hadn't heard, he watched her take her lower lip between her teeth.

"How are we going to get out of this?" she asked.

He wished she hadn't asked the question. "We're safe

here for the time being." He cast his eyes toward the window. "Where's the car?"

"Around back."

"If it's still running, I'll take it out tonight and get us some new wheels."

"Steal a car?"

"I don't think I have much choice."

"Where are we going?"

"I've got friends in Baltimore. They'll help us."

"Won't they think you went berserk when you got mixed up with me?"

"No."

She looked over his shoulder again. "I'd better check on Teddy."

Together they made their way down the hall. The boy was crouched over his drawings with his back to them. As Laurel hunched down beside him, Sam heard her make a small, distressed sound.

Moving as fast as he could, he joined them on the floor, staring down at the picture. It was done in five-year-old terms, but it clearly showed three big stick-figure men holding guns at a much smaller, cowering figure.

Sam's chest tightened painfully. Teddy might be acting calm on the outside, but the past few days had obviously taken their toll on him—climaxing with the scene last night.

"Oh, honey," Laurel murmured, sliding her arm around the boy's shoulder.

"Is that your dad and the men who were with him last night?" Sam asked.

Teddy nodded.

There were several sheets of paper on the floor. Sam picked them up and shuffled through them. The scenes were graphic depictions of Teddy's recent experiences. He and Laurel together in a motel room. Laurel leading him across a porch roof. A truck bearing down on a car. And one more picture—of a woman lying down with her eyes closed and her arms folded across her chest.

Apparently the boy had caught the reference to his mother last night. Sam was careful to keep his face neutral as he felt the boy's questioning gaze on him.

"Are you mad?" Teddy asked, his voice so low that it was barely audible.

"Why would I be mad?" Sam said.

The boy shrugged.

"Of course I'm not mad. You've had a pretty rough time lately," Sam answered.

"Yeah."

There were tears in the boy's eyes now. Tears in his voice.

Sam reached for him, held him close. "And you're probably wishing everything could go back to the way it was," he whispered.

Teddy's body was shaking now.

"I know what you're feeling," Sam murmured. "I know it because I lost my own little girl. So I know how you feel about your mom."

The boy nodded against his shirtfront.

"And you can't go to your dad, because he's acting so strange."

Teddy was crying in earnest now. All Sam could do was hold him, rock him.

The boy's muffled voice came through his sobs. "I was afraid about my mom. But I was afraid to ask Laurel. Then last night…"

Sam hugged the youngster close. Judging from the pictures he'd drawn, the kid was probably going to need some sessions with a shrink. But first things first. And the primary order of business was keeping him alive.

When the sobs had eased, Sam gestured toward the pictures. "I'm glad you drew these for us."

"You are?" Teddy asked, sounding astonished.

"It's good for you to let us know what you're feeling."

Teddy sighed, relaxed a fraction.

"And Laurel and I are going to keep you safe."

The boy nodded.

Finally, Laurel broke into the conversation. "So maybe we should all go have something to eat. There's French toast in the freezer and maple syrup in the refrigerator. How does that sound?"

"Good."

She led the way to the kitchen. Sam organized Teddy into helping him set the table. Laurel got out a carton of frozen French toast and warmed the slices in the oven while she heated the jug of syrup in a saucepan full of water on the stove.

Sam picked at his breakfast. But Teddy and Laurel each polished off two pieces of toast. Still, he was thinking things were running on a pretty smooth track when he heard the crunch of gravel outside.

His head jerked to the window, and he saw a car pulling to a stop in the driveway.

Chapter Six

"Eric," Laurel whispered, her face white.

Teddy began to shake and make small, whimpering sounds.

"Not necessarily," Sam answered, moving to the side of the window so that he could look out without being observed. "Does Eric have a gray Toyota Camry?"

"No," Laurel answered.

A large man with thick salt-and-pepper hair had gotten out of the car and was staring at the house. He returned to the car, popped the trunk and retrieved a hunting rifle.

"Oh great," Sam muttered, his head instantly beginning to pound in reaction. He beckoned Laurel to the window, holding her to the side so she didn't reveal herself. "Do you recognize that guy?" he asked.

She gulped. "Mr. Ripley."

"The owner?"

She nodded tightly. "Why did he…" She let the sentence trail off as she glanced quickly back at Teddy, but Sam was pretty sure he knew what she'd been about to ask: Why had Ripley gone for his gun?

"I guess he was wondering why the lights were on when he got here," he answered the unspoken question. "And I guess you'd better take Teddy in the back," he added. "You and he get yourselves into a closet."

Laurel looked as if she might have protested, if she hadn't been worried about Teddy's welfare.

The man was still standing beside his car, and Sam pegged him for a hard-ass type prepared to defend his turf by himself instead of doing the smart thing, which would have been to call the police. That was good. Because if reinforcements arrived, their goose was cooked.

"What are you going to do?" Laurel whispered.

"Keep him from hurting us without doing any damage to him." *I hope,* he silently added.

Laurel eased Teddy out of his seat and moved quickly down the hall. As soon as their backs were to him, Sam started opening kitchen drawers, found a large knife and wrapped his fingers around the handle, the throbbing in his head growing stronger by the second. If he stopped to analyze his own actions, he'd make himself sick.

But he'd already discarded the idea of reasoning with Ripley. Not when he could see the kind of guy he was dealing with. And not when Laurel's and Teddy's lives were at stake.

A quick look out the window told Sam that the jerk was advancing on the front door with the rifle cocked.

Terrific move! Probably he assumed kids had broken into the house, and he was going to give them the scare of their lives—or maybe blow their heads off and claim self-defense.

Defying the pounding in his skull, Sam sprinted to the side of the door and flattened his shoulders against the wall. Every muscle in his body tensed as he heard the key slip into the lock and turn.

When Ripley stepped into the room, Sam thrust the blade against his back. "Hold it right there!" he growled.

The man jerked, started to turn, and the rifle discharged, blowing a hole in a sofa cushion.

Sam had only a split second to react. He could thrust the

knife into the guy's side, which might damn well kill him, or he could try to take away the gun. He chose to drop the knife and reach for the rifle barrel, twisting it upward. Ripley was as strong as an angry bear. He held on to the weapon, the second barrel discharging.

The rifle was now empty, but neither man could loosen his hold on the weapon. They turned in a circle, so that Sam was facing the open door, the sunlight piercing his eyes.

Ripley grunted, gave a mighty tug on the weapon.

Bending at the waist, Sam tried to throw the guy over his shoulders. But the other man twisted to the side.

Behind him he sensed a rush of movement. Before he could figure out exactly what was happening, he heard a dull thud followed by a groan. In the next moment, Ripley sank to his knees and collapsed in a heap, his body still curled around the rifle.

Whirling, Sam found Laurel standing over the man, a Remington table statue in her raised hand—a bronze figure of a horse and rider.

Slowly, she lowered her arm, and the bronze dropped to the wooden floor with a clank.

"I told you to stay with Teddy," he growled.

"I think it's lucky that I didn't."

They stared at each other across several feet of charged space. He wanted to throttle her for disobeying orders, and at the same time he wanted to sweep her into his arms and hug her to himself. God, she had guts. But he'd known that all along, even when he'd assumed the worst about her.

Still he wasn't going to tell her she'd done the right thing. Turning away, he wrenched the gun from the home owner's limp fingers, then shoved it under the sofa. When he turned back to Laurel, he saw that she still looked stunned by what she'd done.

"We've got to tie this guy up," he muttered.

Her gaze snapped back to the man on the floor. "Can we use duct tape? There's some in the utility room of the kitchen. I saw it when I was prowling around."

"I'll get it. Go back to Teddy," Sam told her. "He needs you. And stay out of sight. I want Ripley to think I'm the only one in the house."

She nodded, but stood where she was with a distressed look on her face as she stared down at the man.

"Go on," Sam urged. "We'll talk about it later."

After retrieving the tape, he stopped at the coatrack near the front door and grabbed the Pennzoil cap he'd seen hanging there. After jamming it onto his head, he pulled on a jacket and pulled the collar up around his face. Not much of a disguise, but better than nothing, he decided as he knelt over the unconscious man and quickly secured his hands behind his back. Then he searched Ripley's pockets and took out a wallet, car keys and a cell phone.

So the guy had been able to call in help all along and he'd elected to do things the dumb way. Well, he was getting what he deserved.

Ripley's moan had Sam quickly securing his ankles. He moaned again and tried to move his arms. When they remained inoperable, his eyes snapped open and focused on Sam.

They stared at each other for several seconds. Then the man's lips moved and he tried to wrench his hands free. "You bastard."

"Take it easy. You don't want to hurt yourself."

"You're scum." Ripley spat out the words.

"Maybe. But consider yourself lucky. I could have slipped a knife between your ribs as soon as you walked in the door, but I didn't."

The guy thought that over. Then his eyes narrowed. "You look too puny to have gotten the drop on me."

Sam spread his hands. "No dishonor on you. It's my black belt in kung fu."

He waited tensely for the guy to contradict him, to say something about a woman rushing into the room and braining him. When he didn't, Sam decided to go with the best possible scenario: Ripley hadn't seen Laurel or didn't remember seeing who'd hit him over the head.

As Sam opened Ripley's wallet and extracted a wad of bills, the man sounded a protest.

"What are you going to do—leave me here to die?"

"So you're not expecting company. Good," Sam answered.

Ripley grimaced. "Maybe I am. But I'm damn well not going to tell you about it."

Sam stared down at the immobilized man. He didn't like him, but he knew who was in the wrong here. "Just sit tight for a while," he said. "When I'm in the clear, I'll call 911."

"Sure."

Sam thought about taking the rifle, then decided it was only going to make things worse if the cops pulled him over. Without prolonging the conversation, he turned and trotted down the hall to where the others were waiting.

LAUREL'S GAZE SHOT to Sam as he stepped into the bedroom and closed the door.

He looked shaken, but his voice was even as he said, "Is there a back way out of the house?" he whispered.

She pitched her voice low to match his. "Just the front door and the kitchen door."

"Then we're going out the window."

Teddy's eyes were round. "Why?"

Sam was the one who answered. "So the guy in the living room doesn't see us."

"I heard a gun," the boy said. "Did you hurt him?"

"No. I just tied him up. He assumes I'm the only one here, and that's what he'll report to the cops. So we're going to make a little mess back here, then leave through the window." As he spoke, he opened a drawer and started tossing the contents on the floor.

"What about fingerprints?" Laurel asked.

"Wipe off every hard surface. Doorknobs, countertops, the bedposts, the bathroom fixtures. Anything you might have touched. If we make this look like a simple breaking and entering, we've got a chance of keeping them from knowing we were still in the area as of last night."

"Okay," she answered, turning her face downward.

"What?"

"I shouldn't have brought us here."

He crooked his finger under her chin and tipped it up. "You did the right thing. We needed a place to stay. It's just bad luck that Mr. Macho decided to show up." He turned to Teddy. "You put all your pencils and papers in here. And anything else you used."

"'Cause we don't want anybody to know we were here?"

"Right." Laurel pulled the boy to her and hugged him tightly. "We're going to be fine, Teddy."

"If the police don't catch us."

"What do you know about that?" Sam asked.

"I could hear you talking."

"Well, I used to be a policeman before I became a private detective. So I know how they think."

Teddy nodded gravely, and Laurel felt her heart turn over.

She wanted to throttle Eric Frees for damaging this child, for taking away his mother. But there wasn't much chance of that, so she simply followed Sam's lead.

Fifteen minutes later they were all standing on the lawn,

next to the window Sam had smashed. As he raised his head and scanned the area, he scowled.

"What?" she said.

"I'm not functioning on all cylinders. I believe I was about to overlook a major detail. Where did you say you left the car?"

She led him around back, and Sam whistled as he took in the missing front bumper, the obliterated fenders and the long gash in the side.

"We drove in *that*," Teddy marveled.

"Yes. Cross my heart and hope—" She stopped short as she realized the last word of the saying wasn't what she was hoping for at all.

Sam looked under the chassis and muttered something about oil. Then he opened the driver's door.

"Can I ride with you?" the boy asked eagerly.

"No, you stay with Laurel. I don't even know if I can get this contraption to run."

She held her breath as he turned the key. At first the ignition made a grinding sound. Then it turned over, and a huge plume of smoke puffed out the back.

"I don't think we're going to get too far," he observed dryly. "But five or ten miles would be nice. Which way should I turn if I want to stay off the highway?"

"Left. There's a series of back roads you can take."

"You follow me in the Camry."

Laurel trailed the rattling car, staying well back from the smoke that puffed out the exhaust.

Sam stuck it out for about five miles, then pulled onto what might have been an old logging road and plowed into a honeysuckle thicket.

Laurel had followed him up the road. As he walked back to the Camry, he said, "One of us should lie down in the back. So we don't stand out as the armed-and-dangerous couple the cops are looking for."

"I can drive," she volunteered.

"You sure?"

"You get some rest."

"I wish."

Sam stretched out in the back seat of the Camry. Laurel and Teddy took the front.

She glanced at him over her shoulder. "The only problem is that I don't know where I'm going."

"Out of the state. Western Pennsylvania."

THERE WAS NO POINT in his staying up in western Maryland, the grieving father had told the authorities. If Lassiter and the nanny were going to contact him with a ransom demand, they would probably be looking for him at home.

That had given him the excuse he needed to repair to his mansion. But as he paced the length of the elegant sitting room, he clenched his hands at his sides and cursed his run of bad luck.

He was really on a roll! His problems had started months ago when one of his biggest distributors, Steely Turner, had been arrested. Not long after that, one of his most trusted men had betrayed him, leaving him twisting in the wind. Then he'd thought of a foolproof way to make things come out right. It had all been going according to plan. So good that he'd let down his guard.

Last night everything had gone sour again at the motel where he'd cornered the fugitives.

With Lassiter on a rampage behind the wheel, the manager had called the cops, and they'd arrived with sirens blaring, leaving Eric to explain what was going on.

The recent memory sent him into a spasm of curses. He'd been sure his plan to get rid of his biggest problems—Lassiter, the nanny and the boy—was foolproof. He hadn't counted on his men screwing up, or on Lassiter still being able to think straight with that much liquor in him.

But the P.I. had played it cool. Very cool. He had to give the man his due. He was one tough son of a bitch.

He squeezed his eyes closed, clenched and unclenched his fists, cursing the damn local cops. Why couldn't they just have handled this by themselves? But no, they'd called in the FBI. And there hadn't been any way he could protest. Not when he was supposed to be so worried about his kid.

His only choice had been to peddle the story of the boozed-up kidnapper. And now he was stuck with it—stuck with the news media and the publicity he'd hoped to avoid.

There were TV trucks parked down on Holly Thicket Pass right now. He couldn't go in and out of his own driveway without being harassed. But that was going to end soon one way or the other. He was already making contingency plans. If the cops or the FBI didn't bring down Lassiter and the woman in a blaze of gunfire pretty damn quick, Eric Frees was going to have to do a disappearing act. He'd be gone in a convenient puff of smoke.

He let out a bitter laugh. He could do it. But the cost would be high after all the plans he'd made. And before he folded up his tent, he was going to arrange a nasty surprise for Mr. Lassiter and Ms. Coleman.

"ARE YOU AWAKE?" Laurel asked.

"Yeah."

Sam sat up, stretched and looked around at the rural scenery. They were passing a stone building with a Dutch-style windmill out front. Pennsylvania, all right. "How far are we from the scene of our latest crime?"

"Seventy-five miles. And we're getting low on gas."

"You might as well stop at a station where there's a convenience store. We can get something to eat and drink."

"Do you think they have HoHo's?" Teddy piped up from the passenger seat.

"Maybe, but you're going to have a sandwich before you

have dessert," Laurel informed him as she turned onto a business road.

"Can't I have any fun?" the boy asked.

Sam leaned across the seat and whispered loudly into the boy's ear, "Fun is good. We'll see if we can get around Laurel."

Apparently, she heard him because she shot a narrow-eyed glance his way.

He rolled his eyes, then repeated the message more loudly, "Fun is good."

After a few seconds, she gave him a tight nod, bowing to his unspoken suggestion: *Cut the kid some slack. He's having a pretty rough time. He's lost his mother and he's being chased by his dad's hired killers. If HoHo's will make him happy, then let him eat dessert first.*

A few minutes later they pulled into a gas station.

"I think we're far enough away to spring Ripley from bondage. Let me make a call before I do anything else," Sam said as Laurel stopped at the gas pump.

"Okay."

He stepped out of the car and found himself staring across the street at a liquor store. Suddenly an image leaped into his mind. An image of himself crossing the street, going inside and buying a pint of bourbon. He could almost savor the taste of it in his mouth, the warm feel of it sliding down his throat and pooling in his stomach, the buzz in his brain.

The fantasy was so vivid that he found himself licking his lips. When he realized what he was doing, he went rigid.

Squeezing his eyes shut, he stood on the oil-stained concrete for several seconds, fighting for control. When he was sure he wasn't going to bolt across the street, he pulled out the cell phone he'd taken. After activating the unit, he called 911.

In a rough, scratchy voice, he said, "I'm calling to report a crime committed at the Ripley residence near Frostburg, Maryland."

"What is the nature of the crime, sir?"

"Breaking and entering. Mr. Ripley was left tied up in his house."

When the operator tried to get more information out of him, he clicked the off button. Then he tossed the phone into the trash can beside the paper-towel dispenser.

He was just unscrewing the cover on the gas tank when he felt a prickly sensation at the back of his neck.

Now what?

Glancing casually around, he saw a police cruiser pulling into the station.

Sweat broke out on his forehead, and he resisted the urge to wipe it away. Lord, had the cops somehow picked up on the call?

Impossible, he told himself. This was simply a random piece of bad luck. With only seconds to react, he bent quickly toward Laurel's window.

"Police. I'm going inside. You get gas, then meet me around the back where he can't see me getting in the car. Hopefully, he won't realize we're together. And have Teddy get on the floor so he can't be seen."

For a moment she looked as if she was going to freak out. Then she nodded tightly.

The cop car had pulled up near the door and the uniformed officer was eyeing him.

Hoping he looked like a guy who'd walked in off the street, Sam stepped into the store and found the snack department where he scooped up several bags and boxes of junk food and a couple of comic books for Teddy.

As he brought his purchases to the counter, he judged Laurel's progress. He wanted her to finish her gas purchase before he ducked out the back.

"Where's the men's room?" he asked after pocketing his change.

"You've got to go out the back door. Then to your right."

Perfect, Sam thought as he exited through the rear door. Outside, he saw Laurel's car pull around the side of the station.

She stopped short when she saw him. Climbing into the back seat he ducked low as she lurched away with a jerky motion.

"Drive normally," he hissed as he felt her speeding up.

"Oh, sure," she muttered, then swore.

"What?"

"He's right behind me."

Chapter Seven

"Can I have a HoHo?" Teddy asked.

"What?"

"A HoHo."

"Have anything you want," Laurel answered, her mind on the cop who was staying behind her as if the two of them were attached by an invisible cord.

"Wow!"

Her gaze shot to the rearview mirror as she tried to read the cop's expression. Then she decided she'd better keep her focus on the road ahead.

But she felt the patrol car rolling relentlessly along behind her. God, what if he went after her for some dumb moving violation? Or what if he ran the license plate they'd picked up this morning and found it had expired or something?

Behind her, Teddy was tearing open the cake wrapper, and she wanted to scream at him to be quiet. But she kept her lips pressed together because there was no point in taking out her anxiety on him.

Finally, the cop turned off onto a side street, and she felt as if an enormous weight had just been lifted from her shoulders. "He's gone," she called out softly.

"Good," Sam answered from the back seat.

"Now what?"

"Let's put a few more miles on the odometer. Do you want me to take over?"

She glanced in the mirror again. Teddy was munching his way through his second cake roll or maybe his third. And Sam looked as though he'd spent the night in an all-night movie theater.

"I don't mind driving. Where should I go?"

"Find a highway with a lot of motels, then pick something that looks moderately priced. If you can, look for something near a low-end department store. We need clothing, toilet articles."

"Okay." She made her way down the road for twenty miles, until she came to a place where two highways crossed.

There were plenty of motels as well as several shopping areas.

When she pulled into the parking lot of a one-story motel, Sam leaned forward. "This is fine. I'll go in and register."

He got them a room around the back, a room that was much nicer than the one up in western Maryland, with new carpeting and a big bathroom. Then he conferred with her on a shopping list. She would have preferred to get her own underpants but she saw the wisdom of not appearing in public with him and Teddy.

"Will you be okay?" he asked as he pocketed her list.

"Of course," she answered because there was no alternative.

"Don't open the door to anyone."

She wanted to ask what she should do if the police came knocking, instead she said a silent prayer that it wouldn't happen.

The next two hours were agony. Every time she heard footsteps outside, she tensed. And inside, there was Teddy to deal with. She'd already given up on letting him eat the junk food, but she wasn't going to cave in on the television, not when there might be news of the supposed kidnapping. Not when there might be something about his mother. He'd cried when he'd learned she was dead. But since then he hadn't mentioned the subject. Probably—to use some psychological jargon she'd picked up at her therapy sessions—he was repressing his feelings. But she wasn't equipped to deal with feelings right now. So she spent most of her time reading him the comic books that Sam had bought at the gas station, struggling to concentrate on the words and pictures. When she finally heard a light tap at the door, every muscle in her body went rigid.

"It's me," Sam called, then turned the key in the lock.

When he stepped into the room, she wanted to leap across the carpet and throw her arms around him. But she hung back because she knew Teddy was watching them. The boy showed no such restraint. He streaked past her and caught Sam in a bear hug, making him drop some of the shopping bags he was holding. So much for loyalty, Laurel thought with a little pang. She wasn't jealous, she told herself. She was glad that Teddy had bonded with Sam.

Over the boy's head, Sam caught her eye, and she knew there were things he wanted to talk about.

"Teddy, could you get me a couple of towels from the bathroom so we can use them for a tablecloth?" Sam said.

When Teddy rushed off to carry out the mission, Laurel looked questioningly at Sam. "What happened?"

"We're all over the TV news and the papers," he told her in a low voice.

"Ripley?"

"They haven't tied us to him. Not yet."

The boy came rushing back, cutting off the conversation.

"You were talking about me," he accused when he saw Laurel's face.

She swallowed, unsure of what to say.

Sam came to her rescue. "There are some things that adults need to talk about between themselves. It's about all the stuff that's been happening. It's nothing you need to worry about, though."

The boy scuffed his shoe against the carpet. "I can't help being worried."

Sam came over and knelt beside him. "Yeah, I understand that. But try to turn it over to me and Laurel. Okay?"

"Okay."

"So let's eat dinner."

He'd stopped at a chicken place and gotten food that was slightly more nutritious than the junk from the gas station.

Laurel had been too nervous to eat any of the cakes or chips, and she didn't feel much better now. But she knew that eating would be a good way to show Teddy that everything was under control.

Sam spread the towels on the bed. While they were tucking into the fried chicken, he grinned at the boy. "Have you ever heard the phrase 'Blondes have more fun?'"

"Yeah," Teddy said.

"Well, I'm going to test the theory." He reached in one of the bags and pulled out a package of hair dye.

"That's for girls!" Teddy said as he eyed the woman on the box.

"Not just girls. I can use it to make my hair the color of yours."

"Really?" Teddy marveled.

"Yeah." After they finished eating, Sam took the package into the bathroom, but he left the door open.

"Have you ever used this stuff?" he called out.

"Never," Laurel answered.

"It says you've got to strip out the color first." He was quiet for a few minutes, then made a disgusted sound. "You do it with blue goop."

Teddy giggled. "Can I see?"

Sam stuck his head through the door, and the boy laughed and pointed.

Sam grimaced and returned to the bathroom. When he emerged more than an hour later, he looked like a different person.

Teddy's mouth fell open. "You look like a rock star."

"If I tried to sing, you'd run screaming from the room."

Teddy made a game of it, trying to persuade Sam to sing something, and Laurel sat on the bed smiling as she watched them fooling around together, thinking that they really could pass for father and child with their matching blond heads, although the stubble of Sam's dark beard did show on his lean cheeks. He'd have to keep it shaved, she thought.

Finally the child started yawning.

"I think you need your beauty rest," Sam said.

"I don't want to go to bed."

"Kids never do," he answered easily. "But why don't you lie down and see what happens? And you can wear the new Batman pajamas I got you."

"Batman! Okay!"

Sam was so good with Teddy. So natural. He wasn't just giving the boy what he needed at the moment. He was laying a foundation of warmth and trust.

Her heart squeezed when she remembered how he'd sounded when he talked about losing his own child. Seeing him with Teddy this evening, she could only imagine what the loss had done to him.

Twenty minutes later they both kissed Teddy good-night and Laurel shut off most of the lights. But she felt Sam's eyes on her.

She stepped into the bathroom where they could talk, and he followed.

"Your turn," he said.

"I'm going to have more fun, too?"

"Yeah. But first we're going to give you a trim." As he spoke, he took a large pair of scissors out of the bag with the hair dye.

"We?" she asked, gripping the porcelain of the sink. It felt cold and smooth against the fingers she'd burned. "Have you ever cut a woman's hair?"

"Once. My sister's. She was five and I was seven."

"And you made a mess?"

He nodded.

"That's not very reassuring."

"I'm a lot more experienced now."

"I hope so," she answered, hearing her voice suddenly crack. Teddy had said earlier that he couldn't help worrying. She identified completely with that observation. And now that they'd gotten the boy to bed, she didn't have the energy to keep up the chipper front that she'd been projecting.

Sam must have seen the change in her because he murmured, "Hey, don't give out on me now."

"I'm scared. I didn't want to say that in front of Teddy," she whispered.

"I know. You've been super. You've given him just what he needed."

"So have you. More than I could do."

"Don't sell yourself short."

"I'm nothing special."

"Of course you are!" He reached for her, and she came into his arms, sighing as his warmth enveloped her. Closing her eyes, she pressed her cheek against his chest, feeling the steady beat of his heart.

His hands stroked up and down her back and into her hair.

"You've got beautiful hair," he whispered.

"Do I?"

"Uh-huh. And I hate the idea of changing it. But we've got to look like a Beach Boys Family."

"At least you didn't say Barbie and Ken."

"Doesn't Ken have dark hair?"

"If you say so." She tightened her arms around his waist and snuggled against his shirtfront. For years the idea of getting this close to a man had terrified her. But slipping into Sam Lassiter's arms felt comforting. More than comforting. Good. In ways she'd never let herself feel because she'd been too afraid.

"You're wonderful with Teddy. You know exactly what to do and say with him," she murmured, because that topic seemed the safest at the moment.

His reaction wasn't what she might have expected.

"Don't make me into a hero," he cautioned, his voice turning sharp.

She sensed his sudden tension, caught his self-deprecating tone. With insights gained from her own sense of self, she understood what he was doing. He was dismissing anything good about himself and focusing on the negative. And she knew what that meant for Sam Lassiter. He was worried about last night.

She lifted her head and met his eyes. "You're thinking about Eric forcing you to drink, aren't you?"

He made a rough sound in his throat that might have been an acknowledgment.

"You can't blame yourself for what somebody did to you," she pointed out. "My shrink taught me that."

His face contorted. "Maybe. But what about right now? If you knew how much I wanted a drink, you'd tie me to the bed."

"No, I wouldn't. And stop acting like it was your fault."

He gave a small shrug, and she knew there was nothing she could say to wipe out the negative image lodged in his brain. She'd been thinking about what she needed from him. But it went both ways. She understood that now.

The realization was empowering.

Without conscious thought, she raised her hand, stroking a path along his cheek to his lips then back up again, mesmerized by the contrast between the softness of his lips and the dark stubble that covered his cheeks. She loved the way it abraded her fingers. Loved the way it sent prickles of sensation along her nerve endings.

Her hand trailed lower, along the side of his throat. Under the slight pressure of her fingers she felt his pulse accelerate. His response gave her a little thrill of power. And the power fueled her own need.

She stared up at him, stared into his eyes.

Her lips parted. So did his as he sighed out her name.

He was the one who moved first, lowering his head so that his mouth touched down on hers, brushed back and forth over soft, warm flesh.

She made a tiny incoherent sound, and her hands moved to circle his shoulders, anchoring him to her.

"Laurel?"

"You don't have to treat me like glass," she whispered. "I won't break."

"I don't want to frighten you. I don't want to hurt you."

"You don't. You won't."

She brought her mouth back to his, pressing, deepening the contact, drinking in the wonderful taste of him in huge gulps. When he finally raised his head, they were both trembling and breathless.

She sighed. "That's so nice."

IT WAS SO TEMPTING to take more of what she was so generously offering. But he knew how selfish it was to simply follow his impulses, especially when he was holding a woman who had been hurt so badly.

He raised his head and stared down at her. "If we keep this up, I'm going to want more than kisses."

"I know."

"That doesn't worry you?"

"It worries me some. But what you're making me feel is stronger than the worries. Sam, I've never imagined I could have anything like this."

She was so tough in many ways—from her early experiences and then prison. But when it came to relationships with men, she seemed so damn innocent, so trusting, when he hardly trusted himself.

Better to stop this now, he decided. But when he started to pull away, he felt her hand in his hair, pressing him to her, urging him closer. Unable to deny himself the sweet pleasure of her mouth, he lowered his head again.

This time, restraint was harder to summon, not when most of the blood from his brain had migrated to the lower half of his body. He was helpless to stop himself from feasting on her, first with his tongue and teeth.

Softening the kiss, he traced the outline of her lips with his tongue, feeling her shivering reaction like an electric charge through his body, jolting his heart.

Through the fabric of her T-shirt and bra, he felt her breasts straining against his chest. Her nipples had become hard points that tantalized him almost beyond endurance.

"Laurel, can I touch you?"

She nodded.

Shifting her in his arms, his movements slow and deliberate, he gazed down into her eyes as he slipped his hand under her shirt. She went very still as he cupped her breast through the bra. The feel of her tightened nipple against his palm was intoxicating.

Reaching around her, giving her time to pull away, he stroked the silky skin of her back, then unhooked the bra and pushed it out of the way under her shirt.

Her eyes were closed, her lips parted, but he watched her face as he took her breasts into his hands. He was instantly mesmerized by the soft feel of her skin contrasting with the hardened tips. They seemed to beg for his attention. And he brushed his fingers back and forth across them, feeling them bud even more tightly. His own body tightened in response, even as she made a low sound of pleasure.

Her eyes stayed closed, her face stayed dreamy. It held such a combination of arousal and wonder that he felt his heart turn over.

He was suddenly struck by the realization that she hadn't had much pleasure in her life. And the knowledge that he was giving it to her now humbled him.

"Laurel, sweetheart," he murmured.

"Oh, Sam. For such a long time, I thought that touching was bad. I didn't know it could be like this."

His attention was focused so totally on her that a sound in the other room barely registered.

Then the door pushed open, hitting his shoulder, and every muscle in his body went rigid as he waited to hear the words, "Police. Freeze."

It wasn't the police.

Laurel's eyes snapped open just as Teddy stepped into the room, rubbing his eyes in the light.

"Sam? Laurel? What are you doing in here?" he asked sleepily, blinking at the adults.

It took seconds for Sam to adjust his thinking. His throat felt so thick he could barely speak, his brain was so logy he could hardly think. Somehow he managed to say, "I have to cut Laurel's hair and help her dye it."

"Well, I've got to pee," the boy said.

"Sure." He backed out of the room. Laurel followed. When they were both on the other side of the door, she reached behind and snapped her bra.

"Sorry," he muttered as they stood awkwardly facing each other in the dim light.

"Not your fault. I think we were both kind of carried away."

"Yeah."

Teddy emerged from the bathroom and stumbled back across the room to his bed.

Laurel followed him and kissed his cheek as he snuggled under the covers. Then she made her way back to the bathroom. "I guess we'd better do my hair," she said briskly.

"Are you angry with me?" he asked.

"No."

"We weren't doing anything wrong," he said. "Unless you think we were."

She didn't reply.

He crooked his finger under her chin and lifted her head. "Laurel?"

She ran her tongue over her lips, a movement he followed with his eyes. "Okay, if you insist on an answer, I guess I feel like I *was* doing something wrong."

"Why?"

"Isn't it obvious?"

"Not to me."

"I'm supposed to be keeping Teddy safe, not…not losing track of everything except what you were doing to me. What if that had been the FBI? We'd be on our way to jail."

He didn't tell her the same line of reasoning had occurred to him. Instead he asked, "Is that what happened? You forgot about everything besides us?"

She gave him a tiny nod.

"Laurel, you have the same wants and needs as everyone else. You're allowed."

He saw from the expression on her face that that was a novel idea, and he felt his heart stutter.

Reaching for her, he pulled her close, held her against him, but very gently. At first her arms hung at her sides, then they came up to clasp him.

"You, too," she whispered.

"Me, too, what?"

"You're allowed to ask for what you need."

The words made him go very still. It had been eighteen months since he had thought in those terms. He'd simply been dragging himself through one day at a time. Until he'd met Laurel Coleman and Teddy Frees.

He fought against the lump rising in his throat. Lord, what irony. What timing. He'd found a woman who made him feel alive again. And the two of them were being chased by a ruthless killer bent on their destruction. Not just a killer. The police and the FBI.

And he and Laurel weren't simply trying to save their own lives. They had a little boy in their charge as well.

He must have made some sound, because her expression changed.

"What?"

"I was thinking about our timing."

She nodded solemnly.

"We'd better do your hair, then get some sleep."

"Okay," she agreed. He was disappointed by the note of relief that washed through her voice. But he didn't push her or himself.

Instead he reached for scissors. "Do you want to cut or shall I?"

"You do it."

"You trust me that much?"

"I think your hand is steadier than mine. Besides, it's easier for someone else to do it."

He took that at face value and reached for a strand of her hair, feeling the silky texture. He had intended to give her a very short cut. But as he stood there starting to work, he found he'd lost his nerve. So he settled for a trim, cutting her shoulder-length hair off a couple of inches below chin level.

He knew they were both reacting to the intimacy of the service he was performing. He knew, too, that both of them were struggling to maintain some distance.

And when he'd finished cutting, he withdrew from the bathroom and let her take over.

SAM WAS LYING on the bed, his eyes fixed on the bathroom door when Laurel finally emerged, wearing the large T-shirt he'd bought her instead of a nightgown. She paused there for a moment, lit from the back, standing tall and straight, the curves of her lithe body hidden by the shirt. But he knew they were there, and he felt his whole body tighten as he watched her take a tentative step into the room.

In the dim light, he couldn't get a good look at the haircut and the dye job. But from what he could see, the effect looked amazingly natural. And amazingly sexy.

He had the feeling that everything that had to do with her was going to turn out to have a sexual connotation for him.

He saw her look toward him, and he wanted to call out to her, to ask her to come sleep with him. Only sleep. Because he wanted the pleasure of holding her close in the night. Just once.

He'd made some difficult decisions while she was in there. And they didn't involve dragging her and Teddy all over hell evading Frees and the cops and the FBI. Tomorrow he was going to find a safe place to stash her and the boy. Then he'd set out on his own to get evidence against Frees.

But he wasn't going to open that topic for discussion tonight. So he kept his lips pressed together as he watched her wordlessly cross the room to the bed where Teddy lay and slip under the covers.

SAM WAS UP with the sun the next morning.

Looking over at Laurel and the boy cuddled together in the other bed, he didn't have the heart to wake them. Instead he left a note saying he was getting breakfast.

Thankful that Ripley's gray Camry was a very common car on the road, he found a convenience store and bought several papers, including the *Baltimore Sun*. To his relief, there was still no tie-in between the hunting lodge and the fugitives. But there were several paragraphs about the death of Mrs. Frees. He tossed the papers in the trash before crossing to the pay phone and calling Randolph Security. Randolph worked closely with the Light Street Detective Agency because Jo O'Malley, one of the Light Street Partners, was the wife of Cam Randolph, C.E.O. of the security company.

Next he tried out his new blond head of hair on the kid at the drive-through window of a fast-food restaurant that served breakfast sandwiches. The kid didn't give him a second look.

When he returned to the room, Laurel had Teddy up and dressed.

She gave him a shy smile as if to tell him she'd been thinking about their discussion in the bathroom last night. The smile made his heart squeeze, because he was pretty sure she wasn't going to like his further thoughts this morning.

"The bathroom's all cleaned up from the hairstyling session," she said. "We just have to throw out the evidence."

"Good."

"You look cool," Teddy said, then dragged them both over to the mirror so he could look at himself standing between the adults. "We all look cool." His eyes met Sam's in the mirror. "Where are we going next?"

Sam had hoped to choose the time to introduce that topic. Now he felt trapped, but he didn't want to start the precedent of lying to the kid.

"I was talking to some of my friends this morning. Friends who have a real neat house," he said. "With a playground and a swimming pool. Two children live there—Anna and Leo. And I thought you'd have fun staying with them for a while."

The boy looked alarmed. "Without you?"

"The house has a high wall all around it and a security system. The mommy at the house is named Jo O'Malley. She's a private detective, just like me. So she knows as much about keeping you safe as I do. And she's more fun," he added for good measure.

"I like *you!*"

"What about Laurel? You like her. And she's going to be with you."

In the mirror, she shot him an astonished look and started to open her mouth. After a quick glance at Teddy, she shut it again. But as they ate their picnic breakfast on the bed, she kept glancing at him with narrowed eyes.

When they were finished eating, she told Teddy he'd better go to the bathroom before they left. As soon as the bathroom door was closed, she rounded on Sam.

"I understand why it's dangerous to keep dragging Teddy around," she said in an angry whisper.

He pitched his own voice low. "It's dangerous for you, too."

"You think Teddy is going to like being left with strangers?"

"It's in his best interests. And we can stay long enough to make sure he's comfortable... I want you safe," he said with more force than he intended.

She stood with her hands on her hips. "I run my own life. I won't have you making decisions for me."

It flashed into his mind that she hadn't made such a great decision when she'd let Oren Clark talk her into kidnapping that child five years ago. But he had sense enough not to fling that in her face. Instead he observed mildly. "You let me get you away from Frees."

Her response was instantaneous and hot. "That was an emergency. This is long-range planning."

"We'll see," he answered.

"Are you saying you've changed your mind?"

He stared into her fierce, questioning eyes, thinking how much he wanted her with him and at the same time how bad an idea he thought that was. He would have said more but the toilet flushed, and they both made an attempt to loosen their postures. When Teddy came back into the room, Sam was bagging the breakfast litter and Laurel was opening the blinds.

The silence continued during the first half hour of the ride. Sam drove. Laurel sat beside him. Teddy was in the back.

Finally Laurel sighed. "Where are we going, exactly?"

"Hagerstown. To a Park and Ride lot on the south side of town. Matt Forester from Randolph Security is going to meet us with a van. Then we drive to Owings Mills."

Laurel nodded, but her rigid posture didn't relax.

Sam found himself becoming more wary as they crossed into Maryland again, although he knew the reaction was irrational. Maryland wasn't any more dangerous than Pennsylvania, now that the FBI was in on the case. But they might be thinking that he'd head back this way, back to his home base. On the other hand, they might just as well have decided that he'd cut out for parts unknown, he told himself.

He had no problem following the Randolph directions to the parking lot.

Or in finding the burgundy van at the far corner of the lot.

After cutting the engine, he stepped out—then froze.

The man sitting behind the wheel wasn't Matt Forester from Randolph Security. Instead he saw the dark hair, chiseled jaw and lean profile of Alex Shane, a Howard County, Maryland, cop.

Lord, he'd thought Randolph's phone lines were secure. But maybe the police had been listening all along!

A kaleidoscope of overlapping thoughts swirled in his brain.

He and Alex had worked together to rescue Cal Rollins, another Howard County detective, from a serial killer.

Now what were his plans? Was he here on his own? Or here on police business?

Once again, Sam cursed his lack of a weapon, then conceded it wouldn't do him any good. Alex was a friend. He couldn't pull a gun on him. Which was maybe why the police had sent him to this meeting.

But Sam wasn't going to stay around to find out what they had in mind. With lightning reflexes he leaped back behind the wheel and threw the car into reverse. But the van was already pulling out in back of him so that the two vehicles came together with the rending sound of crumpling metal.

Chapter Eight

The car was still reverberating from the impact when Alex jumped out of the van. One of his hands was raised in the air. The other was fumbling furiously in his pocket.

"What...what's happening?" Laurel screamed.

Sam answered with a curse, his eyes on Alex. He watched the cop pull out a white handkerchief and raise it over his head, waving it vigorously. At the same time, he was shouting something, his gestures exaggerating his words.

"Stop, you damn fool!"

Sam caught that much. At the same time it registered that Alex appeared to be alone, although that could be a trick. The van could be full of cops.

But Alex was an honorable guy. He wouldn't hold up a flag of truce unless he was serious about it.

So Sam took a chance and slammed the gear lever into park.

"Don't," Laurel whispered as he started to open the door.

"I think it's okay," he answered, praying that he'd made the right decision as he stepped back outside.

Alex strode toward him, still with his hands in the air. "I get the feeling you don't know I resigned from the Howard County Police Department and joined Randolph Security a couple of weeks ago,'' he said in a mild voice.

"No, I guess I wasn't in the loop."

Alex lowered his hands. "A memo went to your office."

"I haven't been paying much attention to my mail." Sam sighed. "So you're not the cops after all. Why not?"

"I liked working with Randolph Security when we rescued Cal Rollins. I liked the way they did things."

"No problem about red tape."

Alex laughed. "That's part of it. I guess I'm a cowboy at heart."

"Well, you took about ten years off my life when I saw you in that van. I thought I was meeting Matt Forester. Where is he?"

"We've got a rush security job down in Virginia. It looks like the equipment is defective. Since that's his area of expertise, he and Cam Randolph went down there to troubleshoot the system, and I got sent up here. We would have called you to tell you about the change in plans, but there was no way to get in touch with you."

"Right," Sam answered. "My cell phone's back in the motel where Eric Frees took us captive." He eyed the dent in the side of the van. "I assume Randolph has insurance."

"I assume so."

Sam watched Alex looking over the parking lot and realized that the two of them would have aroused considerable interest, if there had been anyone around to observe the crash. Luckily, they were alone.

Except for Laurel and Teddy who were staring at them wide-eyed.

Sam motioned to her, and she climbed out of the car, holding tightly to the boy's hand.

"Laurel, Teddy, this is Alex Shane, formerly of the Howard County police. He's with Randolph Security now, a fact that I wish I'd known five minutes ago. Alex, these are my traveling companions. Laurel Coleman and Teddy Frees.''

Teddy inspected him with interest. "Why did you stop being a policeman?" he asked.

Alex grinned at the boy. "I worked with Randolph Security on a job and realized that I liked the way they worked. Plus, they've got more neat equipment than the cops.''

Teddy nodded.

"We shouldn't be standing around talking," Sam advised.

Alex nodded, then ushered them into the van for the trip to the Randolph estate.

LAUREL FELT HER NERVES stretching tighter the closer they got to Baltimore. But she sat calmly in the van, trying to convey to Teddy that there was nothing to worry about.

In the front, she could hear the two men talking, their conversation guarded. She supposed they were being careful not to worry Teddy. He'd been through so much since the two of them had climbed out the window and down the tree, and she wished the running and hiding could be at an end.

Which was why she'd agreed to let him stay with Jo O'Malley and her husband Cam Randolph. At least she'd tentatively agreed. She was reserving the right to make a final judgment until after she met Jo O'Malley and saw how she interacted with her children. Laurel still didn't know whether Sam had oversold his proposition to get her to agree.

At least security looked pretty impressive, she mused as they pulled up in front of a walled estate, the driveway blocked by a wrought-iron gate. Before they were admitted, Alex stopped beside a video camera and punched a code into a keypad beside an intercom. Then the gate swung open and they drove through.

Laurel was even more impressed as the van rolled up the wide driveway. She'd thought that the Frees estate was luxurious, but as she gazed around at the manicured greenery and the sprawling mansion beyond, she decided that the Randolphs were in another league entirely.

Eric Frees had gone for a house and garden that showed off his wealth. The Randolphs obviously had plenty of money, but they seemed more interested in understatement.

After they all got out, Sam introduced Laurel and Teddy to Jo O'Malley and her son and daughter, Leo and Anna, five and three, respectively.

Laurel glanced from Teddy to Sam. She could see the boy was a little uncertain. She was jittery herself, actually. She didn't know whether Sam had said anything about her background to this woman with a mop of red curls and twinkling blue eyes who was making friendly chatter to the newcomers.

Would she be so welcoming if she knew she was entertaining an ex-convict? Laurel wondered. She wished she'd had a chance to ask Sam some questions. But the only private moment they'd had was when Teddy had briefly disappeared into the bathroom.

If she'd been alone she might have stuck close to Sam. But since she had Teddy to think about, she acted as if she were perfectly comfortable in this new environment.

Jo invited them inside.

Laurel slung her arm around Teddy and felt him pressing close to her as they went down a long hallway and into the kitchen. It was difficult not to start babbling to Jo—about how he liked to play with Lego blocks and Matchbox cars and puzzles. That his favorite board game was Sorry! That he was learning to ride a bike with training wheels. But she held the words back because she didn't want to come marching in here and start making demands. She felt better when Jo offered the kids juice and cookies.

As they ate their snack, the youngsters started to get comfortable with each other. And it struck her then how normal this scene was. It seemed as if they'd been running and hiding all their lives even though it had been less than two weeks. But here was Teddy in a warm country kitchen with other kids, enjoying a snack.

After a half hour here, she was pretty sure that staying with Jo and her children was the right thing for him because it could give him the stability he'd been lacking. And it would make him feel safe. That was important after everything they'd been through.

Safety. The concept had a seductive appeal for her, too. But she couldn't give in to her own weakness. She had to keep control of her life. And the way to do it was to help Sam get the drop on Eric Frees.

She couldn't do it if she was hiding in this mansion, she told herself. But she knew there was more to her feelings than the need to validate herself. Something had happened between herself and Sam. Something that for her bordered on magic. He was making her feel things she'd never thought she'd feel. Making her want things she'd never thought she'd want. And she couldn't stop herself from worrying that if they broke the contact now, it would never be the same again.

A child's voice interrupted her musings. It was Leo. "Can we take Teddy out to the playground?" he asked his mother.

Teddy looked at Laurel. "Is that okay?"

"Yes. Do you want me to walk outside with you?"

He nodded.

The play equipment was only a few yards from the door. Crossing the stretch of grass, she smiled as Teddy climbed into a fort made of garden ties then slid down the rope that dangled in the middle of the floor. He was having fun, and as she watched him, she felt herself smile. Yet she didn't take his tranquillity for granted. She was pretty sure he needed to know where she was.

"I'll be right inside," she told him. "I'll sit where you can see me through the window."

"Okay."

Stepping back into the kitchen, she pulled the French doors closed. The adults were drinking coffee, and the guys were finishing off the cookies that the children had left. Yet the room was strangely silent, and she had the feeling she'd interrupted an important conversation. A conversation about her, she suddenly realized, from the way everyone was managing to avoid her gaze.

Old instincts urged her to back out the door again. Instead she made herself cross the room, pull out a chair and sit down at the table.

Alex looked down into his coffee mug. Jo turned to watch the children out the window.

There was a mug with coffee at the place where she'd been sitting. Assuming it was for her, she took her seat again, then added milk and sugar to the coffee.

Stirring it with her spoon, she asked, "Did I interrupt something?"

Sam was the one who finally spoke. "Well, Jo was pointing out that there's no reason I can't stay here and use the house as a base of operation."

That should have been a big relief. Sam wasn't going to leave her here. Yet her tension didn't drop off. "What else were you talking about?" she asked.

"I was giving them some background on the case."

"Like what?" she pressed.

"Like your account of what happened at the Frees house."

"And what else?"

"I was telling them about Eric's coming to me for help. And I needed to make it clear why I believed his initial story."

"Oh," she answered in a small voice, thinking about the implications. Then speaking softly, she added, "So you filled them in on *my* background."

"Yes."

She felt her face go hot, felt a stab of betrayal. And yet, what had she expected, after all? It seemed like a lifetime ago that she'd helped her boyfriend kidnap a child. But that episode in her life was five years in the past. In between was the prison term she'd served for the crime and the time she'd spent with Cindy and Teddy. "Are you talking about my little mistake with Oren Clark?" she asked, wanting to make sure they were on the same page. "And my stay at Jessup?"

"Yes."

She didn't trust herself to speak then. All she could do was nod.

The others were looking at her now. Lowering her head, she avoided their gazes. Alex was a former police officer. Jo was a private detective. They'd treated her as a friend when they'd first met her. They'd been thinking of her as a woman in trouble. Now she was an ex-con. And they were probably wishing they'd never gotten involved with her.

The terrible choking feeling in her throat made it impossible to draw in a full breath. She wanted to get up from the table and disappear. But she didn't know where to go.

She raised her eyes enough to look at Sam. His face was rigid. Probably he was having second thoughts about her, too.

Jo laid a hand on her shoulder. "It's okay."

"For you, maybe," she whispered.

"Sam told us what happened."

Her gaze flew to him. "You told them about…about my stepfather?"

That question hung in the air of the room like the scent of rotting vegetables.

"No," Sam answered.

And she knew she'd only made things worse. He hadn't talked about *that*. But her dumb accusation had started them wondering.

It was impossible to stay where she was. With a strangled little sound, she sprang up, knocking over the chair. Blindly she ran out of the room, down the hall and out the front door.

When she heard footsteps behind her, she ran faster.

Sam reached her as she was twisting the knob on the front door. His hand covered hers, and she tried to twist away.

"Laurel, don't."

"Let me go."

"Laurel." He pulled her away from the door, pulled her into a room off the hall.

His arms went around her, and she stood stiffly for a moment, then pushed away.

"Don't touch me."

He backed up, hands palm up. "I'm sorry."

"Yeah, I'll bet."

"It was important for them to understand why I took Eric Frees as a client."

"Right. You needed to make sure you didn't look bad for taking that scumbag's word about what happened the night I ran away."

She heard him swallow. There was a long pause before he said, "You can put it in those terms, if you want."

She made a little snorting noise.

"Jo has asked us to stay in her house. She and Alex needed to have an accurate picture of the case. They know that you've changed since you made that mistake with Oren Clark.''

''That's not how you thought about it when you read up on me and when you first got the scoop from Eric. You were thinking, once a criminal, always a criminal.''

She saw him wince and knew that the observation had hit home.

''Eric made sure I had reason to suspect you. You and Teddy were missing, and Eric had a perfectly plausible explanation for what had happened.''

She turned away, her eyes unseeing as she faced the window. She heard him move, felt his hands settle lightly on her shoulders.

''I told you not to touch me.''

''I need to. For me.''

''Well, I need you not to,'' she said in a tight voice, still with her back to him.

Again, his hands dropped away.

Her legs felt as if they were going to buckle, and she locked her knees to keep herself upright.

''I would never betray your confidence. I wouldn't tell anyone the things you told me about your stepfather.''

''Unless it was relevant to the case.''

''It's not,'' he answered, sidestepping the accusation.

''They why did you make me tell you about it?''

She heard him draw in a breath and let it out again. ''Despite what Frees told me, I liked you. I wanted a reason to trust you.''

She didn't answer, and he was silent for several moments.

Then he cleared his throat. ''We don't have a photograph of Eric Frees, and we want to do a composite picture of him. You could be a big help.''

''You know what he looks like.''

"Not as well as you. You lived in the same house with him for months. Your input would be helpful."

It was hard to speak against the pressure of tears blocking her throat, but she managed. "Maybe. But I can't face your friends. Not now. Maybe never. So I guess you're going to have to do it without me."

Sam waited several more minutes. When she didn't say anything else, he turned and left the room.

Her legs were too unsteady to walk. Reaching out, she pressed her palm against one of the windowpanes, the glass cold and smooth against her skin.

When she thought she could manage to stand on her own, she turned back to the room. There was a couch along one wall and she staggered over to it.

Collapsing on the cushions, she sat there breathing hard. Then she lay down, rolled to her side and pulled up her knees, clasping her arms around them, thinking that she should have listened to him last night when he'd warned her about getting close to him. He wasn't her stepfather, but he was a guy. And guys were out for what they could get.

Eyes closed, she lay in the darkened room, wanting to weep and at the same time thinking she should be laughing at her own foolishness.

Eric Frees and his armed killers were after her and Teddy. Yet during the past few days with Sam, she had been dumb enough to let herself imagine that her life might turn out happy.

A strangled sound welled in her throat. She'd been dead wrong about him. Things were turning out the way they always did.

Tears leaked from her eyes, and she reached to brush them away. There was one good thing. At least it looked as if Teddy had found a place where he was safe and happy. She'd come here wondering if it was all right to leave him.

Now she had to, because she couldn't stay and face these people.

She lay there waiting for evening, thinking that was the best time to escape from this place. If she left, Eric Frees would probably find her, but she didn't much care.

She might have been dozing when a light tap at the door made her eyes snap open.

Then Jo O'Malley was standing in the doorway.

"Laurel? Are you all right?"

She pushed herself to a sitting position. "I realize this is your house and I'm being rude, but I'd like to be alone."

"Yes, I understand. But I hope we can talk for a few minutes." Jo came slowly into the room and perched on the edge of a chair a few feet away.

Laurel ran a hand through her hair, momentarily confused when she found it was shorter than she expected it to be. And blond, she remembered. Like Teddy's and Sam's.

Unable to meet Jo's eyes, she wrapped her arms around her shoulders.

"We could use your help with the composite picture."

"Well, I'm not comfortable being around any of you, so I guess you'll have to do it without me."

"Because Sam told us about the kidnapping?" Jo asked bluntly.

Wordlessly, Laurel nodded.

"Sam also told us how brave and resourceful you've been. He told us that you kept Teddy safe. That you found a place for the three of you to hide out after Frees found you. He says you saved his life when Ripley came in with a rifle. I know that whoever you might have been five years ago, you're not the same person now."

If she'd had the energy, she might have asked if Jo was saying what her guest wanted to hear. Instead she simply shrugged.

Jo studied her for a moment, then added, "I'm hoping that you've got enough spirit to come out and help us now."

The words were a direct challenge, and Laurel found herself responding. Why not? she asked herself. She wasn't going to be here for very long. She'd endured worse things in her life—like a prison strip search, for example. What these people thought about her wasn't going to make much difference in the long run.

Pushing herself up, she looked at Jo. "Okay."

"Thank you."

Her palms were damp as she followed her hostess down the hall. The children were in the family room watching a Disney video. None of them, including Teddy, looked up, and she felt relieved. He was fitting in here, just as she'd speculated he would.

They took another hallway off the kitchen. The men were in a small office sitting in front of a computer screen. They were both trying to look casual as she came in, but she could see the relief on Sam's face.

She didn't say anything to him or Alex directly, only stared at the screen, trying to maintain a certain degree of detachment.

On it was the basic shape of a man's face. It was a square face, with heavy eyebrows over light-colored eyes. She remembered the way those eyebrows had snapped together when he was angry, and those eyes had pinned her with malicious intent more than once.

Despite her vow to keep herself from feeling anything, she gave an involuntary little shiver. Beside her, Sam started to reach for her, then stopped and pulled his hand back into his lap.

Jo pulled up a seat in back of everybody else and gestured toward a chair close to the computer.

Laurel sat, conscious that she was wedged between the two men.

"We were hoping you could help us with the mouth," Alex said as he displayed a set of mouths down the side of the screen. She selected one and watched as he clicked on it and put it into place on the face.

"Not quite right," she said. "It's not broad enough."

Sam agreed. Alex brought up more examples, and she selected another. That one seemed to fit.

They went on to the nose, and Sam made that selection. He got it right on the first try—heavy enough for the aggressive face but not out of proportion. As the feature clicked into place, she privately decided that Sam could have done this just fine on his own. He didn't need her, but he'd gotten Jo to drag her out here—to make a point.

Unconsciously, she took her bottom lip between her teeth, then made an effort to relax as they went on to get the rest of the details. From the corner of her eye she could see Alex tensing as the final face took shape.

"This is Eric Frees?" he asked carefully.

Wondering what he was getting at, she gave him a narrow-eyed look. "That's what we're doing, isn't it? Making a picture of Eric Frees because you said you didn't have one."

"That's right. I did." He looked at Sam. "You agree? That's the guy who hired you to find Laurel and Teddy?"

It was clear Sam was as mystified as she. He looked from Alex to the screen, then said, "Yeah, that's the guy. Have you got some reason to doubt us?"

Alex reached into his coat pocket, pulled out a photograph and laid it on the computer keyboard. It showed the head and shoulders of a man, but she suspected the portrait had been cropped from a larger picture because there was a slightly blurry quality to the reproduction. Still, the man in the photo was perfectly recognizable to her.

"What do you mean you don't have a picture?" she almost shouted. "That's him. That's Frees."

"Maybe," he countered. "But that's not the name I've got for the guy in this photograph. As far as I know, this is Dallas Sedgwick. The crime boss who's been trying to kill Lucas Somerville."

Chapter Nine

Laurel stared from the screen to the picture, trying to take all that in. "Who are Dallas Sedgwick and Lucas Somerville?" she asked.

It was Sam who answered. "Lucas Somerville was a covert agent assigned to infiltrate the organization of crime boss Dallas Sedgwick. Sedgwick had a big smuggling operation across the border from Mexico into Texas. Drugs. *Cholos.*"

"*Cholos?*"

"Chickens—in the northern Mexican vernacular. People willing to pay a big price to have someone lead them illegally into the United States. Lucas was with a group of Sedgwick's men at a meeting to exchange drugs for money when there was an ambush. Everyone but Lucas was killed. He got away with the money, but in the process he cracked his head and ended up with amnesia.

"To make a long story short, he hired one of the other detectives in our office, Hannah Dawson, to help him figure out who he was and where the money came from. He and Hannah got very close when they went back to Texas to investigate Lucas's past," he added, then stopped abruptly, his gaze colliding with Laurel's before dropping away.

She felt a charge of energy in the room. Her mind went

blank. Was he trying to tell her something? If so, she wasn't going to listen to anything besides facts.

"Lucas and Hannah are still on the run from Sedgwick," he was saying. "They're due back here tomorrow or the next day."

"They're not just playing hide-and-seek with Sedgwick," Alex added. "Hannah was involved in a drug bust that went bad. A teenager named Sean Naylor was shot and bled to death on the street. Hannah was with him when he died. The incident led her to resign from the police department. The boy's brother, Jamie Naylor, was going after the officers involved. He killed one of them and he was trying to kill Hannah."

Laurel nodded, trying to take it all in.

Alex continued with the story. "Sam got a message from a guy calling himself Deep Throat who said he wanted to sell information about Sedgwick. Sam was sick and couldn't make the meeting, so our friend Cal Rollins kept the appointment. The informant claimed Sedgwick was in the Baltimore area and that he'd changed his name to Sierra. I guess that name was only temporary, until he was sure he could operate in the open as Eric Frees. Before the informant could say anything else, somebody started shooting. Cal's scalp was grazed and he was in a coma for several days. Deep Throat was killed. We assumed it was one of Sedgwick's men who did the shooting. And we now think there's some connection between Sedgwick and the Naylor case. The Naylor kid was involved in a drug bust. Sedgwick's the prime supplier to the Baltimore drug trade."

"I never saw a picture of Sedgwick," Sam said. "So I didn't know he looked like Frees."

"So, uh, Deep Throat claimed this guy Sedgwick is in Baltimore," Laurel murmured as she considered the implications. "And you're telling me that he's been leading a

double life. That sometimes he was Eric Frees and sometimes he was Dallas Sedgwick?''

"Do you have any other suggestions?" Alex asked.

"Sedgwick's from Texas?"

"We don't know. He worked his operation from there,
but was living in San Diego when Lucas was working for
him.''

"Eric Frees did have a slight southern accent," she said.

"Does his leading two lives jibe with the facts as you
know them?" Alex pressed.

"Well, he was away a lot on business trips. I don't know
if he was away enough to have been leading another life.
What did Lucas tell you?"

"There wasn't any occasion to ask him about Sedgwick's whereabouts back when he was undercover with
him. We just assumed he was at his home base. When the
feds closed in on his operation, they scooped up a number
of his men. But he'd disappeared. So maybe he decided to
run his drug operation from Baltimore, using his Eric Frees
persona.''

Laurel digested that piece of information. "How long
ago are we talking about?"

"Spring," Sam answered. "Was there anything unusual
going on in the Frees household in the spring? Did Eric
seem tense, upset?"

"He was never real relaxed," Laurel answered, "but he
didn't seem any more uptight than usual."

She was about to ask another question when she heard
a high-pitched exclamation from behind her. "That's my
dad!"

It was Teddy, who had come into the room without any
of the adults noticing him. Quickly her mind went back
over the conversation as she wondered how long he'd been
standing there. Getting out of her chair, she knelt beside
the boy, throwing her arm around his shoulders.

"I didn't know you were here," she said.

"I came to find you. I wanted to make sure you hadn't left."

"I would never just disappear. If I were going to leave, I'd talk to you about it first."

The boy nodded solemnly.

Alex, who had been watching them, smiled at Teddy. "How are you doing?" he asked.

"Fine."

Alex picked up the photograph from the keyboard. "Is this also a picture of your dad?" he asked.

The boy stared at the head shot for a long time. "It looks like him," he finally said. "But it looks different, too."

"Different how?" Alex prompted.

The boy shrugged. "I don't know."

"Was your dad home all the time?" Alex asked.

Teddy shook his head. "He was away a lot."

They questioned him for several more minutes, but there was nothing else he could contribute that would help them pin down the Sedgwick-Frees connection.

Laurel took Teddy back to the television room, and Jo got up to check on her own children.

"I can show you which room you're sleeping in," she said to Laurel when the children were settled again.

Laurel swallowed. She wasn't going to be staying here very long, but she didn't plan to confide that information, so she only nodded.

Jo showed her upstairs to a large bedroom decorated with several different calico prints in shades of pink and rose. It was one of the prettiest bedrooms Laurel had ever seen, and she wondered what her life would have been like if she'd grown up in a place like this.

Then she pushed that thought aside. She didn't belong here, and she never would.

"There are towels and toilet articles in the bathroom. I

have a lot of company, so there's a big closet with lots of different sizes of clothes. Take anything you need.''

"Thank you,'' she managed to say, wondering about a household that was prepared for visitors who had come without a change of clothing.

"I've got to talk to the cook about dinner,'' Jo told her.

"Sure.''

They started back down the hall.

Jo paused beside the next door. "I'm putting Sam in here.''

Laurel gave a little shrug. It didn't matter to her where Sam was going to sleep. Well, maybe it did, because it might help her avoid him.

She followed her hostess downstairs again, then found herself wandering back to the television room. Jo had been playing videos for the kids. Convenient, since the kidnapping was probably still a big item on the local news.

Standing in the doorway, she watched Teddy. He seemed fairly relaxed considering everything he'd been through. He'd be okay here, she told herself again, then felt a little pang.

His mom was dead, his father had tried to kill him. Lord, wouldn't it be wonderful if she could adopt him? Make a home for him, she thought as she allowed herself to spin out a warm and wonderful fantasy, just for a few minutes. She loved him. She'd make a good mom.

But she recognized it for the fantasy it was. The courts would decide where Teddy would live, and they certainly wouldn't give him to a convicted felon.

She blinked against the moisture that suddenly clouded her eyes. Turning, she found herself heading back down the hall. As she approached the computer room, voices drifted toward her, and she stopped, listening. It sounded like Sam and Alex were having an argument.

"I say we drop in for a visit at the Frees estate," Sam was saying, "and see what we can find out."

"Too risky," Alex countered. "From what you and Lucas have told me, he's got a squad of goons. I'd suggest you tackle this from the other end and have a talk with Sean Naylor's father. I think he knows more about what was going on with his sons than he was letting on."

"I think that's riskier than breaking into the Frees estate. Naylor is expecting trouble. Frees thinks the lush of a detective he hired wouldn't dare invade his territory."

Out in the hall, Laurel stifled a wince. Whatever she thought about Sam, she hated his referring to himself that way.

Apparently Alex shared her view. "You're not a lush," he said firmly.

"What would you call me?"

"A guy who used liquor for a while to deaden some major pain in his life, then straightened out. But let's not get sidetracked," Alex said. "We were talking about the Frees estate. If Frees—or Sedgwick—is at home, he'll have bodyguards. And there's another problem. We'd want to get in and out quickly, but we don't know the layout of the house. My advice is to stay away from there."

"I'm going this evening. If you don't want to come with me, fine."

Laurel felt her stomach clench. Sam wanted to go to Eric's house tonight? She took a step forward, then stopped. Sam and Alex had their backs to her, and neither one of them knew she was eavesdropping.

Her fingers gripped the molding of the door frame as sounds and images flashed into her mind. Evil sounds and images from the last time she'd been at that house.

The sharp voices outside her bedroom. The sound of Cindy pleading with her husband, her body thumping down the stairs. Then the men searching for her and Teddy.

They'd escaped across the roof, and as she'd fled, she'd known that nothing in the world could induce her to go back to that place.

Now...

Now she backed away from the room, then turned and hurried down the hall, glad, after all, that Jo had provided her with a room, so she could be by herself for a while.

She went into the bathroom, used the facilities, then washed her hands and face.

When she stepped into the bedroom again, she gasped. She'd expected to be alone, but Alex was standing near the door.

He was a large man, larger than her stepfather, and her automatic reaction to being alone with him was wariness. Not that she thought he was going to do anything to her, she told herself quickly.

Still, she'd felt uncomfortable with him since she'd come in from the play area and realized the drift of the conversation.

"I didn't mean to startle you."

Lord, she thought. First Jo had sought her out in private. Now it was Alex. Anxious to get this over with, whatever it was, she blurted, "What do you want? To tell me what you think about having a kidnapper in Jo O'Malley's house?"

He shoved his hands into his pockets. "I don't think you're a kidnapper."

"I served time for the crime."

"From what Sam says, you were duped into it."

"When did you talk about that?"

"A little while ago. I pressed him for details. He wanted to make it clear that it wasn't your fault."

She stared at him, taking that in.

"Earlier, while you were outside, he didn't just start talking about your background. I forced him to do it."

Her head jerked up. "How could you force him? You didn't know anything about me until he told you."

"True. But until a couple of weeks ago, I was a cop. I'm trained to listen to people. I know when a guy is lying— or leaving something important out of his story. And I knew that Sam's tale about Eric Frees hiring him didn't make sense."

When she just stood there staring at him, he went on, "I knew it from what he was saying. And I knew it from his eyes. So I pressed him. I forced him to come clean with us."

She was too shaken to respond. Sam hadn't told her anything like that. He'd simply said that he'd needed to give Jo and Alex the facts. He hadn't shifted the blame for his revelation to anyone else.

"So if you want to accuse someone, accuse me," Alex continued. "He was trying his best to protect you. I wouldn't let him do it because I needed to understand what really happened."

She licked her dry lips, wanting to turn away. But she couldn't do it. She'd made assumptions about Sam's motives and about Alex's attitude toward her—and they were dead wrong.

Alex was apparently as uncomfortable with the conversation as she was herself. Shifting his weight from one foot to the other, he said, "I heard you tell Teddy you wouldn't leave without saying goodbye to him. Give Sam that same courtesy. Better yet, don't run out on him."

She was so startled that she felt her mouth drop open. "How...how do you know that's what I was thinking?"

"Like I said, I'm good at reading people. You look like a woman who wants to bail out." He was silent for a moment. "Which is a very bad idea right now. Eric Frees, or Dallas Sedgwick, or whatever his real name is, is still looking for you. And if you listen to the news, you'll find out that you haven't dropped off the FBI radar scopes. The hunt for you is very intensive. In an ordinary B and E case, they wouldn't get around to checking the fingerprints right away. But they've already run the prints in that hunting lodge. They know you were there. They know Sam assaulted Ripley. They're doing everything they can to find you. You leave this compound, and you'll be caught by somebody. If it's Frees, he'll kill you. If it's the police, they'll turn you over to the feds, and the feds will put the pressure on to get you to tell them where Sam and Teddy are. Is that what you want to happen?''

She hadn't thought that far ahead. Now she winced.

Alex plowed on. ''Even if you don't talk, you'd be doing Sam a world of harm. He's had a rough time over the past year and a half. And he doesn't need to worry about you.''

She bowed her head, unable to answer him.

''I could see how he was with you,'' Alex went on. ''Being with you has made him care about life again. But it's more than that. He—'' He stopped, turned one palm up. ''I'm not here to force my opinion on you. Or to get you to do anything that goes against the grain. I just don't want you to do anything...foolish because you're feeling wounded. And I wanted to make damn sure you didn't condemn Sam without knowing the truth. Just like I didn't condemn you.''

She swallowed. ''I should thank you.''

''But you're still bristly.''

She gave a small laugh. ''It's hard for me to relax with new people.''

''I understand.''

Laurel screwed up her courage and asked, ''Sam is pretty observant, too. Does he know I was planning to leave?''

Alex didn't comment on her use of the past tense. ''He's too tired and too tied up in knots to notice much.''

She nodded, watched Alex leave the room and close the

door behind him. She stayed where she was, feeling the breath move in and out of her lungs, thinking that Alex had probably told her the truth. She'd jumped to the wrong conclusions, and that had made her push Sam away.

And Alex had told her Sam was tied up in knots. Because of her.

She stood in the middle of the floor, knitting and un-knitting her fingers. So many times in her life she'd felt like someone else was in control. Or she'd made the wrong decision and found herself living with the consequences.

Like now. Probably things couldn't be worse between her and Sam. She didn't know how to make them better, but she was damn well going to try.

Jo had said she'd given Sam the room next door. Was he there now? She sucked in several breaths and let them out slowly. Then she stepped quietly into the hall.

The door to the next room was closed. After a moment's hesitation, she knocked lightly.

"Who's there?"

She didn't give him a chance to tell her to go away. She simply pushed open the door and stepped inside, then snapped the lock behind her. The shades were drawn, and it took several moments for her eyes to adjust to the dim light. When they did, she saw that Sam was lying on the double bed.

Every time she saw his dyed blond hair, she was shocked again by the startling difference in his appearance.

But that wasn't the only thing that made her stop in her tracks. She'd pushed her way into his bedroom, and now she saw that the covers were pulled a little above his waist and she could see his chest was bare. His hands were cra-dled behind his head, giving her an excellent view of his muscular arms.

"What are you doing here?" he asked.

"I wanted to talk to you."

"It's been a hell of a day, and I need to get some rest before I go out tonight," he said, his voice tight as he lowered his arms. "I guess I should have locked the door."

Before he went out tonight. Well, she knew where he was going.

"I'm glad you didn't lock the door. I need to tell you some things." Quickly she crossed the room and stood looking down at him, fighting a stab of fear. Then she reached for the snap at the top of her jeans and shucked them off.

"What the hell do you think you're doing?"

"Nothing earthshaking. I just need to be close to you," she choked out. Before she could think about the consequences, she slipped into bed and rolled toward him, pressing her face against his shoulder.

She knew at once that he was nearly naked under the covers. She could feel his bare legs and chest. She could feel his muscles turn rigid, but he made no move toward her—or away.

She kept her head bent and began to speak rapidly, determined to get out what she needed to say before she lost her nerve. "When I was in prison, the women used to talk about what they missed in the outside world. Some of them missed their kids. Some of them missed good food. Pretty clothes. Being able to do what they wanted. I never had any of those things, so I couldn't identify with that." She made a small sound that might have started as a nervous laugh. "A lot of them had a man or men they missed. They'd talk about wanting to be kissed. Wanting to make love. I couldn't identify with any of that, either. Just the idea of being in bed with a man terrified me."

"Then why are you here?"

She laughed. "I guess because I wanted to find out if I was brave enough to do it." She lurched to a stop, swallowed. "None of this is coming out right. I'm not saying

I dared myself to climb in here with you just to make a point. What I really came to do was apologize for getting bent out of shape that you told Jo and Alex about my background. Alex told me he was the one who pried the information out of you. But even if he hadn't, it was relevant, whether I like it or not. My past gave you good reason to believe Eric's story about my pushing Cindy down the stairs and disappearing with Teddy.''

He said nothing, and she knew she'd made a colossal fool of herself for blurting out all of that. He didn't need to hear any of it. He already knew it.

She started to roll away from him, but his hand came up to clasp her shoulder.

"Stay here."

She'd been barely holding herself together, and just that simple gesture was enough to tip the balance.

To her utter chagrin, she started to weep.

He shifted toward her, his hand stroking her hair, her shoulder, his voice low and soothing as he told her to just let go and cry it all out.

She was helpless to do anything else, the sobs wracking her body as she pressed into his warmth.

After a time, his strength and his quiet support helped her get control of herself.

He reached behind her to the bedside table and pulled a wad of tissues out of the box she'd seen there. Rolling to her back, she blew her nose.

"Better?" he asked.

She nodded. "I'm sorry I found a reason to put a wall between us. I've only known you for a few days, but I know you're a good man. Better than you think, actually. And you made me feel things I never felt before. I knew I was safe with you. I mean, I knew you'd fight for me and Teddy, and I knew you wouldn't take advantage of me. So I kind of let my guard down. But see, it's hard for me to imagine that anything's going to work out the way I want it to. So when I came inside and realized what you'd said to Jo and Alex, I felt like you'd betrayed me. Why...why didn't you blame it on Alex?''

"When I thought about it, I realized he was right."

"You're always so damn fair!"

He laughed. "Yeah, I can't help it. Even when it gets me into trouble."

She looked up at him from under her lashes. "You're going to Eric's house tonight."

"Did Alex tell you that?" he asked, his voice taking on a hard edge.

"No. I heard you talking about it. I was in the hall."

"I didn't know you were there."

"I didn't want you to. I wanted to nurse my wounded feelings. Now...I want to go with you."

"I don't much like that idea."

"I figured you wouldn't. But I heard Alex say that you don't have a plan of the Frees house. I know the place. I lived there."

"You can draw me diagrams."

"I'm not that great at putting stuff on paper. It's easier to show you."

"Laurel, I want to make sure you're safe. That cuts out going to Eric Frees's house."

"I feel the same way about you."

"I need information. That's the best place to start."

"We could keep arguing. Or we could change the subject," she said. He had made her desperate, made her bold enough to raise up so that she could press her lips to his.

And once she did, she liked the way it felt. Just for its own sake. She kissed him then deepened the kiss.

"Are you trying for spontaneous combustion?" Sam growled, the words blurred because he seemed unable to break the contact.

"Is that good or bad?" Laurel breathed.

"It depends on your point of view." This time he did ease away from her. "Honey, a bed is a very intimate place—where things can get out of hand real quick."

"You wouldn't do anything I didn't want you to do."

"How do you know?"

"You're too honorable," she said, bringing her mouth back to his for another feast.

"I wouldn't be too confident of that," he muttered when he could speak again. Her sweet kisses were driving him around the bend. In fact, he knew that some men in this situation would take the attitude that they were being teased. He knew that wasn't Laurel's intention. She was too innocent for that. Too caught up in the heady pleasure of letting herself go. And doing it with complete confidence that she was safe in his hands.

She trusted him. And he'd die before he abused that trust. But his iron will stretched only so far, and he couldn't stop his hand from touring the front of her T-shirt, tracing the sweet shape of her breasts. They were soft and quivering, the hardened tips telling him that she was aroused.

He'd touched her before. But now they were in bed, and he knew that had been a threatening place for her. So he moved slowly, giving her time to back away. As he had last night in the bathroom, he reached around and stroked the amazing skin of her back. Then he unhooked her bra and pushed it out of the way, along with her shirt. Bending, he swirled his tongue around one pebbled nipple, then sucked it into his mouth.

"Oh, Sam," she gasped, clasping her hands around the back of his head, winnowing her fingers through his hair. "How can anything so simple feel so good?"

He lifted his head, stared down at her.

Her arms fell back to her sides, and he raised his head. "You've never felt this way before?"

"Only with you. Like when you kissed me and touched me...before you cut my hair."

"Oh yeah," he answered, remembering.

"But not this much. Not like *this*."

"How exactly?" he asked, his voice thick.

"Like my body's on fire. Like there are hot coiled springs inside me, tightening and tightening," she gasped out. "And I don't know what to do with it."

He could identify with the description. Only, he knew what he wanted to do, all right. At the same time he felt overcome by the ragged words. What had happened to her in her childhood had been monstrous—bad enough that she'd been afraid to let herself feel anything physical. She'd never allowed the sweet pangs of arousal to take command of her body.

Until now. With him.

The realization was as close to pain as it was to pleasure. He ached to show her how high a man and a woman could carry each other on this sweet current of need. He'd found a box of condoms in the bedside table—a nice, thoughtful touch—yet he knew there was danger here that had nothing to do with protection. He could panic Laurel if he did the wrong thing. Send her scurrying back to the dark frightened place where she'd languished for so long.

"You trust me, then?" he asked.

She nodded.

He leaned toward her again, stroking her delicate eyebrows, sliding his lips along the tender place where her hair met her cheek, dipping down to nibble along the line of her chin and then the side of her neck.

"Yes," he murmured when she arched to his touch.

When she sighed and sank her head to his shoulder, he kissed the side of her face, then dipped back to her breasts, moving slowly, kneading and stroking, then taking one nipple into his mouth and the other between his finger and thumb, gently sucking and squeezing, building her pleasure with all the skill and care he had ever possessed.

Every fiber of his concentration was tuned to her, to the tiny sounds she made and the ripples of sensation that flowed across her body, until she was half gasping, half whimpering.

"Sam, please. Sam!"

Touching her had set his own blood to boiling. He had never wanted a woman more urgently, more violently. He ached to strip off her panties, strip off his briefs, but he was afraid that might break the sensual spell for her. And that would be a true pity.

So instead of giving in to his own raging needs, he rolled to his back and pulled her with him so that her body was sprawled over his, then slid her downward so that his erection nestled in the cleft of her legs. Two thin layers of fabric separated his heated flesh from hers. But that didn't stop her from moving frantically against his erection. Her breath coming in urgent gasps.

He caressed her, whispered low encouraging words that came from someplace deep inside himself.

"Ah, sweetheart, that's right. Do what feels good to you. Everything that feels good."

It felt good to him, too. Damn good. Her movements quickened, then her body stiffened. When a shuddering climax seized her, she took him with her.

Her body had gone limp as his fingers stroked up and down the damp skin of her back. Turning his head, he slid his lips gently against her hair.

Long moments passed before she raised her head and looked into his eyes, stunned.

He reached to lift a lock of damp golden hair back from her face.

Still staring down at him, she moistened her lips, hesitated, then blurted out, "When I heard women talk about…sex, I thought there was something wrong with me. I thought he had done something to me so that I wasn't normal.''

He felt his chest tighten painfully. "Oh, no. There's nothing wrong with you, love. Nothing at all."

She was still trying to take it all in. "And you felt that, too? That…firestorm sweeping through your body?"

With someone more experienced he might have been embarrassed. Instead, he tightened his arms around her and nodded his acknowledgment. "Uh-huh."

She eased off of him, settled to the surface of the bed. Gathering her close, he nestled her against him then drifted into a calm and peaceful sleep that deepened quickly.

Sometime later, the ringing of the phone jerked him awake. His eyes probed the darkened bedroom, but it took several seconds before he remembered where he was and why Laurel was with him in the double bed.

She raised her head as he fumbled for the receiver. It was Jo on the other end of the line. "Sam, I know you must be exhausted. I'm sorry to wake you up, but we've got a problem."

"Yeah?" he answered, his gaze swinging to the woman who had been sleeping peacefully in his arms. She was sitting up, reaching under her shirt to hook her bra.

"It's Laurel," Jo said, the worry in her voice coming through the phone line. "We can't find her. Alex told me she might have been planning to leave. Cal and Beth are here, too. And Cam. We've all been looking. Maybe you'd better come down so we can figure out what to do."

He knew by Laurel's expression that she'd heard Jo. Suddenly he felt torn between two perfectly valid alternatives. Hours ago, he'd felt compelled to betray Laurel's confidence, and she'd been hurt and angry.

Well, he certainly knew where she was now. In his bed.

But did she want Jo and the others to start speculating about what they'd been doing up here?

Cupping his hand over the phone, he asked, "What do you want me to tell her?"

Chapter Ten

Laurel closed her eyes, fully aware of the implications. Jo and Alex had both been worried about her, and she'd sent the house into an uproar by disappearing. After a moment's hesitation, she held out her hand for the phone.

Sam's eyes met hers as he passed her the receiver.

"Jo?" she said.

"Laurel!"

"I'm with Sam."

"Thank God. We were worried, and trying not to let Teddy know. But he sensed that something was wrong."

Teddy. For the first time in days she hadn't been thinking about him. "I'm sorry. Tell him I'll be down in a little while." She swallowed. "Tell him that Sam and I had some stuff we needed to talk about." She glanced at the clock, seeing that it would have been a pretty long talk. "And…and tell him that we were both really tired and fell asleep," she added, keeping the focus of her explanation on the boy, although she knew full well that everybody down there was going to get the information.

"So everything's okay?" Jo asked.

The question covered a lot of territory, but Laurel was pretty sure Jo was asking about her relationship with Sam.

"Yes," she answered softly.

"I'm glad."

"Thank you," she murmured, not knowing quite what to say. "We'll be down soon." Reaching across Sam, she replaced the receiver.

"There's nothing wrong with you and me being up here together," he said.

"I know."

"But you're embarrassed that Jo knows we were in my bedroom."

"A little. And at the same time, I'm feeling kind of smug about…about…" She stopped, flushed.

"About making love and enjoying yourself doing it?" he said softly, leaning over to stroke his lips against her cheek.

The light touch sent a tingle along her nerve endings. Still, she managed to say, "Not everyone would call it that."

"I would." He punctuated the assertion with more tiny kisses, this time along her jawline.

The flush deepened. "I suspect a lot of guys would feel cheated."

"I don't. I wanted you to know that touching and kissing could be something good."

"You have." Just these tiny kisses were kindling heat again. "Better than I ever imagined. So good that I've started imagining the real thing."

She saw his breath catch. "Unless this is all you want with me," she added quickly.

He shook his head. "I want more. But if we start discussing it now, we may not get downstairs for a long time."

She nodded, knowing he was right. Getting into that discussion would be a mistake at the moment. She couldn't just think about herself and what she wanted. She had to go down and make sure Teddy was all right. And while she was down there, she had to get Alex Shane on her side, because if Sam thought going to the Frees mansion was the right thing to do, then they were going. At least she and Sam were going. And she hoped that Alex would come along as backup.

"We can continue the conversation later," she said.

"Yeah." He hesitated and then asked. "Would you feel more comfortable going down by yourself or with me?"

She laughed. "I guess it's a toss-up. So I'll stick with you."

"I'll take that as a good sign," he said, then added, "Give me a few minutes to get presentable."

"Me too. Ten minutes." She climbed out of bed, snatched up her jeans from the floor and pulled them on. Then she dashed back down the hall to her own room, where she washed, and took advantage of Jo's generous offer of clothing.

When she met Sam in the hall, she could see from his damp hair that he'd taken a quick shower. He'd also changed his clothes.

He gave her an easy smile, and reached for her hand as they descended the steps. She found herself gripping his fingers as they approached the family room. She had said she wanted to come down here with him, but she knew that everyone was going to be wondering what they'd been doing up in the bedroom. Well, probably not wondering. Probably making assumptions. Not exactly the right assumptions, either. But probably close enough for government work, she thought with a giggle.

"What?" Sam asked.

"My nerves are showing."

His hand tightened on hers. "We're partners in crime," he whispered just before they stepped into the family room.

Alex was there, with Jo and a man she didn't recognize who looked like a cross between a college professor and a covert agent. Probably Cam Randolph, Jo's husband, judging from their body language. Another couple stood in the background, holding hands. The woman looked as shy as Laurel felt.

She had been planning to look for Teddy the moment she got downstairs. But as she took in the scene in the family room, she saw that most of the guys were holding glasses of beer.

Sam must have made the same observation, because she sensed his body go tense.

Since Jo's phone call, she'd been worrying about what they would be thinking about her. Suddenly, her full attention was on the man at her side.

"Hey," the guy she assumed was Jo's husband said, raising his glass. "You want a beer?" It was obvious from his friendly offer that he hadn't gotten the full story of what had happened to them two nights ago. And just as obvious that Jo was kicking herself for not having warned him.

"No thanks," Sam said stiffly and very quickly.

The guy's expression changed, as if he'd just remembered why Sam Lassiter might not want an alcoholic beverage.

Jo rushed forward into the conversation gap. "Laurel, this is my husband, Cameron Randolph. Cam just got home from a job in Virginia. And Cal and Beth Rollins have joined us, too."

Randolph stepped forward and held out his hand to her. She shook it. "I'm glad to meet you. Thanks for letting us stay at your house."

"No problem. Sam and Jo work at the Light Street Detective Agency together."

"Yes. Right." Still intent on keeping the focus of attention away from Sam, she plowed ahead. "So are you going to help us break into the Frees mansion tonight?"

Cam blinked. "I didn't know that was on the agenda."

She glanced around the room to make sure that the children were out of earshot. Still, she lowered her voice as she said, "Jo must have told you something about why we're here. Eric Frees killed his wife and went after me and his son. We got away and Sam's been helping us stay out of his clutches. Then we did a composite picture of Eric this afternoon and realized he's a dead ringer for a crime boss named Dallas Sedgwick. Sam thinks we need to go to his house to look around."

Cam nodded. "Let's talk about it." He turned to Sam. "What are you looking for, exactly?"

"I don't know. Anything that will tie Frees and Sedgwick together. You see, Frees has the cops and the FBI convinced that we're armed kidnappers. So it's not just an academic question. We need to find some evidence that will clear us."

"We think it was Sedgwick who ordered that informant killed," Beth murmured. "When Cal got shot."

Her husband linked his fingers with hers. Laurel could see that Beth was shy, but she was making an effort to be part of things and trying to help Laurel feel comfortable as well. They smiled at each other.

"You think Sedgwick would leave evidence like that lying around?" Alex asked.

"No," Sam said. "But I'd like to check out the scene of the crime. And I'd like to find out where he hides stuff."

Before Alex could answer, a clatter of little feet in the doorway halted the conversation. Teddy rushed in and ran straight to Laurel. She went down on her knees, gathering him in her arms and holding tight. Lord, this child had become such an important part of her life, and she wasn't sure how she was going to cope when the authorities finally took him away from her.

"You having a good time with Leo and Anna?" she asked, struggling to speak around the lump that had formed in her throat.

"Uh-huh. But I missed you. And then I could tell that everybody was looking for you and I got worried."

The lump threatened to block off speech altogether, but she managed to say, "I told you I wouldn't leave without saying something to you."

"Yeah. But I was worried," he repeated.

"Teddy, I would never lie to you," she whispered.

She felt him nod. Eyes squeezed closed, she clung to him for several more seconds before easing away. When she looked up, she found that she and the boy were the center of attention.

"Hey, let's go sit in the den for a while, and you can tell me what you've been doing," she managed to say. Then, without glancing again at anyone in the room, she led Teddy down the hall to the room where they caught up on his afternoon.

IT TURNED OUT that the kids had already eaten dinner. So Beth Rollins helped Jo get her son and daughter to bed while Laurel settled Teddy down for the night. Then they joined the men in the dining room.

Sam looked up as she entered, and she felt a thrill at the way his eyes brightened.

Quickly she scooted around the table and took the chair next to him.

"How's Teddy doing?" he asked, clasping her hand under the table.

"Fine," she answered, giving his fingers a quick squeeze before Cam passed her a large platter of marinated steak.

Guy food, she thought with a grin as she helped herself to some meat, then mashed potatoes and gravy.

She found out the reason for the hearty meal as she caught the drift of the conversation. It seemed that in her absence, Sam must have done some fast and persuasive talking, because he had won them over to his point of view about the evening's commando raid.

Once the decision had been made, it sounded as if they were planning to invade a small nation. The operation was going to involve a van that looked as though it belonged to a plumbing and heating company, burglary tools, state-of-the-art communications devices, nightscopes and a whole bunch more toys that the guys seemed positively gleeful about using. As she listened to the men talking, she gathered that Cam Randolph was an inventor, and the assault team was going to be employing some of his inventions—devices that were not available commercially.

"When are we leaving?" she asked.

"What do you mean, we?" Sam questioned.

"I'm going with you."

"I think not."

"You want to get in and out of there fast. There's a fence around the property. It's got barbed wire at the top. But there's a gate around the back."

"How do you know?"

"Because Cindy and I used to go for walks."

Sam was about to object again, when Alex came to her rescue. "I think she'd be an asset. She can show us around the house, show us where Frees is likely to hide important papers."

Sam glared at him.

"But nobody is going in unless the place is empty," Alex added.

Laurel had trouble repressing a grin. Alex was publicly declaring that he was on her side, and that made her feel welcomed into the group in a way that no amount of private conversation could convey. And as she listened to the planning session continue, she was caught up in the excitement. After she'd pulled on black sweat clothes, she went in and kissed a sleeping Teddy, telling him softly that she was going out but she'd be back later.

Jo was waiting for her as she came out of the room he was sharing with Leo.

"If he wakes up, tell him I'll be back in the morning, and that he was sleeping when I kissed him goodbye."

"I will," the other woman agreed.

But the sober expression on her face made Laurel go still.

"I know you want to go on this expedition," Jo said. "But I want you to understand that the trip could be dangerous."

"I know that. Remember, this all started when I escaped from the house with Teddy."

Jo nodded. "Just be careful. You took Frees by surprise when you got away from him. But you're not trained for covert operations the way the guys are. Stick close to Sam and do what he tells you." She forced a smile. "The good news is that the Frees house is the last place the police and FBI will be looking for you, so you won't have to worry about them."

"Yeah, right. Unless something goes wrong," Laurel answered, tucking her blond hair under one of the knit caps the raiding party was wearing.

Beth joined them, and as they walked downstairs, Laurel felt a kind of suppressed excitement. Not just from the mission. From this community of people. Cindy had been her only good friend, but now she was starting to feel her personal world opening up because of Sam and these friends of his who had accepted her, too.

As they reached the van, she saw Cam Randolph was driving, Alex was in the front seat, and Cal was staying behind to man the communications equipment. Laurel climbed into the back of the vehicle with Sam.

In the dim light she could see his face was stony. She knew he was still worried about her going along, and she didn't want to argue about it in front of the others. So, after the light went off, she reached out and covered his hand with hers, wondering how he would respond. When he turned his palm up and knit their fingers, she breathed out a little sigh and settled against him.

For years she had thought that touching was bad. With Sam, everything had changed. So after a few minutes, instead of simply sitting in the dark worrying about returning to the house where Eric had tried to kill her, she began to stroke her fingers against Sam's, amazed at how the simple movement could send ripples of heat to intimate parts of her body. Feeling very bold, she let go of his hand and pressed hers to Sam's thigh. Eyes closed, she explored the firm muscles below the fabric of his sweatpants, wishing they were alone in his room instead of in the van about to reach the Frees estate.

From the corner of her eye she caught sight of the gateposts that marked the entrance to Frees's property. She was sure Sam felt her shiver as they passed the turnoff, then proceeded slowly down the road toward a patch of woods. Cam pulled the van under overhanging branches and pressed a button on the dashboard. Laurel leaned forward, watching him scan some instruments that were unfamiliar to her.

"I'm not detecting any kind of electronic net around the house," he said.

"That's good," Laurel whispered.

"Perhaps not. Maybe it means that Frees wants us to walk into a trap."

She nodded tightly, knowing that she was out of her depths. But she wasn't going to admit that now.

"I'd feel better if you stay here with Cam," Sam said, giving her one more chance to back out gracefully.

"I'm going along," she said firmly, picking up the pack she'd set on the floor.

"Fine," he muttered, shifting his own pack over his shoulder.

The team climbed out of the van and pulled on rubber gloves before putting on night-vision goggles and starting through the woods toward the mansion. Angling away from the road, they headed toward the back of the property.

When they reached the chain-link fence, Sam brought out a device that he used to scan the fence. Next he attacked the padlocked gate with a set of picks.

The sound of the lock clicking open zinged along Laurel's nerve endings, and she clenched her teeth as Alex opened the gate. She'd spent the past several hours telling herself that she could handle coming back to this charming antebellum-style mansion. Now all the terrifying memories of her escape were crowding in around her, and it was too late to back out.

The men were on either side of her. Silently she pointed out the best way to reach the house. It loomed dark and brooding at the other side of a small woods.

Sam pointed to the wide back porch and the tree next to it. "That's where you got down with Teddy?" he asked.

"No. We went across the front portico."

"Is it as high up?"

"Yes."

"I'm impressed," Sam muttered.

As they drew close, Alex pulled another scanning device from his pack, pointed it at the wall and moved it back and forth. Cam Randolph had already explained its purpose to Laurel. It was a heat sensor, and it would tell them if anyone was inside.

She stood with her hands clenched, waiting for the verdict.

"It looks like no one's home," Alex finally said.

When she let out the breath she didn't know she'd been holding, Sam slung his arm around her shoulder. "Let's go," he murmured, his voice pitched low, as though he didn't quite trust technology.

Laurel led the way across the patio to the French doors, which Alex examined carefully.

"The alarm system on the house isn't active," he informed them.

"Why not?" Sam growled.

Alex shrugged, then gingerly began to work on the lock. He had it open as quickly as Sam had dispatched the padlock, then stepped inside.

Laurel came next, followed by Sam.

She stood for a moment in the breakfast room, her eyes and ears probing the shadows and quiet around them.

It was a cozy room. She remembered the mornings she and Cindy had sat here talking, and the many afternoons she and Teddy had played here. Now the room felt devoid of life.

The goggles were heavy and beginning to hurt her head. "Can we take these off?" she asked Sam.

He thought about it for a moment, then pulled his off, stuffed them in his pack and pulled out a large flashlight.

She and Alex did the same.

As they'd already agreed, she led the way to Frees's home office. But as they crossed the front hall she couldn't hold back a small sound.

Sam looked toward the stairs. "That's where he pushed her down?"

"Yes," Laurel whispered, trying not to picture her friend sprawled on the marble floor.

He slung his arm around her, moving her away. The minute they stepped into the office, she knew that somebody had been there first. In the beams from the three flashlights, she saw that file drawers hung open. Papers were scattered over the surface of the desk and onto the floor.

Sam crossed to the window and drew the drapes, then he switched on the light.

They all stood blinking, looking around at the chaos.

"I'd like to know who did this," Alex growled.

"Either somebody else is interested in Frees, or he did it himself," Sam suggested.

"Why would he do that?" Laurel asked.

"To make it look like he'd been burglarized." He shrugged. "That's just a guess." Stepping to the filing cabinet, he began to sift through the remaining contents.

Alex sat down at the computer and booted up the machine. After several minutes, they heard a frustrated curse. "It looks like the hard drive has been wiped. If I had to guess, I'd say that Frees is hiding evidence."

"Like what?" Laurel asked.

"That he's Dallas Sedgwick."

She thought about that. "You think he came back here to remove anything incriminating, then cleared out?"

"Yeah," Sam snarled. "And it looks like he was in a hurry. Which might mean he didn't get everything he was looking for. Where else do you think there might be papers hidden?"

"They had a safe somewhere in the master bedroom," Laurel answered. "I'm not sure exactly where."

"Let's go up there," Sam suggested.

They had started back down the hall when Sam stopped and sniffed the air.

"What?" Alex asked.

Turning, Sam headed for the family room. As Laurel followed, she suddenly realized what he was smelling.

Unconsciously, she grabbed his arm, but he pulled away from her and quickened his pace. The door to the room was closed. When he thrust it open, Laurel gagged as the smell of liquor enveloped her.

Sam made an angry sound as he shone his flashlight on

more than a dozen smashed liquor bottles. With the door open, their fumes were so strong that she thought a lit match might set off an explosion.

Sam's light swung around the room. It came to rest in the center of a pile of glass that was crowned by a full, intact bottle of bourbon.

"The son of a bitch," he growled. "He left that for me. There's not a doubt in my mind who trashed this house."

Stepping back he slammed the door with a curse.

"Which way to the master bedroom?" he asked, his voice low and dangerously controlled.

"Up the stairs and down the hall to the right."

She gasped once more when she saw the master bedroom suite. It was in the same condition as the office. Only worse because someone had taken the time to empty the perfume bottles and makeup on Cindy's dressing table and the floor. The same someone had also pulled her clothing and Eric's off the hangers and tossed them in all directions.

Laurel stared at the destruction. "Why would he do that?"

Alex, who had joined them, answered the question, "He's losing it."

"The safe's over here," Sam said. "And we won't need to break into it. It's already open—and empty." He turned away in disgust, then stopped and stooped down. When he stood, he was holding a large gold cuff link that had wedged itself under the shoe rack. On the burnished surface were the initials DS.

"Looks like that belongs to Dallas Sedgwick," Alex commented, holding out his hand. "He must not have realized he dropped it when he was gathering up his stuff," he added as he inspected the piece of jewelry, then slipped it into his pocket.

Sam nodded tightly.

They looked through the mess for more items that might have been overlooked but found nothing more.

"We should leave," Alex finally said.

They started toward the stairs, with Sam in the lead. Laurel was in the middle and Alex brought up the rear.

Three-quarters of the way down the hall, Laurel stopped.

Sam whirled. "Come on. We're getting out of here. I've got a bad feeling about this place, starting with the alarm system being deactivated. I'm thinking that Frees was hoping we'd come here, and we've obliged him."

Laurel gestured toward the doorway in front of her. "This is Teddy's room. When I took him away, we had to leave without any of his toys. Do you think I could bring him something?"

Sam's eyebrows were knitted as if the simple question were a complicated puzzle she'd just presented to him.

So many rooms in the house had been reduced to chaos, but as Laurel shone the light inside Teddy's bedroom, she breathed out a little sigh. Nothing looked out of place. In fact, his bed was made, and she saw familiar stuffed animals, trucks and a box of snap-together plastic blocks neatly lined up along the window seat. In the middle of the window seat was Mr. Nutmeg, the bear that Teddy had loved best of all. His dad had told him he was too old to be playing with stuffed animals, but Laurel had often sneaked the bear into bed with him.

"Hold up a minute." Sam took a step toward her. From behind her, he shone his flashlight into the room, the beam bouncing off the toys, then focusing along the rug and down toward her feet.

"Just let me get Mr. Nutmeg," she murmured. "Teddy's been cut off from everything familiar. He'll be so glad to have his favorite toy. And maybe I can bring his plastic blocks, too."

"No!"

She had already started through the doorway when she felt something brush against her shoe.

"Get down," Sam shouted.

From the corner of her eye, she saw Alex hit the floor. Sam grabbed her by the shoulders, jerking her back and to the right as he slammed the door in one fluid motion. Twisting, he threw her to the carpet so that she landed underneath him.

"What?" Laurel screamed.

Before Sam could answer, an explosion from inside the room blew the door off its hinges.

Chapter Eleven

The door went flying over their heads and crashed into the
balustrade. Sam was on top of Laurel, pressing her against
the carpet as debris blew outward from Teddy's room and
rained down around them. When the world stopped vibrating, she sat up, staring at the plaster dust that coated Sam's
clothing.

She gasped, coughed as she tried to breathe. She could
see chunks of wallboard and other building materials
strewn around them. And as she craned her neck, she saw
some of the debris had careened over the balustrade and
landed on the marble floor below.

Down the hall, Alex sat up looking dazed. She could
imagine her expression matched his.

"Are you all right?" Sam asked, his breath wheezing in
and out of his lungs.

She gave a small nod, coughed again as she brought her
gaze back to him again. "How did you know?" she choked
out.

He had to clear his throat before he could answer. "I
had a bad feeling about the house. Then the room looked
too perfect. I was thinking it was set up for you. A temp-
tation. Like the liquor was set up for me. Then I saw the
wire inside the doorway."

"The wire," she repeated, remembering that something had brushed her foot.

"A trip wire," Alex clarified, cleared his throat. "Attached to a bomb."

She was staring around her in horror, thinking about what might have happened if Sam hadn't pulled her back and slammed the door, when a low, vibrating sound invaded her consciousness.

She stiffened, then saw Sam pull a phone out of the pack that was still slung over his shoulder.

"What the hell was that?" Cam Randolph's voice came over the speaker as Sam pressed the button.

"A little explosion."

"It didn't sound so little. Are you all right?"

"Yeah," Sam answered. "We're fine."

"I suggest you get out of there. If I heard that blast, you can bet the neighbors are wondering what happened. I don't think it would be such a good idea for the kidnappers to be found at the scene of the crime."

"I had the same thought," Sam agreed as he wiped gypsum dust from his shoulders, then reached to brush his fingers through Laurel's hair. Plaster rained down around her, and she coughed again.

The three of them made their way down the stairs, and as they walked, Laurel could see a trail of white footprints.

"We're leaving tracks. The police will know that two men and a woman were here."

"Yeah," Sam muttered. "Where can I find a broom?"

She led him to the utility closet. Grabbing the broom, he went back up the stairs, sweeping their tracks.

"It's obvious somebody was here and ran into a little trouble," Alex said. "But at least this leaves a little more ambiguity."

By the time they made it out the patio door, they could hear sirens in the distance.

Cam was waiting in the van with the engine running. "You look like you had an altercation with the Pillsbury Doughboy," he said as they climbed inside. Moments later, he was driving down the road at a sedate pace, as emergency vehicles came toward them.

"So tell me what happened," he said, after the noise had abated. "No, wait. Let me get Cal on the speakerphone. I know everybody at home wants to be in on this too."

As Sam slumped in his seat, Alex pulled out the gold jewelry and held it up. "We found a cuff link with the initials DS," he explained for the benefit of their listening audience.

"Not much for all that effort," Sam muttered.

Laurel scowled at him. "I think we found out enough. We know this guy Dallas Sedgwick was living two lives. One in Texas and one in Maryland. I think it's pretty clear he was giving up the Texas identity and moving to Maryland for good." She stopped and drew in a shuddering breath. "And a wife and son didn't fit into the plan. Maybe he's got another family in Texas. So he hatched a plan to get rid of this family. Only, we got in his way. And now he's got to regroup."

Alex turned and looked at her. "That's a pretty fair summary of the situation."

"But the bottom line is that we're no closer to finding the guy than we were a couple of hours ago," Sam growled.

"We will be," Cam said. He asked more questions about the raid, but only Laurel and Alex answered.

Jo, Beth and Cal were waiting for them at the front door of the Randolph mansion, and the look on their faces told Laurel they all looked to be in pretty bad shape.

"We're fine," she said as she watched Sam stalk off.

"You go on up," Beth told her. "I know you want to clean up."

"Yes."

Under a hot shower, she let the water wash away the grime from the explosion. But it didn't wipe away the edgy feeling gathering inside her. With hands that weren't quite steady, she pulled on the white terry-cloth robe that Jo had left for her on the back of the bathroom door.

After tying the belt, she turned and looked at herself in the mirror. Her face was tense but determined.

She practiced a little smile, trying to loosen her features. She couldn't get the smile to look right, so she shrugged and tiptoed out of her room and down the hall toward Sam's room.

This time when she knocked he said, "Go away," without asking who was there.

Quietly, she stepped inside and closed and locked the door behind her. There was only one light in the room, and it drew her attention to Sam, who was sitting in a chair by the window. He had also showered. His hair was wet. And he was wearing only a pair of faded jeans.

Her eyes wanted to explore the wide expanse of his chest. Instead they were drawn to the stark lines of his face.

He was staring at the bottle of bourbon that gleamed in the lamplight on the table next to him.

The bottle was open and not quite full.

He'd poured some into a tumbler, which he clasped in his hand. He was holding it up as though studying the color.

"Where did you get that?"

"I took it from Cam's liquor cabinet. I'll pay him back."

She regarded him for several seconds. "I'd ask you what you're doing with it, but I'm pretty sure I know."

He gave a small laugh, setting the glass down with a clunk. "So what's your theory?"

She folded her arms across her chest. "I think you're testing yourself. Seeing how close you can get to that bourbon without drinking it."

He shrugged, but his eyes told her that she'd given the correct answer.

"You don't have to do that," she said.

When he didn't respond, she walked across the room. Acting as if her insides weren't quaking, she picked up the glass and the bottle and carried them to the bathroom where she poured the contents of both into the toilet and flushed it.

As she came back, she saw Sam was watching her with narrowed eyes. "Now I won't be able to find out if I can do something right tonight."

"We both know you weren't going to drink that stuff."

"You've got more confidence than I do."

"Sam, you've got more strength of character than a dozen other men." When he snorted, she went on. "And if you want an example of what you did right tonight, you saved my life. And Alex's—by shouting at him to get down. I think that counts."

"It was the least I could do after insisting on getting my way."

"You were perfectly justified in wanting to check out Frees's place."

"Apparently not."

"Stop it!"

"Did you come here to make me feel better?"

"No. I came here to make myself feel better."

He raised a questioning eyebrow.

She took her bottom lip between her teeth, wishing he wasn't forcing her to be quite so explicit.

Finally, she worked up the courage to say, "This afternoon you did something else very right. You gave me back a part of myself that was missing. I've been afraid to let myself feel anything with a man. You made that okay for me." She stopped, sucked in a breath, and let it out in a rush. "I'm not very good with words. Every time I try to tell you something important, it comes out sounding wrong. What I'm trying to say is that this afternoon was a lot more than okay. It was maybe…what they call a peak experience. And I was hoping we could, uh, go a little further with it. But if you want to be by yourself, I guess I can understand that, too.''

When he said nothing, she ducked her head and turned quickly, hoping she could make it out the door before she started crying.

But she hadn't taken two steps when she felt Sam's hand on her shoulder, turning her in his arms.

''I'm not fit company for anybody.''

''You're fit company for me.''

When he didn't reply, she closed her eyes and pressed her head against his shoulder. ''I guess from your point of view, it seems like I came in here making demands.''

''No. You're offering me a whole lot more than I deserve.''

She raised her face to him, her eyes fierce. ''Sam Lassiter, I'm tired of hearing you run yourself down!''

To make sure he couldn't talk back to her, she pressed her mouth to his. His reaction was swift and primal. He kissed her hard, a desperate kiss filled with hunger, and she knew in that incandescent moment that he needed her as much as she needed him. The realization was heady.

He needed her!

And suddenly she felt a freedom she'd never felt before. A freedom to feast on him, to angle her head one way and then the other, taking the kiss to a level of intimacy that she once would have found shocking.

She knew then that he had held himself back until now. Knew by the way his hands moved restlessly over her— across her back, down her spine, to her hips, molding their bodies, sealing them with heat.

Except for the few times she'd been with Sam, she was

a total novice at giving and receiving such passion. Yet in this bedroom, with this man, she met his hunger with hunger. Her mouth exploring his, her hands clutching at him, pulling him closer.

She heard tiny, whimpering sounds and knew they were coming from her own throat. She felt her knees buckle, and he took her weight against himself. His hands and mouth feasted, greedy and urgent.

"Anything. Anything you want," she whispered.

She felt him go very still then, heard his indrawn breath.

"What am I thinking? I'm going too fast for you."

"No."

"Yes." He eased away from her, then swung her up into his arms and carried her to the bed. Pulling down the covers, he laid her gently on the bottom sheet. Then he came down beside her and pushed back a lock of her damp hair, his face both serious and passionate.

"I want you," she whispered. "When I think about that, I know it's a miracle. Well, not a miracle. You changed me. Made me want to take the pleasure you give me and return it to you."

In the muted light, he stared down at her, his eyes so warm that they heated her from the inside out. "Oh, Laurel."

She was ready for this. She wanted this. But her nerves jumped as his hands went to the belt of the robe. Gently he untied it, then carefully spread the fabric open, his hands barely grazing her flesh.

The last time they had been together—the only time—she had been wearing a T-shirt and panties. Now...

Now her breath caught as his gaze moved over her body, from head to toe and back again.

Lifting his eyes to hers, he murmured, "You are so beautiful."

"Am I?"

"Oh, yes. You're perfect. And so damn sexy." Lightly his hand slid down the side of her breast, her belly, her thigh; and her body responded to the warm, sensual touch.

It was a miracle, she thought again. A miracle that she could lie here, letting a man look at her body and touch her after everything that had happened to her. But the man was Sam Lassiter, and that made it all right.

Smiling at him, she pulled her arms from the sleeves of the robe, then lifted her hips enough to toss the garment away.

"You, too," she whispered. "I want you naked, too."

"Oh yeah." He stood, shucked off his jeans and briefs in one fluid motion.

He stood before her tall and strong and aroused. Not so long ago, the sight of him would have been enough to send her running from the room. And, in fact, a little bit of anxiety nibbled below the surface of her calm.

She masked it by holding out her arms. Still, she suspected that he understood. Because when he came down beside her and gathered her to him, he moved slowly and tenderly.

Closing her eyes, she absorbed the reality of his naked body pressed to hers, absorbed the pleasure of skin against skin.

He kissed her then, gently at first and then with more heat as she accepted what he offered.

His hair-roughened leg moved between her smooth ones, and she arched against him as his hands began to stroke her breasts, starting at the outer margins, the teasing caress making her nipples beg for attention. She didn't have to tell him what she wanted. He gave her pleasure with a generosity that had her dragging in ragged gulps of air, as she moved urgently against him, her hand splaying across his hips, her fingers digging into his flesh.

The gratification he gave her was exquisite, and the need

to give it back to him made her dare what she would have thought beyond her.

Shifting to her side, she slid her hand down his body and found his sex, closing her fingers around him, moving in ways she knew would please him.

A sense of triumph surged through her as she heard his breathing go ragged.

"Oh, Laurel," he groaned, his hips straining toward her, even as his mouth found one of her taut nipples and suckled.

The sensations built, and she knew she was headed where he had taken her before. "Sam, please. I'm going to... Please," she gasped out, unable to quite say the words, but hoping that her hands clutching at his shoulders would tell him what she wanted.

"We can do what we did the last time," he whispered, his lips against her cheek.

"No." She swallowed, raised her face toward his. "I want you inside me. Please, give me that gift."

"*You* are the gift," he whispered, taking out one of the condoms from the drawer and readying himself before moving between her legs, spreading her thighs as his mouth found hers.

She felt his erection pressing against her, pressing into her. Then a stab of pain took her by surprise, and she cried out, her body stiffening in protest.

Above her, Sam went instantly still.

"Laurel?"

"I'm fine," she managed to say. "Fine." Her arms tightened around him, her hips tilted up to take him deeper. Reaching up, she stroked her fingers against his lips. "Take me where you took me before," she murmured.

He kissed her fingertips, then began to move, his eyes on her face as he set a slow rhythm.

"Oh, Sam. That's so good."

Her hands slid up and down his back, over his buttocks, gathering him to her. And as the pace become more urgent, more demanding, she dug her fingers into his flesh.

He took her higher and higher, his hand sliding between them to intensify her pleasure, sending a tidal wave of sensation washing over her, through her.

"Don't stop," she gasped, her movements becoming frantic as she sought her release. "Don't stop."

And then she felt the first bright burst of ecstasy deep in her belly. The sensation cascaded, took over her body.

Above her, Sam drank in her glad cries, even as his own body convulsed so that they were swept along together in a great wave that locked them together in fulfillment.

She was left gasping for breath, clinging to him, her body still vibrating with rapture and her mind marveling at the gift he'd bestowed on her.

Never until she had met this man had she dared to imagine that her body could give her so much pleasure.

She didn't realize she was crying until she felt him shift off of her, heard his urgent voice.

"Laurel. Laurel, are you all right?"

She nodded against his shoulder, struggled to rein in her emotions. "Fine...I'm fine," she assured him once more.

"What is it? Did I hurt you?"

"No. I mean, only for a moment. Only at the beginning. Then you..." She struggled for some metaphor that would convey her awe. "You carried me over the moon."

"You carried me there too," he answered, his lips stroking her damp cheek.

She felt triumphant, exalted, smug. Because Sam had helped her defeat the demon that had haunted her past.

She ached to tell him that. She ached to overflow with her thanks. And most of all, she ached to know what making love had meant to him.

Certainly not as much as it had meant to her.

But she wouldn't let that make her sad. And she wouldn't place any demands on him. She had no right to make any claims on this man, because she was the last thing he needed. A woman who was a convicted felon. A woman being chased by a killer.

But she had this night with him. And perhaps a few more.

She didn't want to sleep. She wanted to savor this time with him. But the night had been too full of activity. Danger before the ecstasy.

And so it wasn't long before consciousness slipped away.

She woke when the first gray light of dawn invaded the room. Not so many days ago her sleep had been light and fitful.

Last night she hadn't stirred.

Sam was still in bed, but he had drawn away from her. He was lying with his hands wedged behind his head, his profile rigid.

Barely moving her head, she studied his face, wondering if he was regretting their night together. He must have sensed that she was awake, because he turned toward her, and she saw he was making an effort to relax.

"What are you thinking about?" she asked quietly.

"How to set up a meeting with Sean Naylor's father."

"You told Alex that was too dangerous!"

"It doesn't matter what I said. It's got to be done because he's the only link we have to Sedgwick now. What I'm thinking is that if Sean Naylor worked for him, we might have a lead."

"Can't somebody else do it? You told me there were other people involved. Hannah and Lucas. And Cal."

He sighed. "I'll have help—and I don't mean *you*."

"But you got into this mess because of me."

His hand tightened on her flesh, and she winced.

"Sorry." His fingers loosened, and she pressed her hand

over his. "If you're feeling guilty, you can forget it. I got into this months before you escaped from the Frees mansion—when Deep Throat wanted to sell me information about Dallas Sedgwick. He picked me because I was a friend of Hannah's. And she and Lucas were already hiding out. When Sedgwick hired me to look for you, he must have known I was trying to chase him down. You gave him the perfect opportunity to get even with me. He knew he could reel me in because he'd studied my background. He knew I'd be likely to believe his story. I was the perfect dupe."

"No!"

"Then what?"

She gave him a fierce look. "I'd say he knew you were a man with integrity." She swallowed. "A man who'd lost his own family, so he'd be sympathetic to the story of his son's being kidnapped. And don't tell me that makes you a dupe! It makes you sensitive!" she added, the exclamation making her throat constrict.

"Sensitive!" He flung the word at her as if it were a curse.

"Are you saying that's bad? Are you trying to pretend you weren't sensitive with me when we made love." She glared at him in the dim early-morning light. "Are you thinking I could have trusted someone else to touch me and kiss me the way I trusted you?"

She stopped abruptly, thankful she hadn't said more, and worried that she might have given away too much of what was in her heart. In truth, she didn't really want to hear the answers to any of those revealing questions.

She'd already discovered a good way to keep him from answering back. As she'd done the night before, she sealed her lips to his.

There was a moment full of tension when she was afraid he might pull away. Then he gathered her to him, his mouth urgent as it began to move against hers, and she gave herself over to the magic that only he could create.

THIRTEEN HOURS LATER, Sam drove slowly down a block in east Baltimore, intently scanning the area.

The sun was a red ball of flame in the sky, reflecting off the windows on the right side of the street.

Long ago when he'd been a uniformed officer, he'd patrolled this working-class neighborhood on foot. Typical Charm City row houses marched down the block, some with their original brick or wood exteriors, some refaced with artificially formed gray stone that was, for some unfathomable reason, a building fashion statement.

The house he sought was in the middle of a block. The home of Arnold Naylor, father of Sean and Jamie Naylor.

Sean was dead, shot during a drug bust nine months ago. Jamie was in prison for murdering Ron Wexler, one of the officers involved in the incident. He'd also gone after Hannah Dawson, but Hannah had, thankfully, gotten away.

The senior Naylor had refused to give any information to the police. Now, suddenly, he was willing to tell what he knew. And he'd agreed to talk to only one person—Sam Lassiter.

Sam's hands clenched on the wheel. He didn't much like this setup. But he couldn't see any alternative to the meeting.

Of course, there was always the question of why the senior Naylor was willing to talk when he'd kept his lips buttoned up until now. Was he out for revenge, the way his son Jamie had been? Or maybe it was nothing personal. Maybe Sedgwick was simply paying him off to lure Lassiter into a trap. Because Sedgwick's Baltimore connection had gone sour and Lassiter was on his case now. And maybe Cindy Frees had found out that her respectable husband was a drug dealer—and that was why he'd knocked her off.

That made a kind of horrible sense. Bump off the witness. And bump off Sam Lassiter. But he was prepared to take the risk of being set up because he needed information if he and Laurel were ever going to get the police, the FBI and Sedgwick off their backs.

As he pulled into a parking space around the corner, an image floated into his mind. An image of Laurel lying on his bed, holding out her arms to him.

Cutting the engine of his rented Dodge, he sat with his skin suddenly feeling too tight for his body as he remembered what it had been like making love with her last night and this morning. Incredible.

All that sensuality and generosity had been frozen up inside her. And he had been the one to release it. He was awed by that realization. Awed that she'd trusted him so much. He'd wanted to tell her that, yet the words had stayed locked inside him because he had no right to make any claims on her. Not when the Eric Frees situation was hanging in the balance. And not when every bottle of booze he saw set up a craving inside him that was like a ticking bomb.

His hands tightened on the wheel as he squeezed his eyes shut, fighting off the fear that was always ready to pop into the open like a goblin released from a box. The fear that the craving would swallow him up.

He took a couple of deep breaths, then climbed out of the car and locked the door.

The sun had dipped below the row of houses at his back, plunging the sidewalk into twilight. Although the street looked deserted, he felt as if he was being watched.

Shoving his hands into his pockets, he made his way along the side street and into the alley that ran between two rows of houses. A good spot for an ambush, he thought as he scanned the rooftops and the fenced backyards of the row houses.

He resisted the impulse to check the special equipment he was wearing under his shirt. Cam Randolph had checked it out before he'd left. If it wasn't working now, he'd find out soon enough.

Several of his fingertips were covered with plastic-bandage strips. He used one of those fingers to lift the latch on the gate, stepped inside and made his way up the short sidewalk. Naylor had asked him to knock twice, wait five seconds, then knock again. Feeling like a character in a spy movie, Sam did as he'd been bidden.

Arnold Naylor peeked out through a slat in the venetian blind, then opened the door and stepped back for his visitor to enter. Once he had been a large, buff man. In the months since his older son's shooting and his younger son's rampage of vengeance, he seemed to have shrunken inward.

His blue eyes were red-rimmed and watery. His medium-brown hair was thinning, and in the dim light, his complexion looked like wet cement.

Sam stepped into a small, neat kitchen. Renovated some time within the past five years, he decided as he scanned the maple cabinets and new appliances.

"Thanks for seeing me," he said, wondering if he was going to end up taking the words back.

"I guess it's time," Naylor answered with a lift of his shoulder, leading the way down a Berber-carpeted hall, through a chrome and glass dining room and into a living room that was small but plush.

Naylor dropped swiftly to a blue velvet couch. Sam took a matching chair opposite him.

"So what did you want to tell me?" he asked.

"I wanted to explain about Sean."

"Why?"

"Kind of a confession," Naylor said, his eyes cast downward, his hands clenched at his sides.

"All right." Sam leaned forward, thinking that it was best to let the man start where he wanted, as long as they ended up talking about Sedgwick.

"See, I've been doing my own investigating," Naylor said. "I know now that my son, Sean, wasn't in the wrong place at the wrong time. He was on that street to buy drugs."

"Did drugs pay for all this?" Sam asked, sweeping his hand around the room and back toward the kitchen.

Naylor stiffened. "I had a good business until I got in trouble with the city."

Sam already knew about that—how Naylor had been brought into court for numerous housing violations in the slum property he owned—but he only nodded.

"Sean was planning to get out."

"Uh-huh."

Naylor raised his eyes to Sam. "See, he'd gotten his girlfriend, Denata, pregnant and he knew he had to get out of the business. But he wanted a big score one more time. To provide for her and the kid. Instead he got himself killed. And Denata, she won't let me have nothing to do with that child."

"I'm sorry about that," Sam allowed. "But none of that information is relevant to me."

"I'm sorry too in a way. I wanted you to understand," Naylor said. "I needed the money to buy Denata's goodwill and to buy a decent lawyer for my boy, Jamie. He was crazed by his brother's death. He didn't know what he was doing when he killed that cop."

Sam shifted in his seat. "Oh yeah?"

He saw Naylor's gaze flick to the closet bin back of him.

Sam was out of his seat in time to feel the barrel of a gun jammed against his spine.

"Raise your hands slowly," a familiar voice said.

It was Bo, one of the two goons who had shown up at the motel with Frees. The one who brought the bourbon.

A mixture of anger and fear rose in Sam's throat.

Chapter Twelve

"Hands up," the thug repeated.

Sam pressed his arm firmly against his side, feeling the plastic container under his shirt begin to depressurize.

Then, knowing he had no choice, he raised his hands, keeping his gaze fixed on Naylor. His job now was to keep the conversation going for a few more critical moments, and to keep Bo from frisking him and finding out what he was carrying.

No point in getting himself shot at this stage of the game, he thought with a strange sense of calm.

"So you need money. And Sedgwick paid you to set me up," he said to the grieving father.

"It's nothing personal. Not like Jamie going after those cops."

"Am I supposed to feel better about that?"

Naylor shrugged.

"We're getting out of here," the gunman behind him growled.

I wouldn't be too sure of that, Sam thought as he stood between the two men, taking shallow breaths. These guys were both in for a big surprise.

Specifically, the knockout gas that he'd carried in here with him. Too bad he had to take a dose of it along with the other victims. But after considering all the angles, he and Cam Randolph had concluded that carrying the stuff on his person was the most reliable delivery system. At least Cam had assured him that there would be no permanent effects.

With a kind of clinical detachment, his mind turned inward, focusing on his own physical sensations. He felt his chest tighten and his vision begin to blur, the room going from sharp focus to fuzzy. The rest of it happened quickly.

One moment he was on his feet. In the next, he was slumping to the floor, consciousness slipping from him, his mind drifting toward Laurel.

"Hey," Bo exclaimed. "I feel sick."

"Don't throw up on Naylor's nice new carpet," Sam muttered.

HE WOKE with a pounding headache and a mouth as dry as a desert island. Probably he'd been out for no more than fifteen minutes. At least that was what Cam Randolph had told him to expect.

"Sam's coming around," a voice said. It was Lucas Somerville, the cowboy turned secret agent.

Cautiously Sam cracked an eye and winced as the dim light in the room stabbed at his eyeballs.

"Just lie there for a few more minutes," Lucas advised. "Cal gave you the antidote as soon as we got inside, but it hasn't taken full effect."

Cal was on a leave of absence until Sedgwick was put out of commission, so he wasn't acting in any kind of official police capacity. He, Sam and Lucas were here together. They all shared something important in common—a need to put Dallas Sedgwick away so they could lead normal lives.

Sam tried to nod, but the movement sent what felt like an ax blade slamming through his head. He felt bad, but he knew it wouldn't be nearly as bad as the other two men who had been gassed along with him because he'd taken medicine to reduce the effects.

"The others?"

"They'll come around in a minute. You got the cure first."

"Thanks." He cautiously moved his shoulder muscles, then pressed his hands into the thick fibers of the carpet, feeling the plastic strips on his fingers, a reminder not to touch any hard surfaces without their protection.

After a few more minutes, he pushed himself up and rested his back against the chair.

Across the room, he could see Cal kneeling over Naylor's limp body. From behind the chair in back of him, he spotted a pair of legs protruding. That was Bo, the goblin who had popped out of the closet in the middle of Sam's conversation with Naylor.

Too bad Sedgwick hadn't shown up. But that would have been a lot to expect.

At least they had one of his bodyguards, and the guy should have some information about the boss.

"Naylor doesn't look so good."

"Cam said he might take longer to come around because of his age. So we'll just have to wait." He looked toward Lucas. "Better see about Bo. We don't want him waking up and going for his gun."

"I've got his gun," Lucas said as he crossed to the dining room and brought back a captain's chair. Then he picked up the thug, set him upright and started tying his hands and feet to the chair's arms and legs.

Cal had stood up and was calling Cam Randolph on his specially encrypted cell phone to give him a progress report.

Sam switched his attention back to Bo, watching the man's eyes blink open, then close again in reaction to the light.

"Wha...the hell..." he muttered.

"Surprise," Sam answered. "We wanted to ask you a few questions, and we figured a quick dose of knockout gas was the best way to invite you to the party."

Bo glared at him, then looked around at the other men in the room. "Rollins and Somerville," he muttered.

"Since you recognize us, you probably know that we want information about Sedgwick."

The man licked his lips. "I ain't talkin'."

Sam smiled at him. "I think you will. You're feeling pretty sick at the moment, aren't you?"

"About as sick as you," the man snarled.

Sam shook his head. "Actually, no. I took something before I came here. Something to counteract the effects."

"Goody for you."

"My friends have brought a whole pharmacy with them, actually. Stuff that combines with the gas that's in your system now."

On cue, Lucas reached in a leather carrying case and brought out a hypodermic.

Sam took the needle and held it up to the light. "We give you this stuff, and you're going to feel like your head is exploding and your arteries are pumping fire. Is protecting Dallas Sedgwick worth that?"

A sheen of perspiration had broken out on Bo's forehead. "He kills anybody who crosses him. He'll kill me."

"We want you to testify against him, so we can offer you protection."

"How can I be sure of that?"

"The Howard County P.D. is willing to keep you in protective custody."

"Trust the police? Right."

"If you want to do this the hard way, that's fine with me," Sam said, holding up the hypodermic and staring at the slightly milky liquid inside the glass cylinder. "Roll up his sleeve," he said in a flat voice. "I'm going to enjoy giving you something to remember," he said to Bo. "More than you enjoyed giving me that bourbon."

Bo's face took on a look of panic. "No, wait!"

"Tell us about Sedgwick. Is that his real name?"

"His real name is Ellis Rushing!"

"You can do better than that!"

"It's true," the man insisted, his voice rising in panic. "His father was Avery Rushing, the eccentric millionaire. The guy with the big ranch down near Austin, Texas."

Everybody's attention riveted on the thug.

"Avery Rushing. Didn't he die recently?" Lucas asked.

"Yes! That's right."

"You're saying Rushing's son was a criminal."

Something flickered on the man's face but was quickly gone.

Before Sam could press him, the sound of a shot rang out from across the room, and Bo slumped back as a bright circle of blood bloomed on his shirtfront. They all whirled to find Arnold Naylor sitting up, his back braced against the couch, his face a study in concentration and a gun in his hand.

"Stay right there," he ordered.

Cal cursed. "You were out cold."

"I snapped out of it all of a sudden. So I went for the gun I hid under the sofa," he said, the weapon wavering in his hand.

He was in bad shape, Sam thought as he looked at the man's sweaty, gray face.

"Give me the gun," Sam said.

"Not until you hear what I've got to say. Yeah, I set you up. But I did it because I wanted to get Sedgwick. He was the one shipping drugs into Baltimore. He was the one who ruined my boys. Sean was just a kid, but he was one of Steely Turner's top dealers, and Turner worked directly for Sedgwick. Sean got suckered in by the easy money. Then I couldn't stop Jamie from going after the cops who were there when Sean died. I thought Sedgwick would come here to get you. Too bad it was only his errand boy." He sighed. "I'm sorry I got you involved. Truly. But I wasn't going to let you end up in Sedgwick's hands."

Sam watched the man carefully. He looked as if he was ready to pass out. "I understand why you killed that scum. I would have liked to do it myself," he said. "But you'd better give me the gun before someone else gets hurt."

"Stay where you are or you're next. See, I don't have anything else left to live for. Sean's dead. Jamie's as good as dead. My marriage went to pieces, and my wife left me. Even my mistress jumped ship. The irony is that all that stuff I told you about needing money was a lie. The same lie I told Sedgwick's guy. All the money in the world isn't going to help me." In one swift motion, Naylor raised the gun toward his own head.

Sam leaped toward him, but he was too late. Before he was halfway across the room, Naylor pulled the trigger.

Behind him, Cal uttered a vehement curse. "I should have stayed with him."

"We all thought he was out cold," Lucas reminded him. "And nobody knew that Naylor had a gun hidden under the sofa."

Cal nodded, then looked from one dead man to the other. "I've got to report this."

"I assume you're not going to put your job on the line and identify yourself," Sam answered. "This sting operation could be a little difficult to explain."

The police detective thought about it for a minute, then gave a tight nod.

"Can you live with that?" Sam asked.

"Under the circumstances, yeah."

"Then let's get the hell out of here," Sam said, "in case the neighbors heard the shots."

"Give me a moment," Lucas interjected, moving around the sofa again and reaching inside Bo's coat pocket, where he pulled out a canvas bag about the size of a large envelope.

He looked inside and nodded his head. "Here's the payoff money. Catch." He tossed the bag to Sam, who caught it easily. "Keep it. You earned it. And if you need expense money for tracking down Avery Rushing's son, you've got it. A nice little twist of fate. Sedgwick pays the tab."

Sam grinned. "Yeah, thanks," he answered, tucking the bag under his arm.

They all checked carefully to make sure nobody had left anything in the room. When they were finished, they moved to the back door and slipped into the darkness.

Sam walked rapidly down the alley, then around to the street where his car was parked. His head still felt as if it might split in two, but he was sure he could drive.

LAUREL PACED back and forth on the wide front porch of the Randolph house. Beth Rollins and Hannah Dawson were inside, showing more restraint.

But when the two cars came up the curved driveway, the two other women rushed outside to join her. The first car stopped, and Lucas and Cal climbed out.

"Sam?" she asked around the lump clogging her throat.

"Back there," Lucas said, pointing to the second vehicle, then turning to embrace Hannah. Cal and Beth were similarly occupied.

But the activity barely registered with Laurel. Unable to think about anything but Sam, she ran to the driver's door and yanked it open before leaping inside, her arms sliding around him.

"Are you all right?" she breathed.

"If I weren't, you'd finish me off." He laughed, even as his arms tightened around her.

She closed her eyes, absorbing the feel of him, the steady strength, all the things that she had come to love.

Because she did love him. That was what she was feeling, although it was an emotion that she'd never in her life expected to experience. Well, at least with a man. Loving Teddy had been easy. He was such an endearing little boy that it hadn't taken him long to win her heart.

But a man—that was quite a different thing. Men were dangerous, aggressive. They did things to you that you loathed. At least that was what she'd thought until she'd met Sam Lassiter. Everything he'd done to her had been wonderful.

Now she lifted her head, found his mouth. It sent a surge of new wonder through her that he seemed to crave the contact as much as she did.

Then she stopped thinking and just gave herself over to feeling.

He angled his head, deepening the kiss, feasting on her as if she were the source of everything good in the world.

His hand moved to her breast, stroking, kneading, playing with the nipple that had instantly hardened at his first touch.

For long moments, nothing existed in the universe besides Sam Lassiter. She wanted him. Right here, right now. She was about to change her position in the car, about to straddle his lap, when the sound of a scuffing shoe made her body go rigid.

Raising her head, she found herself staring into the inquisitive eyes of the last person she expected to see at this time of night. Teddy—standing in the driveway staring at them. He was wearing his Batman pajamas and Winnie the Pooh slippers.

"Laurel?"

Feeling her face heat up, she eased her way quickly out of the car. Damn, the door had been open, and the light was on. She might as well have aimed a spotlight at herself and Sam.

"What were you doing?" the boy asked.

Glad that darkness now hid her heated skin, she tried to think of what to say as Sam got out of the car and stood beside her.

Without missing a beat, he turned the conversation away from them. "What are *you* doing out of bed so late?" he asked Teddy.

"I was lying in my bed, and I heard the cars coming back. I wanted to find out what happened."

"Well, Laurel was waiting for me, too. And she kissed me. People who miss each other kiss when they get back together."

"I missed you," the boy said.

"I missed you, too." Sam knelt and gathered Teddy close, kissing him soundly on the cheek.

"Did you get Sedgwick?" Teddy asked.

Laurel stiffened, but Sam kept his voice easy. "What do you know about Sedgwick?"

"I know you're looking for him. I know you think he's the same guy as my dad."

"Yeah," Sam answered. "So you were listening in on our conversations."

Teddy scraped the toe of his slipper against the pavement. "Not on purpose. But sometimes you all are talking when we come in, so I hear stuff. Me and Leo talk about it. Are you angry with me for ease dropping?"

"It's called eavesdropping. And of course I'm not mad at you."

Sam stood and slung an arm around the boy's shoulder. "Let's go in. You should go back to bed."

"Are you going to be here in the morning?"

"Yes."

"Are you and Laurel going to be in the same bed?"

His gaze shot to Laurel.

"Yes," she answered, "we are."

"In bed, big people can do more than kiss. They can make babies. And I know how they do it. The man—"

"Um, we don't need to get into that discussion now," Sam interrupted him.

Laurel blinked her eyes shut, then opened them again.

"We're not making any babies," Sam continued, with a quick glance at Laurel, "so you don't have to worry about that."

"I'm not worried."

"Good. Then you can get some sleep."

"I want both of you to kiss me good-night."

Laurel's throat felt tight, but she managed to say, "Okay."

They accompanied the boy to his room, tucked him back into bed, then hugged and kissed him goodnight.

Out in the hall, Laurel followed Sam toward the steps. "You handled that better than I did."

He shrugged. "Kids ask questions."

She nodded, thinking that his own daughter might have asked him something similar.

Again, her throat constricted. There was so much she wanted to say now. Like, she wanted to tell Sam that the thought of having his baby made her go all soft and warm inside.

But he'd lost his wife and child, and she knew that nobody could ever replace them—least of all her.

So she didn't volunteer.

She simply walked beside him down the hall, feeling a great weight pressing against her chest.

Most of the adults were gathered in the den, arranged

around the computer monitor while Lucas did a Web search, looking for references to Avery Rushing and his son.

THE MAN WHO HAD STARTED off life with the last name of Rushing, but had long since changed it to Sedgwick, slapped his right fist against the palm of his left hand.

He'd gotten the bad news about fifteen minutes ago, and he was mad enough to spit nails.

Almost mad enough to shoot the messenger who'd come to tell him that the ambush had gotten all screwed up—because Lassiter, Somerville and Rollins were all working together.

Naylor was dead and so was one of his best men, Bo Wilson. Bo who'd had the loyalty of a Saint Bernard, the fighting instincts of a pit bull and the cunning of a mutt. His loss would be significant, and so would the loss of the money he'd brought along to pay off Naylor.

Dammit!

Dallas grimaced. Fifty thousand dollars. Hardly anything. But with the business reverses he'd encountered lately, money was getting tight. Thanks to Somerville and Lassiter and Rollins. This time he'd been sure he had one of the bastards—Lassiter—and he'd slipped away again.

He got up and crossed to the window, looking out at the view of an apple orchard and low mountains. He'd decided as soon as he'd gotten back from western Maryland that he'd better not stay at the Frees estate. The police had been asking too many questions about his dear wife and her good friend Laurel Coleman that he found inconvenient to answer.

That alone was enough to prompt a disappearing act. But he'd suspected that Lassiter would be paying him a visit. He'd told himself the guy should be running away with his tail between his legs after that evening session with the bourbon. Instead he'd regrouped and counterattacked.

Dallas cursed under his breath.

Lassiter might be his chief antagonist now. But this whole mess all went back to Somerville, who'd wormed his way into his organization, then taken a million dollars of his money and disappeared. Just his luck that the covert agent had gone to ground in Baltimore and ended up hiring a private detective from the same agency where Lassiter worked. Then Lassiter had gotten the cop Cal Rollins into it.

Rollins was another loose end. Another thorn in his side. It wasn't just a matter of security—of what the cop knew. It was a personal matter. A matter of vengeance, because he wasn't going to be satisfied until he got all three men— Lassiter, Somerville and Rollins.

Now he knew where they were holed up, because one of his men had been able to trail them back to their lair. They were all staying on the estate owned by Cameron Randolph of Randolph Security. Too bad, because there was no practical way to storm that stronghold.

He brought himself up short, aware that he was mentally rambling. Aware that he was letting emotion, and his deeply buried fears, rule him. Not good. But the crap that had happened to him recently was enough to try the patience of a saint.

He laughed. A saint! What a comparison.

More like the devil.

Lips pressed together, he spun away from the window. He'd keep the Randolph estate under surveillance twenty-four seven. Sooner or later someone would have to leave. And he'd get whoever did.

LUCAS FOUND a number of references to Avery Rushing, but not as many as they might have thought, given his millionaire status. Apparently the man had worked hard to keep a low profile. And worked hard to keep his son out of the limelight, because, incredibly, there were no references to the Rushing family.

"I think this means a trip to his home base—Austin, Texas," Sam muttered.

"Just you?" Lucas asked.

"I think we're better off not conducting a small invasion. The less attention we draw to ourselves the better."

"If you're going, so am I," Lucas muttered.

"Well, then just you and me."

Laurel stood near the back of the room, listening. If she'd ever known anything in her life, she knew that Sam wasn't going to Austin without her. But she wasn't dumb enough to start an argument about it in front of everyone else when Sam would feel as if he was losing face if he gave in to a woman.

So she waited. Waited while Jo served hearty deli sandwiches. Waited while the men took themselves off to another room to consider strategy, even though she was inwardly seething at having been excluded. Dallas Sedgwick concerned her as much as he concerned anybody else. But she saw that the other women were staying out of the planning session. So she said she was tired, excused herself and went up to the room that Sam was occupying.

Only it was her room too now. Because while he'd been away, she'd moved her toilet articles and clothing in with his.

It was several hours later when he came to bed, and she watched him standing in the shaft of light from the hallway. She knew he was staring at her lying on the far side of the bed. But she didn't move, didn't let him know that she was awake and naked under the covers, until he quietly slid in beside her.

Then she rolled toward him, reached for him.

As soon as her body touched his, all the hot, frantic currents that had fused them together in the car came flooding back. Only now they weren't awkwardly jammed behind the steering wheel. Now they were in a nice big bed, in a private bedroom where they could do anything they wanted.

And what she wanted was Sam Lassiter—all of him. She rocked against him, kissed him, feeling his hot mouth devour her and his skillful hands slid up and down her back, over her hips.

He'd come to bed in his briefs. She got them out of the way in seconds, then silently showed him how ready she was for him to love her.

Neither of them spoke, but groans and sighs came from their lips as the heat between them built rapidly to unbearable proportions.

And then he was rolling her to her back, plunging into her, and she was lifting her legs to take him as deep as he could go.

They drove each other to a quick, sharp climax.

She longed to stay this way, one with him. But what she had to say was even more important. So she let him settle beside her, let him relax before hitting him with the message that had been simmering inside her. "I've been waiting for hours to tell you that I'm going to Austin with you."

His automatic reaction was a sharp denial.

"I'm sorry, Sam. You're not going to leave me out of it again. Too much bad stuff has happened in my life, and there was never anything I could do about it. I felt small and weak and powerless. But I'm not going to feel that way again. I'm tired of having things done to me. It's my turn now, and I'm not going to let you take that away from me."

He swore, the curse echoing through the room. "You're not playing fair."

"Why not?"

He sucked in a breath, huffed it out again.

Raising up on one elbow, she looked down at him, saw his tense features in the light from the bathroom. Sensing that he didn't want her eyes on him, she rolled to her back, pressed her shoulder to his and found his hand under the covers.

She lay there listening to the pounding of her heart until he spoke.

"You don't understand, do you? You don't know how I feel when I remember that my wife died because of a decision I made. If I had been driving that car, she might be alive now. Instead I was sitting in the passenger seat."

He'd told her about them before, and she'd been too timid to raise any questions. Now she asked, "Were you in any shape to drive?"

"I didn't think so at the time."

"Then if you'd been behind the wheel, maybe things would have come out worse."

"How could they be any worse?"

"You could have been killed too. And then Teddy and I would be dead, because Frees or Sedgwick or whoever he is would have found us."

When he didn't answer, she went on, "You keep telling me you were a drunk. Why don't you tell me why you stopped?"

"Because I almost did the same thing that bastard did who killed my wife and child. I was driving under the influence, and I wove across the white line and almost hit another car. That woke me up."

"So you woke up. So did I."

"What the hell do you mean?"

Her voice quavered as she said, "I mean, you might have crawled inside a bottle for a few months. But I crawled inside my head for years and tried to disappear. And then I crawled inside a prison cell. Only, I didn't exactly crawl. Somebody else stuffed me there. Maybe what you did was more dramatic. For me it was dying a little bit every day. And now I'm alive again.'' She stopped, gulped. "Because of you.''

His hand clenched on her arm.

"You gave me my life back, and I won't let you take that away from me again. So our goals may be in conflict. I'm sorry about that. Sorry that I'm forcing you to worry about me. But I won't be a victim again. I won't do it for you—or anybody else.''

Chapter Thirteen

"We're under surveillance. Sometimes there are cars in the woods. Sometimes they're on the shoulder. I've run the plates. They're all recently bought on used-car lots. The ownership seems to be under several assumed names. I'd say that Sedgwick knows where we are, and he's waiting to nab one of us." The news came from Cal Rollins, who had access to the Motor Vehicle Department's computers.

Laurel waited for Sam's reaction.

"I guess we're not leaving here by car," he said.

"I have a helicopter standing by," Cam advised. "It will take you to a location near BWI airport. From there you'll take one of the Randolph jets to Austin."

He and the Randolph operatives had been planning the trip to Texas. Laurel had invited herself to the sessions, but she'd just listened. Two nights ago she'd pushed Sam pretty hard, and now she was easing up because she understood that his worries were valid. She was taking a risk. Under most circumstances, it would be an unacceptable risk. Yet she was incapable of backing down. Her reasons were the ones she'd given him, and they still stood.

She'd stayed in the background at the business meetings, but she found she was fitting in with the group better than she'd expected. Hannah, Beth and Jo were inviting her to hang out with them. And to her surprise, she'd gotten closer to Alex Shane. From the things she'd overheard, she'd gathered that he was in the middle of a messy divorce. Now that she knew him better, she could tell it had made him bitter. Yet he was careful not to let it interfere with his job.

Her main problems seemed to be with Sam. He was only talking to her when he had to.

When he broke into her thoughts to ask, "Are you packed?" she raised her head slowly and gave him a direct look. "Yes."

"Then get your bag."

She stood, started for the stairs, hoping her anxiety didn't show on her face. Sam's tone of voice had made it obvious to everyone that the two of them weren't getting along.

That was bad enough, but it wasn't the only thing making her stomach knot. In a few minutes she was supposed to climb into a helicopter, and she wasn't sure she could go through with it. Well, that wasn't really true. She would make herself do it. Because she understood perfectly why Randolph Security had chosen that mode of transportation.

As she came back down, she saw Teddy waiting at the bottom of the steps and struggled to compose her features.

"I don't want you to leave," he said.

She looked behind him, saw Sam standing there regarding her. The expression on his face asked how she could abandon the child who had become so important to her. She felt a surge of guilt, yet she managed to say, "Did Sam tell you to say that?"

The boy shook his head.

"I'll be back in a few days," she said, coming down to Teddy's level. "You like it here with Leo and Anna, don't you?"

"They're okay. But I like it here with you."

"I'll be back," was all she could say.

Then she eased away from the boy, gave his shoulder a final squeeze and stood up.

Without speaking, Sam strode out the door and followed Lucas Somerville across the lawn where the helicopter had already landed. Laurel trailed along behind them.

When Lucas and Sam ducked under the blades to open the back door, she followed their example. When Sam strapped himself in, she did the same, her fingers feeling as if they were wrapped in layers of gauze.

As the chopper lifted off the ground, she felt her throat close. Maybe the look of stark terror showed on her face, because Sam reached for her hand.

She clamped her fingers on his, held tight as the helicopter rose into the air. Then when she realized they weren't going to fall out of the sky, she found herself relaxing and marveling at the scene spread below her. It was like looking down on a toy city, complete with highways and cars. Only it was real.

Sam eased his fingers away from hers and turned so that he was studying the view out the opposite window. She didn't try to reach for him again. He'd probably hold her hand again if she wanted, but he wouldn't really be there. Like last night when he physically hadn't been there.

She'd spent the night in his bed, but he hadn't joined her. Maybe he'd been at an all-night planning session. Or maybe he'd slept somewhere else. But she'd forced herself not to ask about it, because she'd known if she did, her voice would crack.

DALLAS SEDGWICK HAD BEEN sitting beside the phone. When it rang, he snatched it up.

Instead of saying hello, he barked out a question, "You have news from the Randolph estate?"

When the man on the other end of the line hesitated, Dallas clenched his hand around the receiver. "Just spit it out!"

"A helicopter landed on the grounds, then it took off again. What do you want us to do?"

What indeed? Not so long ago he'd commanded an army of loyal men. Now his troops were dwindling, and if his organization didn't have an infusion of cash soon, he was going to be in trouble. If his father's will would just clear probate, he'd be in clover. He knew the terms. The old man's fortune was going to him.

But it was too soon for that yet. Which meant that a lot was riding on his next drug shipment to Baltimore. Really, he'd like to ship the stuff somewhere else. But he couldn't pick some other city at random because then he'd be stepping on the toes of some other distributor. He knew that could be a fatal mistake. Just like when other guys had tried to muscle in on *his* territory. So expanding or changing his operation would have to wait until he could build up his power base again.

"See if you can figure out where they land and where they're going from there. Then get back to me."

When he hung up, his heart was pounding. He'd had a run of bad luck and it looked as though it was getting worse.

But he was going to come out on top. He had to.

He stood, paced to the window, then back to the chair, the portable phone still clutched in his hand.

There were only so many fronts on which the Somerville–Lassiter–Rollins coalition could attack him. They could prowl around Baltimore. They could prowl around his old stomping ground in San Diego. Or they could start digging into his background in Austin, assuming that they'd picked up on the Texas connection.

He hated the idea of hiring someone else to do his wet work. But it saved on expenses. You only had to pay for the hours when the troops were actually out on a job.

He dialed rapidly. "Go to plan C," he told the man who answered.

"You want men covering Baltimore, Austin and San Diego?"

"That's what I said," he growled.

"A full team? That's going to be expensive."

He ground his teeth. "Okay. Not a full team." He thought for a moment. "Four in each city."

"You got it."

He hung up, angry that his hand was trembling, angry that he'd lost control of the situation. But he'd get the control back. He'd done it from childhood and he could do it now.

He had to think. Had to put himself into the shoes of the men who were trying to destroy him. The weak link here was Sam Lassiter, he decided. Lucas Somerville had worked with him for two years and kept his true nature hidden. Cal Rollins was a cop, which made it dangerous to go after him. Look what had happened when that psycho Damien Hardon had scooped him up. The whole Howard County police force had rallied round and they'd gotten him back against tremendous odds.

No, he'd save Rollins for last—when he was up to full strength.

Meanwhile, he'd go after Lassiter.

Crossing the room, he opened a drawer and took out the thick dossier he'd acquired on the man.

HER FIRST JET FLIGHT. And in a luxury craft piloted by a man from Randolph Security—Steve Claiborne. To Laurel's surprise, Lucas turned out to be the copilot. She hadn't realized that he could fly a plane. But she already knew from the strategy sessions that he was going to be working the same territory as she and Sam—interviewing former employees of Avery Rushing and seeing if they could get anybody to talk.

The rest of the group had stayed in Baltimore to see if they could scrounge up any leads there, of course from inside the Randolph estate.

After the plane had reached its cruising altitude, Laurel got up to explore and found that there were two separate cabins. The one in front had several groups of comfortable seats arranged so that they were facing each other. In back was a bedroom.

Not your typical jet, she thought, unable to repress a grin.

Since Sam still didn't seem inclined to talk to her, she told him she was tired and that she'd like to rest. When she lay down, she didn't expect to actually sleep, but she did drift off, until a shuddering thump jolted her awake. Her eyes snapped open, and she looked around, momentarily disoriented.

Then she remembered—she was on a plane on the way to Austin. The bed lurched again, lodging her heart in the middle of her windpipe.

The door opened and Sam came in. "We've hit some rough air. You'd better come forward and buckle up."

She nodded and pushed herself off the bed. As she started to stand, the plane bucked again, and Sam caught her and wrapped his arms around her.

"Oh," she gasped. "Are we going to crash?"

"No." Sam leaned back against the bulkhead, holding her close.

"It's just rough air, like I said."

He could have turned her loose and led her to the front cabin. Instead he remained where he was with his legs braced against the floor and his shoulders wedged against the bulkhead.

She closed her eyes and melted into him, her arms around his waist, her face pressed to his shoulder.

"Sam," she breathed.

His embrace tightened. Then he loosened one hand, worked it under her chin and tipped her face up to his.

Her eyes blinked open, and for a moment their gazes locked. Then he lowered his mouth, claiming hers in a greedy, consuming kiss. The power of it stunned her. And when he finally eased away so he could gulp in a draft of air, her head was swimming.

"Sam?"

He didn't answer.

"I thought you were mad at me," she said.

"I am mad at you."

"How can you kiss me like that if you're mad?"

"I'm asking myself that same question. I guess I can separate out the anger. At least I can right now."

"Separate it from what?"

His jaw firmed. "Other feelings."

"What other feelings?"

He looked around the small cabin, at the door separating them from the others on the plane. "I'm afraid this isn't the time or the place for a personal discussion."

"When is the time and the place?"

"When Sedgwick is dead or in custody. Until then, it would be premature to make any decisions about my personal life."

So logical, she thought. So like Sam Lassiter. She wanted to press him, to force him to tell her what decisions he might make. More than that, she ached to tell him that she loved him. But she wasn't going to lay that burden on him. So she kept the words locked in her throat as she clung to him more tightly. Then, when that wasn't enough, she lifted her head again and found his mouth, claiming one more searing kiss before the intercom buzzed.

"Sam, Laurel." Steve Claiborne's voice rang out from

a speaker somewhere above her. "I'll need the two of you to come forward and buckle up."

Caught again, she thought. She was glad Steve and Lucas were facing forward as she and Sam slipped into side-by-side seats.

After they'd landed at the airport, Sam got out his cell phone and confirmed the transportation arrangements they'd made. They weren't using regular rental cars, which would have been easy to spot. Instead, Randolph had arranged to borrow some vehicles from a used-car lot.

In order to blend in as much as possible, they all changed into casual western outfits that had been scuffed up and washed half a dozen times to take off the shine of newness.

Lucas, who was from southwest Texas, had made the selections. They all had western boots, jeans and shirts. The men added ten-gallon hats.

Lucas looked as if he'd been born wearing the outfit. She hoped that she and Sam would pass for natives. A least until they opened their mouths.

And the gun Sam wore under his jeans jacket was certainly an authentic touch.

Before leaving Steve at the plane, they checked their lists of former Rushing employees. The men and women had been separated by sections of the city. Lucas was taking the north and east quadrants, while she and Sam were covering the south and west.

And the plan was to meet up at a motel that evening at the interchange of Highways 1 and 183, a location where the traffic was heavy and three more people would draw little attention.

Laurel tried to relax in her seat as Sam consulted a map, then nosed their green SUV out of the airport and turned north, his destination the modest neighborhood where a man named Pedro Estrada lived. Estrada had been the head gardener at the Rushing estate for ten years and had retired eight years ago.

When they reached his street of low stucco houses, Sam drove around the block first, checking out the area.

Laurel noted his cautious approach. "You don't think anybody's waiting for us here, do you?"

His eyes continued to scan the houses and the cars along the street. "It depends on whether Sedgwick is trying to duplicate our thinking. He might have come to the conclusion that we'd try to get information about him by questioning former employees of his father. If he did, his men could be waiting for us."

The neighborhood looked so peaceful that Laurel didn't want to believe it. But now she felt prickles at the back of her neck as she inspected the area.

When Sam finally pulled to a stop, he made her change places with him and left her in the driver's seat with the engine running.

All set for a quick getaway, she thought as she inspected Estrada's white stucco house. It was in mint condition, as was the small surrounding plot of ground. Flowering shrubs flanked the front door, and the beds of colorful flowers were carefully tended.

She wrapped her hands around the steering wheel, trying to keep her breathing slow and even as Sam approached the front door and rang the bell.

A strange combination of disappointment and relief surged through her as he rang again. There was no answer.

From the corner of her eye, Laurel caught a flash of movement. Her head whipped around to see a dumpy woman in a flowered muumuu who had been peering at them through her front window. Now she was ambling across the street, making straight for the car.

She didn't look like a hit man, Laurel thought as she curved her lips into a smile.

Belatedly she thought that Eric Frees hadn't looked like a killer, either.

"Can I help you?" the woman asked.

Laurel rolled down the window. "We're looking for Mr. Estrada. Do you know where he is?" she asked.

"What do you want with him?"

Laurel hadn't thought that far ahead. She was casting around for an answer when Sam came back down the walk. He didn't give the appearance of moving fast, but Laurel knew him well enough to see that he was in a hurry.

Instead of getting into the car, he walked around to where the woman stood.

"Howdy," he said, his Maryland accent thickening into a nice approximation of a Texas drawl.

The woman eyed him, then repeated her question. "What do you want with Pete?" the woman asked again.

"Actually, we were trying to locate Jose Lopez," Sam said, his speech still easy. "He and Mr. Lopez worked together a few years ago and we don't have his present address."

Laurel knew that wasn't true. Lopez was one of the names on their list of individuals to visit. But apparently the explanation worked.

"Lopez, you say. And what you want him for?"

"He's been named as the beneficiary on an insurance policy. We'd like to pay him some money."

"Who's we?"

Sam pulled out a card case and extracted a card. The woman eyed it. "Allied Insurance," she read, her lips moving as she pronounced the words. "And you're Samuel Lewis."

"At your service."

So he'd come prepared!

"Well, Pete—he ain't home. He left a couple hours ago,

and he had a suitcase with him, so I don't know when he'll be back.''

"Does he go away often?" Sam pressed.

The woman shook her head. "No. He stay home and take care of his flowers."

"And you don't know where he is now?" Sam tried again. "Because if we had some information leading us to Mr. Lopez, we'd sure be happy to give you a finder's fee."

"How much?"

"A hundred dollars."

The woman's face clouded. "I wish I could help you."

"Tell you what. If you can give me a little more information, I'd be able to advance you half the payment now."

The woman licked her lips.

"Was anyone with Mr. Estrada?"

"No, he was alone."

"And he left in his own car?"

"That's right."

"Well, you keep my card. I appreciate your help. Call if you have any information. And thank you for your time."

"I call."

Sam got into the passenger seat, and Laurel pulled away from the curb. "What happens if she calls that number?"

"She gets a special line at the Light Street Detective Agency. At the moment, it's set to ring over to Randolph Security."

"You think Estrada just happened to split a few hours ago?"

"I think he was warned. Either that we were coming looking for him or that Sedgwick was. Which means that we might run into one of his goons."

Laurel felt a wave of cold skitter over her skin. The last time she'd met up with Sedgwick's goons had nearly been a disaster. Now the enormity of what she'd done hit her; unfortunately, it was way too late to bail out.

Chapter Fourteen

Laurel watched Sam pull out his cell phone and punch in a number.

As soon as he started talking, it was obvious that he was calling Lucas and warning him that something was up.

They conferred for several minutes. Then Sam put the phone back into his pocket.

"Okay, let's go for one of the names way down on the list. Clayton Jones."

"The cook?"

"Yeah."

"He was with Rushing fifteen years ago. Isn't he in a nursing home now?"

"He's a long shot, but I'm willing to try it." Again Sam consulted maps. Again he asked Laurel to change places with him as they started for the nursing home.

It was a two-story adobe building located on a tree-shaded street. Sam pulled into the parking lot and cut the engine.

"Are you going to let me come with you this time?" she asked.

"Under the circumstances, I think that's safest."

Laurel followed Sam around the building and through the front door. Elderly people were sitting in chairs lined up against one wall. Some had wheelchairs, others were flanked by walkers. Most of their faces looked vacant. But down the hall she could hear lively music playing, and she saw a group of more animated seniors doing chair-aerobic exercises.

"Can I help you?" a woman's voice asked. "I'm Andrea Masters, program director."

They had both turned to confront a slightly stocky, cheer-ful-looking woman dressed in a lavender business suit and a frilly blouse.

"We'd like to talk to Clayton Jones."

"Clayton Jones," she repeated. "And you are?"

Sam fished out another one of his cards. "I'm Samuel Lewis. And this is Ms. Cole," he said, abbreviating her name. "We're from Allied Insurance. Mr. Jones was named as the beneficiary on an insurance policy."

Ms. Masters wasn't quite as ready to give out information as their previous contact. "Whose policy?" she asked.

"His sister. Eva Bradley."

"I don't remember a sister by that name."

"That's why it's taken us so long to locate Mr. Jones. Eva Bradley was estranged from the family for many years, but it turns out she remembered her brother on her insur-ance," Sam went on glibly. "It may be that Mr. Jones doesn't even know about her, since he was quite young when she left home."

Laurel was impressed with his ability to spin out a story that he was obviously making up as he went along.

Apparently the tall tale was convincing enough for Ms. Masters to give them access to the man. "Well, Clayton has his good days and his bad days, so you might not be able to tell him about it," she said.

"Yes. Thank you."

"He's in the solarium. Let me show you where it is."

She led them down a wide corridor to a sunny room with

a floor of terra-cotta tiles, groups of large potted plants and more seniors arranged in conversation areas or alone.

In one corner, a nurse was carrying a tray full of cups with pills and glasses of water. "Mr. Jones is over there," she said.

Laurel followed the woman's outstretched arm and saw a man hunched in a wheelchair. He looked so small and alone that Laurel's heart turned over. "Thank you," she murmured, then crossed the room a few steps ahead of Sam who had paused to scan their surroundings.

As she came around to face Mr. Jones, she saw his skin was crisscrossed by deep lines and his blue eyes were vague. But his rheumy eyes focused on her as she pulled up a chair beside him.

"Mr. Jones?"

He didn't answer.

"Are you Mr. Jones?"

He gave a small nod as if he wasn't actually sure.

"The Mr. Jones who used to work for Avery Rushing?"

The name seemed to penetrate his fog. "Mr. Rushing. He made demands, he did."

"He was hard to work for?" she asked.

Clayton's face took on some animation. "Yes, sir! You got fired if you didn't come up to the mark. A high mark, let me tell you."

Laurel glanced at Sam, but he motioned for her to go on.

"You were with him for many years. And you knew his family. His son."

Again the eyes clouded in confusion. "His son?"

She felt a stab of disappointment. "Didn't he have a boy? Well, he's grown up now. He'd be in his mid-thirties," Laurel amended.

"He didn't have any *son!*" Clayton said adamantly.

Laurel swallowed. Now what? "I thought that he did. That's what I heard," she said.

"Don't you know anything? He didn't have just a son. He had twin boys! Like peas in a pod. Dennis and Ellis."

"Twin boys?"

The sharp question came from Sam, because Laurel was too startled to speak.

The old man's expression had turned fiery. "Yes, sir! Didn't I just say that? Are you deaf?"

"Sorry. What can you tell us about his sons?"

"He was hard on those boys. Demanding. You hear twins are friends with each other. Not those two. He made sure they hated each other! There wasn't anything one of those boys wouldn't do to get the better of the other. I heard he even set up his last will and testament so only one of them would inherit—the one who was top dog. Like they did in olden times. Only, he didn't care if it was the older one or not. Just the one who did the best, you know."

Laurel was trying to take that all in. Two boys who looked exactly alike. Dennis and Ellis. Did that mean they were Dallas and Eric? Two different men!

Sam squatted down beside the old man. "You hear what happened to the boys?" he asked.

"What boys?"

"Rushing's boys."

The old man's expression turned vague. "Rushing was a hard man to work for," he repeated one of his earlier statements.

"I'd love it if you could tell me some more about the Rushing boys," Sam pressed.

"Twins. He had twins. Like two peas in a pod. Good-looking boys. But mean as cat poop. You'd better watch out for them."

Sam looked as if he was going to ask another question. Then Laurel saw his body stiffen.

Her head jerked up, and she saw a large man coming

down the hallway where they'd entered the room. As his eyes focused on her and Sam, a gun appeared in his hand.

GRABBING LAUREL'S HAND, Sam pulled her behind a screen of plants where several empty wheelchairs were parked.

This time he was carrying a gun. But it didn't do him a damn bit of good. He couldn't shoot, not in a roomful of people. But he was pretty sure the other guy wouldn't have the same scruples.

"Down! Everybody down!" he shouted as he yanked one of the wheelchairs open, then gave it a swift shove, sending it careening toward the intruder.

Sam was pulling Laurel out the door when he heard the gunman yelp as one of the metal legs hit him in the knees.

They didn't stay around to listen to the curse that followed, or the chaos in the solarium behind them.

"Call for help," Sam shouted over his shoulder to the nurse on duty.

Laurel stumbled as the door slammed shut behind them, and he struggled to hold her erect. In the solarium, he heard a blast from the gun and then another as bullets slammed into the door behind them.

Getting his bearings, he saw that they were in a service corridor. Several tall rolling metal racks holding various pieces of equipment stood against the wall. One was full of bedpans.

"Go!" Sam shouted to Laurel.

She gave him a wide-eyed look, but took off down the hallway.

He shoved the rack with the bedpans into the middle of the hall and tipped it. As he sprinted after Laurel, he heard metal clattering to the tile floor of the hallway, followed by the cart crashing. Before the sound had stopped reverberating, there were more gunshots.

But he and Laurel had already rounded a corner, putting a wall between them and the gunman. They charged into a room with more rolling carts, these holding stacks of canned goods and packaged foods.

A woman in a white uniform stood up to block their path. "Just what do you think you're doing?" she demanded.

"There's a man with a gun," Sam shouted. "Right behind us. Get down."

She stood there dumbly, staring at him.

"Sorry," he mumbled, shoving her unceremoniously to the floor.

When he turned back to fling the racks in their pursuer's path, he found that Laurel was already doing it, sending cans and boxes flying.

Nearby sat a large plastic bucket of gray, soapy water. For good measure, he spilled that out onto the tile surface.

"Sam!"

He had just made it to the door Laurel was holding open when the gunman came barreling into the other side of the room. Sam had the satisfaction of hearing him scream and seeing his feet slip out from under him as he hit the slick floor, then landed in a pool of dirty water. Maybe he'd banged himself on a can or two on the way down.

Outside, he took a moment to figure their location. By his calculations, they must be opposite the door where they'd originally entered. The parking lot was to their right, he hoped. But they couldn't head straight for it because of the walled garden in the way.

"Duck," he instructed as they rounded a corner of the stucco wall. Then, "Hurry."

It was awkward moving fast and bending over at the same time, but they managed it. He breathed a sigh of relief as they rounded another corner and saw their rental SUV.

Just then, the gunman emerged from the building, spotted them and got off a shot.

Laurel dropped to the ground.

Taking a chance that no one else was coming out the door after the guy, Sam crouched behind a rosebush, pulled his own weapon and returned fire. Getting off what he considered a lucky shot, he hit the shooter's gun hand.

With a scream, the thug dropped his weapon.

Sprinting to Laurel, Sam reached for her arm and jerked her up, pulling her across the remaining stretch of grass to the parking area.

They fell into the rental SUV, and Sam gunned the engine. They had just pulled out of the lot and were on the street when they heard the sound of police cruisers speeding to the scene.

Sam took several twisting turns, his nerves like taut wires until he'd put several miles between themselves and the nursing home.

Beside him, Laurel sat white-faced and still. When he glanced at her, she murmured, "Do you think we should offer to pay for the damage?"

Sam pulled to the curb and turned disbelieving eyes on her. "We almost got killed back there, and you're worried about property damage?"

When she answered with a helpless shrug, he reached for her, and the car lurched forward. Cursing under his breath, he pulled up the emergency brake, then dragged her into his arms. She closed her eyes and held tight.

"Okay, we'll send the nursing home a check from the Naylor payoff," he growled, "if that's all you can think about."

She couldn't help laughing, then sobered as she tightened her hold on him. "No. I was really thinking about how scared I was."

He held her for long moments, then eased away. "We can't stay here. There's a chance the bastard got away. And if he did, he's gunning for us."

She flopped back in her seat as the car started moving again. "How did that guy know where to look for us? Does Sedgwick have an army of men looking for us?"

"Maybe. Or maybe he's thinking the way I would," Sam growled. "Jones was a long shot, but he figured out I'd take it."

"Great."

"That gives us an angle of attack."

"What?"

"I've got to work on it for a while."

He pulled out his cell phone and handed it to her. "Punch one. That's Lucas. Tell him to meet us back at the plane, pronto. Tell him that Estrada's disappearance was no fluke. Sedgwick has agents in town looking for us, and they're working from the same list we're using. And one of them just shot up a nursing home trying to nail us."

She pressed the number, then waited for an answer.

Sam flicked his eyes from the road. "It's ringing?"

"Yes."

Finally, Lucas came on the line. "What's up?"

Laurel conveyed the message. Then Sam held out his hand for the phone and she gave it to him.

"Sam here," he clipped out, then pressed the speaker so that she could hear the whole conversation.

"Did you find out anything interesting before your hasty departure?" Lucas asked.

"Yeah, get this," Sam answered as he pulled up at a red light and began explaining about Dennis and Ellis Rushing. "I'm thinking one of the boys had taken the name Dallas Sedgwick and was living in San Diego. His brother, calling himself Eric Frees, was living in Maryland. So when Sedgwick's operation got shot to hell and he needed to disappear, he decided the perfect hiding place would be in his brother's life. Only he was afraid that Eric's wife and son and the boy's nanny would realize something was fishy."

Laurel tried to imagine a man so evil that he would murder his own brother then the people closest to the brother. Then she tried to imagine what his father had been like. She'd thought she had a hideous home life. Dennis and Ellis Rushing had been savaged, too—by their own father, with his treatment of them and the terms of his will, if Mr. Jones was right about that. Apparently, he'd turned them into monsters.

Well, perhaps Ellis hadn't been as bad as his brother. He hadn't killed anyone he was supposed to love, as far as she could tell. But now that she looked back on the way he'd treated his wife and son, she could understand his behavior a lot better.

Her attention snapped back to the conversation. "Do you think Eric was in on his brother's business?" Lucas asked.

"I doubt it. Not if Mr. Jones is remembering things right. The father turned them into bitter rivals. Jones isn't exactly in tip-top mental shape, but he was sure about the brothers' relationship. Either it made a big impression on him, or he's in a total fantasyland."

"No, the explanation makes sense," Lucas said. "If you're going to off your twin brother, you damn well better hate him. What do you think he did with the body?"

"Unless we capture him, we're not going to find out." Sam finished the sentence, then made an angry sound.

"What?" Lucas demanded.

"We'd better stop talking and call the Randolph estate. If Sedgwick thinks we're poking into his background here, he can figure the same thing about Baltimore."

"I'll do that," Lucas agreed, his voice turning urgent. "You phone ahead to Steve and tell him we want to take off as soon as possible."

Sam clicked off, then contacted the plane and made arrangements.

An hour and a half later they were in the air again.

This time Laurel stayed with the men, fascinated as they arranged for a closed-circuit picture phone call that allowed Cal and Hannah in on their conversation.

"Are you all right?" Hannah breathed as soon as she saw Lucas.

"Yes, are you?" Luke answered, looking as if he wanted to leap through the monitor and embrace her. Probably they were both wishing they were alone so they could make the conversation more personal, Laurel thought as she reached out to clasp Sam's hand.

He wrapped his fingers around hers and pressed tightly. With an effort she focused on the sound of Lucas's voice as he filled everybody in on recent events.

"If Sedgwick is trying to think like we do, then we need to capitalize on that," Sam said.

"Maybe we can lure him into a meeting and set up a trap," Cal proposed. He was sitting with his shoulder pressed to Beth's. Below the level of the screen, Laurel figured they were holding hands the way she and Sam were.

"He'd figure out what we were up to."

"So we have to let him think he's outsmarted us," Lucas suggested.

Laurel took her bottom lip between her teeth as she listened to the others propose various schemes. Probably it would be prudent to keep her mouth shut, but when had she ever been prudent? Finally she cleared her throat. "Can I make a suggestion?"

"Sure," Lucas answered.

"Okay, we have to give him a good reason for thinking he's got the edge."

"Like what?" Cal asked.

She shot Sam a guilty look. "Like he thinks I've gotten tired of Sam's getting me into danger, so I've switched sides."

Before she'd finished the sentence, Sam's face darkened.

But she pressed ahead. "Well, I don't mean Sam's really responsible for getting me into danger. I mean, I have to make Sedgwick think I'm fed up with...getting shot at and I'm coming to him for help. Then when you set up a meeting, I can tell him what to watch out for, only I'll be steering him wrong."

"Unacceptable!" Sam growled.

She could see Cal and Lucas exchanging glances through the television screen.

"Maybe she's on to something," Cal said.

Sam's retort was immediate as he looked from Cal to Beth and back again. "I seem to remember that when you were worried about your wife, you stashed her at the Randolph estate where she'd be perfectly safe."

"I wasn't suggesting that Laurel do it," Cal said. "I was volunteering, actually."

"Right, and he's going to believe a police detective has switched sides!" Lucas answered.

"Maybe. If I convince him this mess has ruined my career, and I'm looking for retirement income."

Laurel gripped the arm of her chair. "I see I've caused some dissension in the ranks, so I'm not going to sit here arguing the merits of the proposal." Pushing herself up, she stalked toward the bedroom in the back of the plane, aware that she was following another one of her old patterns—bailing out when she couldn't take what was going on around her.

After flopping down on the bed, she lay there stiffly, her nerves stretched as tight as an overinflated balloon.

A brusque knock on the door took her by surprise. Before she could call out, "Come in," Sam had stepped into the cabin and slammed the door behind him.

"Are you insane, or are you trying to put me in the nuthouse?"

"I'm trying to solve a major problem that we seem to be having."

He strode to the bed and stood looming over her. "By volunteering for a suicide mission?"

She wanted to duck away from his fierce gaze, but she kept her head tipped up. "You and Randolph Security will figure out how to keep me safe."

He uttered a low curse, then came down on the bed and pulled her against him, holding her in a death grip.

"Laurel, I never thought I'd love anyone again after I lost Jan and Ellen. Then I met you."

It was hard to take in what he had said, but she thought she caught the gist of it. He loved her. Even if he couldn't say it straight out.

"Oh, Sam," she breathed.

"Do you know what it does to me when I think about your putting yourself in danger? Or like today when I see some bastard shooting at you?"

"He was shooting at you, too."

"That's different."

She eased a little away and raised her head. "You think I don't die inside when you're in danger?"

Before he could respond, she went on, "Both of us know what Sedgwick's capable of. We both know that neither one of us can lead a normal life until we get him off our backs. Don't tell me that isn't true. Are you thinking that we're going into some kind of witness protection program? Not just you and me. Lucas and Hannah and Cal and Beth too."

His expression remained tight.

"Sam, I haven't lived a normal life since I was ten years old. Do you understand how much I want that now?"

He answered with a tight nod.

"Let's at least explore the possibility of setting a trap for him."

"You mean you're coming back out to join the discussion?"

"No. Not now. When we get to Baltimore." She pushed herself off the bed, walked to the door and locked it. She had told him two days ago that their goals were in conflict, and it was still true. But she wasn't going to let it spoil this moment in time.

While she was still standing, she reached for the buttons of her western shirt and started undoing them. Her jeans went next. Then she shucked off her bra and panties, her gaze riveted to Sam's face.

It was gratifying to see the look of passion that bloomed there as he stared at her. Even more gratifying to hear his deep, needy groan as she came back into his arms.

Chapter Fifteen

Laurel stood near the brick wall that surrounded the Randolph estate. Her pulse was thrumming in her ears, her mouth was dry and so many thoughts were swirling in her head that her temples pounded.

She was alone, dressed in black, knowing that her next action might be the dumbest thing she'd ever done in a long string of dumb stunts.

But she had thought her plan through, considered it from every angle—along with her motivation. She'd been a victim more than once, and she'd vowed that would never happen again.

And she sure as hell wasn't going to spend the rest of her life hiding from Dallas Sedgwick. If she and Sam had any chance at all to make it together, they had to do it in the sunlight, not hiding in some dark, unlit cave.

Which was why she was leaving the estate—alone. Because Sam didn't see it that way.

When they'd gotten back from Austin, they'd started making contingency plans. They'd come up with a whole scenario for how she'd approach Sedgwick, tell him she'd escaped the estate and offer to sell him the information he needed to avoid the trap Randolph Security was setting.

Only after they'd blocked it all out, Sam had exercised his veto power. When they'd started kicking around a bunch of other ineffective ideas, she'd found herself getting angry and frustrated.

Tonight she and Sam had had a fight about it.

He didn't understand her point of view. He seemed to think she was volunteering for a suicide mission, based on guilt feelings about her past.

Well, she wasn't that dumb.

She wasn't thinking about her past. She was thinking about her future—with Sam. Only now he might be so angry with her that they didn't have a future.

She took her lower lip between her teeth as she pictured his tense, drawn face. But as she had an hour before, she couldn't let that make any difference,

After their fight, she'd waited until he was locked into one of his plotting sessions with Cal, Lucas, Alex and Cam. Then she'd climbed out of bed, written him a note and changed into the clothes she was wearing now. Next, she'd tiptoed into Teddy's room and wakened him.

"I'm leaving for a few days," she said, "and I'm saying goodbye like I promised. But I'll be back."

"Where are you going?" the boy asked in a sleepy voice.

"I have something I've got to do. It's a secret mission."

"Is Sam going with you?"

"Sam's here. And I don't want you to tell him I came to say goodbye until tomorrow morning, okay?"

The boy hesitated, then nodded and reached out his arms for her.

She hugged him fiercely, and eased away.

The day before, she'd pretended great interest in the estate's control room, getting Cam to show off his special equipment. Now she used her newly acquired knowledge to disconnect the monitoring equipment for a twenty-five-minute time period. That way the sensors would come back on after she'd left, and nobody would be endangered by her impulsive actions.

But she'd already used up ten of her minutes. And now she'd better hustle if she was going to escape.

For a moment she hesitated, shifting her knapsack on her shoulder. Her plan was risky. She wasn't going to deny that. But nobody had come up with a better alternative.

So she willed her hands to steadiness, made a loop in the rope she'd brought along and tossed it upward toward one of the corner posts that extended above the top of the wall. Her nerves were so unsteady that it took several tries to get it into position. The dumb lasso kept falling back on top of her. Too bad she couldn't ask Lucas to do this for her.

But finally, after what seemed like an eternity of frustration, the loop caught and held.

With a little indrawn breath, she began climbing, bracing her feet against the wall as she pulled herself up hand over hand. She reached the top, rested for a moment, then started down the other side. It took another couple of minutes to detach the rope, which she tossed back over the wall so nobody on this side could use it.

She stood, sucking in air, knowing there was no turning back now. With one last glance at the wall, she start walking down the road.

Twenty minutes later a black car glided to a stop beside her. Lord, she hoped it was one of Sedgwick's men and not the FBI or the police.

Reminding herself to keep breathing evenly, she raised her head and looked into the small, dangerous eyes of the man who jumped out and pulled a gun.

"I take it you're from Dallas Sedgwick," she said with as much calm as she could muster.

"You'll find out soon enough."

"Well, I came out here to hook up with him, so I hope that's where we're going," she answered, surprised that she could keep her voice steady.

The man pulled the back door open and hustled her inside. She had barely slid across the seat when she smelled a cloying odor. In the next moment, he pressed a handkerchief saturated with chemicals over her nose and mouth.

She gagged, struggled. But it was no use.

The last thought she had before consciousness slipped away was that she'd been a fool to think she could meet Dallas Sedgwick on equal terms.

SAM BRUSHED BACK a lock of the blond hair that still surprised him every time he looked in the mirror. He was dead tired and thinking of calling it a night when a movement in the doorway made him glance up.

Teddy was standing there in his Batman pajamas, his face looking pinched.

Sam was around the table and squatting beside him before he took his next breath.

"What's wrong?"

"Laurel's gone!"

He struggled to keep his panic in check and his voice calm. "How do you know?"

"She told me." The boy scuffed his foot on the carpet. "She told me not to tell you. But I thought I should. Did I do the right thing?" he asked anxiously.

"Exactly the right thing! When did you see her?"

"A little while ago."

"Okay. Let me go look for her." His fatigue forgotten, he sprinted from the room and up the stairs. Laurel wasn't in their bed, nor in the bathroom. But there was a folded piece of paper lying on the vanity beside the sink.

It said:

Dear Sam,

Sedgwick keeps outsmarting us, and I know the only way to get the drop on him is to go with the plan we discussed. So I'm forcing your hand. By the time you get this, I'll be off the estate. I don't think hooking up with him will be too difficult. All I have to do is make myself available.

Even as the words swam in his vision, he heard other feet on the stairs. Alex made it to the bedroom first, followed by Cam, Cal and Lucas.

He saw their eyes zero in on the paper clutched in his fist.

"She left you a note?" Lucas asked.

He handed over the note. "Yeah. She's left the house. She's planning to hook up with Sedgwick and run the scam we've been kicking around."

"Well, she's got guts," Cal muttered.

"Or she left her brain back here!" Sam snapped.

In moments, the corridor was full of sleepy-looking people. Hannah, Jo and her wide-eyed children, and Teddy, who had followed the men up the stairs.

"What's going on?" Cam demanded.

"Laurel's playing Wonder Woman. She's gone off to hook up with Sedgwick." Sam turned back to Teddy. "How was she dressed?"

"In b-black," the boy stammered.

"We've got to spread out around the grounds. Look for her," Sam ordered.

Nobody disagreed.

Jo took the children back to bed. Some of the adults returned to their rooms to pull on shoes and clothing. Others left the upper floor half dressed. In the equipment room on the first floor, they stopped to get flashlights or night-vision goggles. Then they fanned out around the estate.

"Over here," Lucas called out.

Sam's heart was pounding as he raced toward his friend. His spurt of hope faded away when he saw Alex standing beside the wall—and a length of rope lying on the ground.

"Looks like she went over," Alex muttered.

"That little fool!"

"Maybe not," Lucas answered.

Sam shot him a murderous look. "How can you say that?"

"Because we came up with a good plan to trap the guy. Then you vetoed it."

Sam whirled, grabbed his friend by the shoulders. "Because it was too damn dangerous. Because I couldn't cope with the idea of losing her." The fear was so great that he wanted to scream out his rage. Instead he managed to say, "Not now. Not again. I can't go through that again."

Lucas reached up to cover one of Sam's hands.

"I know."

"Damn her!"

"I think what you really mean is let's make sure we save her," Lucas said quietly. "And I think I know how we can do it."

Sam struggled to contain the sudden surge of hope that flashed within him like a shooting star. "How?"

Lucas shifted from one foot to the other. "Well, I have a confession to make," he said. "You know how I got into this Sedgwick mess in the first place?"

"You were working for a spy agency called the Peregrine Connection, some super-secret organization that takes on the government's dirty work. I know that much. And not a lot more."

"Yeah. Well, they're pretty low profile. I still work for them. I mean, this is my last assignment."

Sam's eyes narrowed. "What do you mean—an assignment?"

"My boss, Addison Jennings, asked me to keep him informed on our progress in nailing Sedgwick. Jennings has had to stay officially out of the investigation because of congressional pressure. He was warned that if he had any further involvement, his funding would dry up. But he wants Sedgwick as much as we do. Remember, I originally went undercover to stop Sedgwick from funneling drugs and illegal aliens into the country. So I think Jennings can be persuaded to help us with the sting operation.''

''Are you saying you've been spying on your friends for months?''

''You could put it that way.''

Sam took a step back. ''And I'm supposed to trust you when you kept this little detail to yourself? Does Hannah know?''

''Not yet. But she's about to. Come on back to the house, and I'll arrange a conference call with Jennings.''

LAUREL WOKE feeling like a spike was sticking through her head, starting between her eyes and exiting through the back. Cautiously she cracked her eyelids and found she was lying on a narrow bed in a room with barred windows.

For several heartbeats she had no idea where she was. Then memory came flooding back, and she groaned.

The wall…the car…the chloroform, or whatever it was.

The goon had drugged her and probably brought her to Sedgwick's house.

Panic threatened to swallow her whole. With shaky arms, she pushed herself up and looked around the room that was little bigger than a prison cell.

The comparison brought a little moan to her throat.

Pressing her shoulders against the wall, she licked her lips, grimacing at the sour taste in her mouth. There was a bottle of water beside the bed. She grabbed it in a trembling hand and fumbled with the top. But her fingers were weak, and it took all her effort to break the seal.

She heaved a sigh when it gave, then dribbled some water onto her chin as she took a swallow. She had just wiped it away when the lock clicked.

Her whole body went rigid as a man walked into the room. A man whose face she knew all too well. She studied his heavy eyebrows, light-colored eyes and substantial nose. Feature for feature, he looked a lot like the Eric Frees she remembered. Yet now that she understood he was someone else, she could see subtle differences.

Eric Frees had been a harsh and angry man who had ridden roughshod over his wife and son. And the person standing in the doorway certainly projected those qualities. Yet there was a degree of malevolence glowing in his eyes that went deeper than what she remembered.

He stepped into the room and closed the door. Suddenly she was alone with him in the confined space, and she was sitting on a bed. She had thought Sam had banished her fear of beds. Now she felt a shiver travel over her skin and knew that it was only with Sam.

There was something else she knew, too. Sedgwick had picked this place for their interview because he knew how much the environment threatened her.

He stabbed her with his gaze as he sat down in the leather chair by the window and crossed one leg over the other.

She sat up straighter, pressing her shoulders more firmly against the wall, thinking about what she'd do if he made a move toward her.

"I assume you know who I am," he said.

She nodded. "Dallas Sedgwick. But you were born Dennis Rushing."

No trace of surprise flickered in those pale eyes. "Very good. So Lassiter and company figured that out."

"But not much else," she said.

He smiled. "You've caused me a lot of trouble. Why did you allow my men to capture you now?" he asked.

Here was the first hurdle she needed to jump, and her head was still so fuzzy that she could barely think. "Because I know you'll pay me a great deal of money to tell you how to get Sam Lassiter, Lucas Somerville, Cal Rollins and their friends off your back."

"I thought they were *your* friends. You've been holed up in that estate with them for days. Except for your trip to Austin."

She raised her chin. "Lassiter wants—" She stopped. "Lassiter thinks that because he rescued me, he has the right to, uh, use my body. I don't give that right to any man."

"Ah, you mean since your stepfather."

She felt the blood drain out of her face as she realized he'd been playing with her all along.

"I see you're shocked. You think I wouldn't have done a great deal of research on you?"

"I don't much like that!" she snapped.

"You're in no position to object."

She struggled her way back to calm, telling herself that his knowledge of her background might be just what she needed to convince him of her sincerity. Looking him in the eye, she said, "But I'm in a position to help you. And to get back at that ham-handed bastard Lassiter. Do you want to deal or not?"

"You took a pretty big risk letting *me* get my hands on you."

The way he said it made her skin crawl, but she answered in the defiant tone of voice that had served her well in the past. "I'm tired of being pawed. If you touch me, I'll kill you." She had the satisfaction of seeing him blanch. "I just want to strike a deal with you," she continued. "Five hundred thousand dollars for the information you need."

"That's a lot of money."

"You can afford it. And I can disappear into the woodwork."

"How do you know I'll let you go?"

"Not because I trust you. I've written a letter to an attorney that he'll deliver to the police if I disappear. So you'll deposit the money in an account for me before you go to the meeting with Lassiter. That way, I'll already be paid."

"You can still talk to the police."

"But I'd be implicating myself in three men's deaths."

"You do have a point."

"So let me tell you enough about what they're planning so that you can decide whether we can do business."

"All right," he agreed, his voice bland but his gaze too hot for comfort.

She resisted the urge to wipe her hand across her face. "Lassiter and company are planning to set up a meeting with you. At an abandoned warehouse on the east side of the city. They're going to offer you a deal. You agree to leave the country, leave them in peace, and they'll pay you a very large sum of money."

"How much?"

"The million dollars Lucas Somerville stole from you, for starters. And part of the money he got for the sale of his dad's ranch. They'll offer you three million to get off their backs."

She paused.

"Go on."

"But it's a trap. They'll have all kinds of special equipment in the warehouse. It will be sort of like what happened at the Naylor place, only on a larger scale."

"What *did* happen at Naylor's?"

Laurel didn't blink. When she and Sam had talked about her sting operation, they'd rehearsed this answer. Unfor-

tunately, in her present state, she was afraid she was going
to get the details wrong. "It's kind of technical for me,"
she allowed. "They used something from Randolph Security. A high-frequency sound-wave thing that made everybody in the place unconscious," she lied, giving him the
gist of the false explanation.

"Let me get this straight. You're telling me that they
want to set up a meeting but they're planning to zap me
with high-frequency sound waves? Why should I come to
their party?"

They had talked about what story Sedgwick might believe, and it had all seemed to make sense at the time. Now
she was going to find out if it would really work.

She licked her suddenly dry lips. "Okay, I've been thinking this through. I know where the meeting is being set up.
First you insist that they bring the money when they come.
Then you check out the warehouse and disable their special
equipment. When you arrive, you send a guy in ahead to
make sure the money's there. They won't object because
they think they're gonna trap you."

Sedgwick's eyes narrowed, and she tensed, waiting for
him to say he didn't believe a word she'd just said.

He made her wait several seconds before asking, "Why
won't they know I've disabled their equipment?"

"Because you get an electronics expert that can make it
look like it's still on-line."

"Is that possible?"

"I'm betting that it is."

"You mean you're betting *my* life."

"If the guy you hire can't do it, you can back out."

She could see him thinking it through. "It looks like I
have nothing to lose," he finally murmured.

She blew out air.

"And your half mil—it's a cut of the money?"

"No. I told you I want my payment up front."

Sedgwick shook his head. "Sorry, honey. If I'm gonna take a risk like that, so are you. You're coming to the meeting with me. And if I find out you double-crossed me, you're dead."

"STAND STILL, dammit. Your pacing back and forth is making me feel like I'm watching a tennis match."

Sam stopped in midstride, whirled and glared at Alex Shane who was sitting in front of the computer screen going over the specifications for some of tomorrow's special effects. "Listen, maybe you're down on women, but I happen to care about Laurel," he growled. "So pardon me if I pace."

Alex tipped his head to the side, but his expression didn't change.

Sam closed his eyes for a moment. "Sorry," he muttered.

"No offense taken."

Sam ran his fingers over his face, feeling the stubble he hadn't bothered to shave in a few days. He'd been too damn busy. "I'm jumpy. Never mind saying this nutball scheme was my idea in the first place. Now that we're actually doing it, I can't stop comparing it to the action climax of a James Bond movie. Only this is real life. Laurel's life."

"Not just Laurel's life," Alex said quietly. "You, Lucas and Cal are going to be right in the middle of the action."

Sam gave him a tight nod. Right, his friends were risking their lives, too.

"It's gonna work." Alex spoke with confidence.

"How do you know?"

Alex started ticking off reasons on his fingers. "Sedgwick took the bait and agreed to meet us at the warehouse. We've left nothing to chance. We've had a team of electronics experts working around the clock since Laurel left. We've been working from a remote location so Sedgwick thinks we haven't been tampering with the equipment at the warehouse." He paused for breath, then added. "And Laurel is smart enough to keep Sedgwick thinking he's got us outfoxed."

"But we can't communicate with her! We can't tell her how we've modified the original plans."

"It's essentially the same. We've just added refinements. She'll do what she's supposed to."

Sam nodded, wanting desperately to believe his friend. Then a noise in the doorway made him swing quickly around. When he saw Beth Rollins peering at him, he glanced at his watch and gave her a tired smile. "It's two in the morning. What are you doing up?"

"Jo sent me over to tell you that if you don't get some sleep, you're going to screw things up tomorrow."

"Jo said that?" he asked.

"Yes. See, I'm supposed to lure you out the door, where Lucas is waiting with a tranquilizer gun."

"You're kidding."

"About the gun, yes." She came over and laid a gentle hand on his arm. "But I do have some sleeping pills. Sam, I know you're worried. Nobody knows better than I do what it's like to be frantic about a hostage. When that madman had Cal, I thought I would go crazy. But I can tell you, you won't do Laurel any good if you blank out from lack of sleep."

He clenched his teeth, then made an effort to relax his jaw. "Okay. Maybe you're right. Give me the damn pills."

She handed him a plastic bottle, which he accepted and slipped into his pocket before continuing, "But I want you to wake me up again in four hours. That's all the time I have for sleeping because we're supposed to meet Sedgwick tomorrow. And I want to personally check every piece of equipment one more time."

"Okay."

He stood there staring at her and finally forced the request hovering in his mind past his lips. "Beth, I know you don't like to talk about your psychic abilities. But...is there anything you can tell me about how Laurel is doing? Or about tomorrow?"

"Oh, Sam." She gripped his hand. "If I could tell you anything, I surely would. I don't predict the future. I can only sense things that are happening now—or just about to happen. And yes, I've tried to send my thoughts to Laurel..." Her fingers tightened on his hand. "I'm sorry. Maybe if I had talked about my abilities to her, prepared her for it, I'd be able to communicate with her now. But you know I hate for strangers to...look at me like I'm different."

He squeezed her hand. "I didn't mean to push you."

"I understand what you're going through, Sam. Believe me, I understand. But there's only one thing you can do for Laurel now. Go up and get some sleep, so you can do your best for her tomorrow."

Chapter Sixteen

Laurel felt her jaw clenching and made a deliberate effort not to give away her reaction. But the closer the sleek black car drew to the warehouse in east Baltimore, the more certain she was that she'd done the wrong thing.

Every instinct toward self-preservation urged her to reach for the door handle, yank it up and bolt from the car.

But escape was impossible. Even when the vehicle slowed, she knew that running away would only get her a bullet in the back.

She'd made her choice two days ago when she'd climbed over the wall at the Randolph estate.

Now she closed her eyes and said a silent prayer. A prayer that Sam had gotten her note. That he hadn't been too angry to see the logic of her unilateral decision. That her harebrained scheme was going to work out.

"Carter, go check on the money. If it's there, come straight back to me."

The driver climbed out of the car, squared his shoulders and headed for the warehouse. She and Sedgwick sat in the back seat, both staring straight ahead, both making an effort not to give anything away. Laurel wondered if his heart was beating as fast as hers, if his palms were wet.

Carter was gone for a century, it seemed. Finally, when

he came walking rapidly back, Sedgwick rolled down the window.

"Well?"

"It's there. They held a gun on me but they let me see it. Then they hustled it into the suitcase again."

"You examined the stacks of bills. They weren't dummies?"

"Yes."

"Then wait for me here as we planned."

While the driver walked around the car, Sedgwick opened the door.

"Come on!" he commanded Laurel.

His voice cut through her thoughts like a knife through tender flesh.

"Not yet."

"I'm calling the shots here."

"I'm not getting out of the car until I know you've deposited my money in the bank."

"You don't have a choice."

She firmed her jaw. "I think I do."

His eyes narrowed. "Your money has been transferred to a Swiss account."

"Then hand over the account number. You must have it with you."

He gave her a long look, then reached into his pocket and pulled out a slip of paper.

Trying to keep her hands from trembling, she unfolded it and read the string of numbers. "Okay. But remember, if I don't walk out of this alive, evidence of your identity goes straight to the cops."

His jaw tightened, but he only said, "Let's get going. We have an important appointment to keep."

He stepped out of the car, and she slid across the seat and joined him on the sidewalk, thinking that the piece of paper he'd given her proved nothing. The account could be completely bogus. And she'd have no way of knowing. But she pretended that she was satisfied because if Sedgwick had come this far, he must think that he had Sam and the others outfoxed. That he'd disconnected the crucial electronics equipment.

But what if he'd gone further than that? What if he'd set up some equipment of his own?

She felt the hairs on her arms stir. But all she could do was follow orders.

"One wrong move, and you're dead," he warned as they marched toward the warehouse. "So don't do anything stupid."

She nodded tightly, wondering what her chances were of getting out of this alive.

In Sedgwick's prison cell, she'd had plenty of time to think about her rash actions and examine her motivations from every angle. The night she'd climbed over the wall she'd told herself she was thinking about the future. But now she wondered if that was really true. Maybe deep down she didn't believe in a future for her and Sam. Didn't think a woman with her past deserved a man like him. So she'd arranged to do him two last favors—get Sedgwick off his back and get herself killed. To make sure she wouldn't have to deal with rejection. Not just from Sam, but from the courts. Because she knew one thing for sure: They would never give her Teddy.

Now she felt as if she was sleepwalking. She could barely feel her feet touching the ground as Sedgwick marched her toward the warehouse. They stepped into the building.

The interior was cavernous, dimly lit. The drug lord's voice echoed eerily off the bare brick walls as he spoke. "Okay. I'm here. Where the hell are you bastards?"

The breath froze in Laurel's lungs as she waited for something to happen.

Then Sam stepped from the shadows and she felt every atom of her body yearn to go to him. All she could do was stand there, stunned, when what she wanted was to run to him and throw herself into his arms.

She'd never experienced a feeling so powerful. Never been more sure that the thing she wanted most in the world was lost to her.

Pulled by an invisible link, she took several steps forward.

"Hold it!" Sedgwick growled, but she took two more steps, until she was standing at a place where some chemical spill had stained the floor.

The drug lord caught up with her, pulled her against his body.

"Don't move again," he ordered.

She gave a tight nod, but her gaze was still riveted to Sam. His eyes were hard, unreadable. And when he spoke, his voice was like ground glass.

"So the little bitch switched sides."

She cringed at the harsh sound of his voice.

"It looks that way," Sedgwick replied.

"Turn her over to us so we can make sure she gets what she deserves."

Sedgwick shook his head. "I'm betting that she still means something to you. She's my ace in the hole. Give me the money and then I may give her to you."

"That's not what you promised!" Laurel wailed as if it had just dawned on her that this whole thing was going rotten.

"I don't owe you anything, honey."

It was true. The drug lord owed her nothing. Neither did Sam.

Sedgwick was speaking again. "Where the hell is the cash? Carter said he checked it. I want it now. Then I disappear. And I don't go after you. That's the deal."

"My associates have it."

Cal and Lucas stepped forward. Lucas was carrying a medium-size suitcase. Laurel had heard the story of how he'd woken up in a hotel room with no idea who he was, and with a suitcase stuffed with a million dollars. Cash that had belonged to Dallas Sedgwick.

Now it looked as if the story had come full circle. Lucas had a wad of bills again, only he was about to hand it over to the drug lord.

Behind her, she could feel waves of hatred coming off Sedgwick. She knew from her talks with the crew at the Randolph estate that for months Lucas had been the focus of his anger. Then Sam and Cal had entered the picture when they'd tried to help Lucas and Hannah.

As he stood there glaring at the trio, she was suddenly certain that he had no intention of keeping his end of the bargain.

She wanted to shout out a warning, but there was nothing she could say because she had no idea what Sedgwick had planned.

All she could do was play the part that they'd discussed—before Sam had vetoed the plan.

She tried not to tense, tried not to give herself away. But she knew that the time to make her move was coming up.

"Stop right there," Sedgwick ordered Lucas. "Put the suitcase down, then back up."

The only hint that emotions might be seething through him was the gritty quality of his voice.

Lucas did as he was directed, then moved back to stand with Sam and Cal.

Laurel was hoping Sedgwick would ask her to get the suitcase. Instead he shoved the muzzle of the gun against her back without letting go of her.

"Move."

Together they shuffled forward.

"Pick it up."

She bent at the waist, her nerves screaming as she thought this might be her chance. But the gun stayed pointed at her back, and all she could do was drag the heavy case across the floor.

Sedgwick pulled her backward beyond the spot where they'd been standing previously.

Laurel set the money down, expecting Sedgwick to pick it up. Instead he reached into his pocket and pulled out a black rectangular object that might have been a cell phone. But she knew what it was, because she'd seen something like it at the Randolph mansion. It was a transmitter.

God no! He hadn't just disabled Sam's equipment. He had set up something of his own.

"You thought you had it all figured out. Well, you're wrong. I've screwed up your plans with some of my own. Goodbye, suckers," he said, pressing the buttons on the device.

A sound like machine-gun bullets filled the air, and Sam, Cal and Lucas collapsed on the floor, their bodies limp, red stains blooming on the front of their shirts.

A scream tore from her throat. It wasn't supposed to happen that way.

"Sam! God, no! Sam!" she cried out, breaking away from Sedgwick and rushing across the floor, sinking to her knees beside Sam.

"You didn't really believe I thought you were going to betray your boyfriend?" Sedgwick shouted, raising the gun. "And even if you were, it didn't matter that you were going to give away my identity to the police. I can't use it anyway. You were stupid enough to think you had me fooled. Now you can die with him."

Before he could fire, she heard a quick, sharp noise and knew what had happened.

Bulletproof plastic walls had dropped into place, separating her from Sedgwick, and Sedgwick from the exit. But it was too late. Too late for the men lying on the floor in a pool of their own blood.

Sobs wracked her. She'd been so afraid that this was going to happen. And now—

To her amazement, Sam sat up, brushed back his blond hair. Beside him, Lucas and Cal were getting up, too, all of them taking off their bloodstained shirts and throwing them onto the floor.

It had been a trick. It had all been a trick!

She heard the sound of gas hissing. Then a roar of anger. "You bastards! You won't get me."

Jerking around, she saw Sedgwick with the gun in his hand, the gun pointed at his own head. Then there was an explosion of sound, his hand fell away and he toppled to the floor. Lord, he was the second man who had executed himself in this gruesome way. First Arnold Naylor. Now Sedgwick.

She could only stare at Sam in dumb-eyed shock as he climbed to his feet. Helpless to do anything else, she launched herself into his arms.

He caught her, held her against his naked chest when more sobs shook her.

"Sam, oh God, Sam, I was so scared."

"I hope so. What were you trying to do—take ten years off my life? I thought you were going to end up on the other side of the partition. I thought he was going to shoot you!"

All she could do was cry and nod against his shoulder. "I'm sorry," she finally managed to say.

"Don't apologize, my dear." A gray-haired man had stepped through the doorway and walked toward the three men.

"Well done, everyone," he said. Then he turned back to Laurel. "Permit me to introduce myself. I'm Addison Jennings, Lucas's boss—*former* boss. I was the one who hired him to go after Sedgwick in the first place and set this whole chain of events in motion. Now, thanks to your courage, we've finally neutralized a very dangerous criminal. I saw the whole thing on closed-circuit television. That was a wonderful performance. If you ever want to join my covert operation, you have a job waiting."

"Not on your life," Sam growled.

"It was a pleasure working with all of you," Jennings continued. "I've already arranged with Cam Randolph to purchase some of his electronics equipment for the Peregrine Connection. But I'd better fade back into the woodwork now, before a certain senator finds out I was in on this operation."

He had disappeared through a side door before Laurel could get her jaw to work again.

"What was that all about?" she breathed, incredulous.

"He was waiting for an opportunity to take care of Sedgwick. And we provided it for him." Sam's voice had turned hard.

"Sam's still a bit shaken up," Lucas said as he brushed off his clothes. "Where are your manners, son? Thank the lady for risking her life."

"Thank her! I'm going to give her what she deserves."

"What?" she whispered.

"I'd like to let you worry about that for a while," he grated, taking her by the hand and pulling her through the door where he'd entered the warehouse. They were in a small room jammed with television screens showing both the inside and outside of the warehouse, as well as banks of equipment that looked as complicated as mission control for a rocket launch.

But it all faded into the background as she stared at Sam standing there with his chest bare and his eyes fierce. A long moment stretched as he glared at her.

"Wh-what are you going to do to me?" she stammered.

"What I'd like to do is take you captive in my bed and make love to you for the next week. But I don't know if I can last that long without a good night's sleep."

Her mouth gaped open. "What?"

He wedged his hands on his hips. "Or are you too chicken to try and work things out with me?"

"I thought maybe you were," she whispered.

"Maybe I was at the start. I decided I'd be a fool to let you go. Then you ran out on me."

"I—I didn't run out."

"What would you call it?"

"Getting Sedgwick to play ball."

He breathed out a gust of air. "Yeah. But don't you ever put yourself in danger like that again."

"I won't."

"How does marriage to me rank on your danger scale?"

She gaped at him again. "Are you saying you want to marry an ex-convict?"

"If she's willing to take a recovering alcoholic," he answered, his face suddenly tense.

She felt hope burgeoning inside her. "Want to make a deal?" she breathed. "I'll stop worrying about my past if you stop worrying about yours. From now on it's just the future."

"Yeah." His face softened as he reached for her, pulled her into his arms again. She knew, as she clung to him, that everything was going to be all right. When she raised her face, her lips met his in a long, hot kiss that left them both gasping.

"Don't scare the life out of me again," he growled.

"I won't."

"You don't have to prove anything to me—or to yourself."

"I wasn't trying to prove anything. I was trying to solve a problem."

"I know you need to take charge of your life, but next time I'd appreciate it if you'd think of something less dramatic."

She laughed, heard the relief and the happiness in her own voice—until she felt a deep twinge spoil the joy.

Sam shifted, looked down into her eyes. "What?"

She took her lower lip between her teeth. "I was so caught up—" She stopped, swallowed. "Teddy. What's going to happen to Teddy? He needs a mother and father who love him."

"I know that," Sam said, his voice thickening. "And I know how much you want to be his mother. So I've talked to some people about it, starting with Dan Cassidy. He's a state's attorney in Baltimore, and he's married to one of our Light Street friends, Sabrina Barkley. He thinks there's a good chance that I can adopt Teddy, especially if I have a wife. And Laura Roswell, a lawyer down at Light Street, will handle the details for us."

"They'd give Teddy to someone like me?"

"Remember, you're not supposed to think that way."

"But—"

"Honey, we've got a lot of important people on our side. The Light Street Foundation is working for us, too. And we've got a lot of character witnesses—everybody who's spent time with you at the Randolph estate. We'll get Teddy, because that's what we both want. I know why you love that boy. I do too. And I want him for our son."

"Oh, Sam!" she exclaimed, throwing her arms around his neck, hugging him with all the strength in her.

TEN BUSY DAYS LATER, Sam blinked in the sunlight of the Randolph gardens where a hundred of his closest friends had assembled to hear him and Laurel pledge their love.

Well, not just the two of them. It was a double wedding, because Lucas and Hannah were just as anxious to get on with the rest of their lives, now that they could all stand in the sunlight without fear.

He'd been angry with Lucas when he'd confessed that he was still working for the Peregrine Connection and feeding them information about their search for Sedgwick.

But he'd gotten over his attitude quickly when he'd found out how much support the agency could give them in the sting operation to neutralize Sedgwick.

The drug lord was dead. And the police and the FBI were off their backs, once they'd learned of Sedgwick's actions over the past few months. One of his men had told them where Eric and Cindy Frees were buried, and their bodies had been transferred to the quiet dignity of Columbia Memorial Park. Even Ripley, the angry home owner Sam had tied up, had agreed to drop charges when Lucas had come forward to pay for the man's car and damages to his house.

Lucas had declined to discuss the amount, and Sam had finally given up trying to get the details. If that's how Lucas wanted to spend some of his millions, then there was no point in arguing about it.

Sam glanced from Lucas to another one of the important people in the Sedgwick drama—Cal Rollins. He stood on his other side, because he was serving as their best man. Little Teddy was the ring bearer.

Teddy had been really excited about wearing a "grown-up" tuxedo. Sam had been less enthusiastic. He wasn't a formal kind of guy, but he'd decided to make the sacrifice for Laurel. He wanted her to have the pride and pleasure of a formal wedding and a reception with all the trimmings. He hadn't kicked up a fuss when Lucas had insisted on paying for that, too. And he'd even let a professional dye his hair back to its natural color so he wouldn't spoil the wedding pictures.

There had been so little ceremony in Laurel's life, so little joy, and he was determined to make this day one she would remember for the rest of her life. Not just because of their own happiness, but because of the way all her new friends had come to celebrate with them.

The violin music swelled, and he saw Cal Rollins straighten and crane his neck. Then Cal's wife, Beth—their matron of honor—came down the aisle, and the expression that suddenly softened the police detective's face proclaimed his deep love for her.

Next came the pint-size ring bearer, proudly carrying two sets of simple gold bands on a green silk pillow.

Teddy was living at the Randolph estate at the moment, along with Laurel and Sam, who had put his old house on the market because he didn't want any reminders of the past to shadow their future. In the hectic week and a half since the Sedgwick/Frees case had closed, he and Laurel had managed to find a brick colonial they liked on a quiet street in Ellicott City, near Cal and Beth. And now it was just a matter of closing the deal, since they were using the Naylor payoff money for their down payment.

Then all Sam's attention focused on the aisle between the seats as the Wedding March sounded, and he found himself straining his eyes for the first sight of Laurel.

She stepped into the spotlight, holding on to Cam Randolph's arm. She looked so beautiful with her hair dark again that for a moment he couldn't catch his breath. The flowing white gown she wore only added to the stunning effect.

She caught his eye through her light veil and gave him a tiny smile, and he ached to come running toward her and take her hand, because he knew her nerves were stretched tight on this important day. But he managed to stay where he was. Finally she was at his side, and he linked his fingers with hers, squeezing reassuringly as he felt her tremble, then steady at the contact.

He was aware that Hannah had come down the aisle on Alex Shane's arm and had joined Lucas, but his attention stayed focused on Laurel.

He knew that Cal was supposed to stand next to him and Lucas, but he couldn't fault his friend for crossing the aisle and joining his own wife, clasping her hand as well.

Then the minister began to speak, saying something about a joyful reward after adversity. Sam knew it was true, but he didn't need a speech to remind him. All he needed was Laurel. He breathed out a little sigh as they got to the important part—the vows.

He said them in a strong voice, wanting everyone to hear him pledge himself to this extraordinary woman who had traveled so far and overcome so much—and risked her life to save both a man and a small boy.

Lucas's voice was just as strong, and he figured his friend was feeling something similar to what he was feeling. Hannah had stood beside Lucas when she had good reason to believe he was a criminal. And she had helped him prove that theory wrong.

Then it was the women's turn. All he heard was Laurel and all he saw was her sweet, serious face as she promised to love and honor him. This woman had saved him. Brought him back to life, although he thought she still didn't fully understand how much she had to offer. Not when she looked totally overwhelmed as she slipped the gold ring on his finger.

Well, he would spend every day of his life making her understand how much she meant to him. That was his silent vow.

Then the minister said, "You may kiss the brides," and Sam took Laurel into his arms, giving her a sweet, short kiss although he longed for something much deeper. But he knew she would be embarrassed by an unseemly display in front of their friends. So he kept his own needs in check, thinking that he was going to have her all to himself in a few hours.

Beside him, he saw his friends Lucas and Hannah looking as joyful as he felt. And he saw the crowd of people in front of them smiling, sharing their happiness.

He focused on Teddy standing a few feet away, eyes riveted to him and Laurel. Grinning, he held out his arm to the boy.

"Come on, son. Come join us," he urged.

Teddy rushed forward and threw his arms around them, hugging hard. When Sam looked at Laurel, he saw tears in her eyes.

They were threatening him, too, if the truth be told. So he took his bride's hand on one side, and his new son's on the other, and they hurried back down the aisle, ready to savor the rich life that he knew awaited them.

* * * * *

HARLEQUIN®
INTRIGUE®
and
DEBRA WEBB

invite you for a special consultation at the

For the most
private investigations!

SOLITARY SOLDIER
January 2002

**Look for three more COLBY AGENCY
cases throughout 2002!**

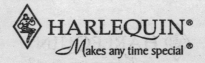

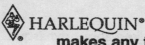

When California's most talked about dynasty is threatened, only family, privilege and the power of love can protect them!

THE COLTONS

Coming in January 2002

TAKING ON TWINS

by

Carolyn Zane

With Wyatt Russell's reappearance in Wyoming, Annie Summers realized the safe life she'd built for herself and her twins had just been blown apart! She'd loved Wyatt once before—until he left her to pursue his ambitions. She couldn't open herself up to that kind of heartbreak again—could she?

Available at your favorite retail outlet.

Silhouette®

Where love comes alive™

CRIMES OF
Passion

Sometimes Cupid's aim can be deadly.

This Valentine's Day, Worldwide Mystery brings you
four stories of passionate betrayal and deadly crime
in one gripping anthology.

Crimes of Passion features FIRE AND ICE,
NIGHT FLAMES, ST. VALENTINE'S DIAMOND,
and THE LOVEBIRDS by favorite romance authors
Maggie Price and B.J. Daniels,
and top mystery authors Nancy Means Wright
and Jonathan Harrington.

Where red isn't just for roses.

Available January 2002 at your favorite retail outlet.

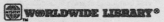

WCOP